ONE IS ONE

It must have been a kind of curiosity that held me back from screaming that night Hodge crashed into my life. Later he said that it was just as well I did not scream or he would have had to 'shut me up'. But I am not so sure. He was in such poor physical condition I think he would have slid off the roof if I had made a sound. What concerns me now is the mental condition I must have been in to react as I did. How many other people would end up feeding turkey sandwiches to a burglar who crashes through their bathroom skylight? Was I *that* lonely? It hardly makes a difference that it was not my bedsit but a house in the adjoining Gardens he intended to burgle.

About the author

Lucy Irvine was born on 1 February 1956 in Whitton, Middlesex. She ran away from school early and had no full-time education after the age of thirteen. A varied and unconventional existence culminated when she was twenty-five in a year spent with a stranger on an uninhabited tropical island. Out of this experience she wrote her first book, *Castaway*, which brought her recognition at home and abroad. *Runaway*, her second book, is also autobiographical, chronicling the events which led up to her island year. *One is One* is her first novel.

She has three young sons and currently lives in a remote part of the Scottish Highlands.

LUCY IRVINE

ONE IS ONE

CORONET BOOKS
Hodder and Stoughton

The author is indebted to Hawthornden
Castle, among whose quiet ghosts
several sections of this book were
written.

The quotation on page 158 is from
The Bronze Horseman, selected poems
of Alexander Pushkin, translated by
D. M. Thomas and published by
Secker & Warburg.

Copyright © 1989 by Lucy Irvine

First published in Great Britain in 1989
by Hodder and Stoughton Ltd.

Coronet early export edition 1990

Coronet edition 1990

British Library C.I.P.

Irvine, Lucy, *1956–*
   One is one.
   I. Title
   823'.914   [F]

   ISBN 0 340 51577 5

Printed and bound in Great Britain
for Hodder and Stoughton
paperbacks, a division of Hodder and
Stoughton Ltd., Mill Road,
Dunton Green, Sevenoaks, Kent
TN13 2YA (Editorial Office:
47 Bedford Square, London
WC1B 3DP) by Cox & Wyman Ltd.,
Reading.

One is one and all alone
And evermore shall be so.

One

Julie

It is almost a year since Hodge went to prison and Daley went into St Bride's. A year, too, since Ann died and I moved here. I would have trouble making her a birthday cake this year if she were still alive. She would laugh if she knew I still only have a single gas ring to cook on. I always said that if and when I moved it would be to a 'proper' home – the sort of place that smells of toast and freshly ground coffee when you walk in through french windows after saying a birdsong-backed hello to the day. Last year, in the old bedsit, I mixed her cake in a washing-up bowl, then whizzed it round to bake in one of my employers' well-equipped kitchens. God knows what I would do now. There are no facilities for baking old ladies' birthday cakes in an all-night sauna.

Daley still writes sometimes; short notes with huge letters in thick black felt-tip wobbling all over the page. The message is always the same; something poignant about Hope. I do not reply these days, having learned that anything I write, however banal, gets him – in Esther's words – 'all worked up'. It is disturbing to be the central subject of somebody else's fantasies.

Hodge does not write any more. He did, once, the letter sent on from my old address when he was first inside and I replied, enclosing tobacco and salami as requested but not letting him know where I am now, because I would not want Hodge in my future as more than a memory. It is easy with the wig, the scarves and the lopsided chignon not to be too conscious of that little scar. If it, or other oddities, had been obvious, I would probably not have got the job at the sauna. Wrong for the image.

What I like best about working there is the walk home in

the early hours. The town, stripped of its essential image of light, bustle and blare, is like another planet then. The last stars peep and fade in a pre-dawn sky that is more lilac than grey and are echoed by glints in the pavement. My footsteps, hidden birds and a distant milkvan make the only sounds. I like the anonymity granted by that time, too, the facelessness. Moving unobserved through lilac-grey stillness I am neither young nor old, scarred nor unscarred, maybe not even a woman. Hodge used to finish his night shift at Perkins & Day at six a.m. He would have been at home, too, in this quiet no-man's-land.

I have Daley's notes and a number of reminders of Ann here, but it is of Hodge that I think most. Lovers, however temporary – or unsuitable – tend to linger in the senses until they are replaced. It ought to be disturbing the way they vanish then, along with memories of moments one imagined were unrepeatable; a private language suddenly extinct. But it is not. Hope and hormones oust wisdom and experience and the dance recommences. It has not yet for me and it is hard to believe at this stage that it ever will. The lines of Hodge's face remain deeply scored in my mind – crevasses compared to my thin crack of a scar – and the soft flap-flap of his plimsoles comes often to my inner ear, as though he is visiting me. There is a memory block, however, between navel and thighs. Those once so hungry other lips are sealed. Is it curiosity that makes me want to open up the memories now? Or perhaps I imagine that by reliving those months I will somehow be purged of their effects.

It must have been a kind of curiosity that held me back from screaming that night Hodge crashed into my life. Later he said that it was just as well I did not scream or he would have had to 'shut me up'. But I am not so sure. He was in such poor physical condition I think he would have slid off the roof if I had made a sound. What concerns me now is the mental condition I must have been in to react as I did. How many other people would end up feeding turkey sandwiches to a burglar who crashes through their bathroom skylight? Was I *that* lonely? It hardly makes a difference that it was not my bedsit but a house in the adjoining Gardens he intended to burgle.

Maybe it was just his face and the fact that I have always been intrigued by chance encounters with strangers. I remember when I was small my mother telling me not to stare at people in the street – or follow them. But I went on doing it and Hodge was the ultimate 'forbidden stranger'. He has one of those faces you might glimpse from the window of a moving railway carriage and that sticks in your memory. I read a lot into that face and, looking back, realise I invested it with qualities that were no more than a reflection of my own needs at the time, nothing to do with the real Hodge. So I did to him what Daley did to me: made him the central subject of my fantasies. The difference was that I worked at making my fantasies real.

I don't know about Ann. Perhaps she simply had a lot of hope where I was concerned. Although the word could just as easily be illusion. My own letters to her, which came back to me in one of her handbags when she died, are further evidence of an odd state of mind. I have the first one in front of me now.

October 15th

Dear Miss Evans,

My name is Julie and I am writing to you as a fellow member of the Treetops Club. Your name was on the Contacts list sent by the secretary.

It's difficult to know how to begin, isn't it? Perhaps it would help if I told you a bit about myself.

A bit about myself. God, how prosaic.

. . . I am twenty-six years old and I live alone in a small bedsitting room. I work three days a week helping to install central heating systems on boats and on Wednesdays and Fridays I do domestic work in private houses. I like the variety of having two different jobs and working on the boats I get the chance of being out in the fresh air some of the time, which is lovely in the summer. It is not quite so pleasant at this time of year of course!

Extraordinary how condescending an exclamation mark can seem.

. . . I am lucky, though, because my boss, Mr Daley, is not the slave-driving type and when it is very cold he always finds me work below decks.

One of the reasons I chose your name from the list is that you do not live too far away from here and I wondered if you might like me to visit you one day. It would only be about a twenty minute ride on the bus. Do you get out much? I hope you will tell me something about how you spend your days.

~~My family~~. . .

Hah. That first crossed out 'family' tells a tale. I bet I pondered for ages before squeezing that whole vast problem area into a few innocuous lines.

. . . My family are rather scattered so I only really see them once or twice a year. I have one sister, who is married and lives in Scotland and a brother at present working in Saudi Arabia. My parents live in the country.

No mention of rows, adultery, schisms, and a neat evasion of the fact that my parents live at opposite ends of 'the country'.

. . . Although my bedsit is small, I am very fond of it. I have been here for three years now and periodically I have to have a rather ruthless Spring clean as there is simply not enough room to allow things to mount up.

Things. How this brings it all back: suitcases on the bed and a dead fridge under the desk in lieu of drawers and cupboards; gumboots, plimsoles and suede stilettos lined up along the skirting board; a broken Wee Baby Belling cooker with a never-used frying pan filled with candles and pencils on top; nylon boilersuits and lacy bras hanging on the walls.

. . . You can't quite see the river from the window but it is nice to know it is there and, high up as I am, the street is hidden by the tops of trees. On a quiet day I can almost imagine I am deep in the country. I don't have a television and for recreation I read a lot and go for walks.

Hoping to hear from you soon, although I will quite under-

stand if you choose not to reply, having perhaps found a suitable
Contact already.

    With all best wishes,

               Yours faithfully,
               Julie Barton (Miss)

I remember grimacing over that 'Miss' but feeling at the
same time it was correct to make my status clear. And that a
lady as old as Miss Evans ('late seventies') might not understand about 'Ms'.

How easy it is to simplify things in letters; to paint a picture
that is true in detail and yet feels like a lie. Who was I trying
to be for Ann Evans? A nice, quiet girl who keeps herself to
herself and makes friends with old ladies? Well I was like that,
or why would I have joined the club in the first place? But
also, I was not.

Three years I had been in that bedsit, three years essentially
alone. I saw Daley, of course, and exchanged any number of
words with the women for whom I charred and strangers met at
bus stops or in shops. I was quite adept, in fact, at the art of
ritual pleasantry, knew how to elicit smiles, my accent changing
in keeping with whoever I was talking to, sliding up and down
the social scale with ease. But none of it amounted to what might
be called 'real' communication. Until Hodge came along the
essential alone-ness remained unbroken. And then I learned to
play new games. Looking back, I see that one of those games
may have been to *imagine* I was no longer so alone.

And I never knew what private games he was playing. For
instance, he claimed that when he was in prison he was popular
with the other inmates, something I would have thought
unlikely. He was not – when I met him anyway – the type to
inspire respect among fellow criminals: he bungled his 'jobs',
rejected the camaraderie of crime outside prison and failed to
look after his bodily needs adequately. Not a villain's villain
at all. And yet I believed him. He was probably as capable of
being a chameleon as I was. As we probably both still are.

Daley was a pushover as far as my games were concerned.
He lived in a permanent shallow depression, occasionally

plunging deeper, occasionally surfacing to a brittle, childlike 'high'. He clung almost lovingly to belief in his own failure in everything: work, his relationship with his wife and as a father. But he enjoyed being distracted, too, and I was good at that. Distracting can be distracting too, another game. "You take me out of myself," he used to say. I have heard the same from men who come to the sauna. As receptionist I am a sort of harmless auntie figure. They butter me up in order to be booked with their favourite girls and sometimes stop for a spot of banter on the way in. On the way out they move differently, more of a scuttle than a strut, but most of them do bother to say good night and sometimes they slip me a few pounds. I like to think that my modestly overalled figure and demure scarf, wig or lopsided chignon make them feel at ease after the sleek, manipulative bodies within. If Daley had been brave enough or had sufficient cash he would have been a typical sauna client, going for the escape, the distraction, the allure of something he 'should not' do.

I met Daley through an advertisement in the local paper when he was looking for temporary student help on the boats. I was not a student but that did not matter and it was just as well as it turned out that I was able to go on working long after college holidays would have ended. He said openly that if I left he doubted he would be able to go on working alone. I forgot that of course when Hodge came along. Or ignored it. When I wrote that first letter to Ann I had been with Daley over a year. It did not pay well but I preferred it to full-time charring or various alternatives I had tried.

I described him in the letter to Ann as 'not the slave-driving type'. That was an understatement. Daley's depression made him easygoing in the extreme, always ready to down tools and brew up tea or wander off to the pub at eleven a.m. and not resume work until three. His clothes, his gestures, his whole bearing said: "What do I care?" And yet he did. Daley, with his never-done-up workboots, his carelessly exposed paunch, frequently nicked chin and grubby hair, was the gentlest, most honest and most dedicated family man I have ever met.

And now shamed, broken, branded a dirty old man and a thief, he sits drugged up to the eyeballs in St Bride's. Did my games contribute to that?

Hodge

Hodge sat on the bed hunched over like a frozen bird, bony hands folded in his lap like claws. Tears of cold wavered in the corners of his eyes and a clear droplet hung from one nostril, trembling with each outbreath. He wore his hair, black and thin, tucked into his collar like a scarf and his legs were crossed, maintaining a sliver of warmth in each thigh. In front of him the dusty honeycomb of an unlit gas fire reflected his stare. He did not have the right coins for the meter.

If it had only been a matter of the cold, he would not have gone out. Instead he would have scraped back the bedcovers and creaked slowly under them in the same hunched position he was in now, plimsoles, clothes and all, and stayed there for an indefinite period. He had done this at similar moments, in similar rooms, many times before. But he could not hibernate without tobacco. His fingers itched to roll.

The front door of The Chalet banged shut on his heel, launching him jerkily into the street. It was the first time he had been out since the Prison Aftercare woman had dropped him at the guesthouse but he remembered passing a corner shop on the way and his plimsoled feet took long, erratic strides in that direction, loose trouser bottoms flapping round his calves. His hands were thrust deep into the pockets of an old RAF trenchcoat, booty from a charity sale the last time he was out. Under this he wore a thigh length grey sweater and two shell pink shirts. He wished he had put on underpants as well: his buttocks and balls were numb with cold, a disturbing lack of sensation.

The owner of the corner shop, Gupta Seth, looked up as Hodge entered and put on a welcoming grin.

"Good morning, sir. Pretty cold today."

Hodge grunted and asked for tobacco, papers and matches

17

which materialised quickly in a little heap on the sweet counter. While he hesitated over a space-age chocolate bar yelling a silent *Kaboom!* at him, Gupta busied himself with a large machine just to the right of the counter. His movements were ostentatious, small fingers fluttering with pride.

"This has been delivered just this morning. Ten weeks I have been waiting and telling all my customers they can soon do half their office work right here in my shop! Are you a businessman yourself, sir?"

Hodge made a non-committal sound and added the *Kaboom!* bar to his purchases. He was bending forward to look at some pencils in a display case under the counter when a sharp blow on the side of the head sent him wobbling sideways over a stand of hairgrips and rubberbands.

"So sorry, sir!" cried Gupta, retrieving the errant top tray of his copying machine. "I had no idea that thing would slide so far. Are you all right?"

"Quite all right," muttered Hodge, although he was a little dazed and his fingers still clutched a packet of hairgrips. "I'll take these as well." He rubbed the side of his head, felt the greasiness of his hair and thought of other things he would need, details of everyday living he had not had to think about for a while: soap, razors. In prison these things were handed out or one was reminded to get them from the canteen.

Gupta apologised again as he was counting out change and followed Hodge to the door of the shop, holding it open for him.

"Is your head aching? I myself always take Anadin." Grinning, he gave a couple to this new customer, free.

Outside, Hodge's long figure hesitated before crossing the road to go back to The Chalet. It had begun to drizzle; light, suburban drizzle darkening the grey of lamp posts and leafless trees. Hodge remained in the shop doorway to roll a cigarette, watery eyes taking in the drizzle and the trees as his tongue slid out to lick the paper. His lips were dry, his stomach empty. He wanted a cup of tea.

Cigarette held between thumb and forefinger, he strode along the cold pavement, lank hair lifting and falling with each footfall. He passed empty gardens with creosoted fences dappling in the rain, a newly painted letter-box, dog dirt and paper in the gutter. A woman with a hat like a pink string bag wheeled a pram along the opposite pavement, a yellow sack of coke nodding in it like a drowsy child. Hodge made diagonally towards her across the road. She looked at him with the lack of interest common in the very tired.

"Excuse me, do you know where I can get a cup of tea?"

The woman stopped and considered, bag of coke stilled. She was unaware of being part of a routine adventure for Hodge, a small voyage of discovery made every time he was released. It involved first pinpointing his needs, then finding ways of fulfilling them. Tobacco and tea were always high on the list. Then there would be beer, painting, burglaries, women, but not necessarily in that order. One of the woman's slippered feet rubbed the toe of the other.

"Place on the High Street might do you one, although it's getting on for lunchtime now."

"Thanks."

He had an idea where it was, having long ago lived in the area, but he waited while she gave directions and nodded thanks again before moving off. She pushed the pram on slowly in the opposite direction, the distance between the two figures widening across the pinkish camber of the road. The drizzle melted fine and sluggish into the grey pavement, on Hodge's hunched, striding form and the patiently plodding woman with the pram.

On the High Street, which stirred only vague memories, the café made its presence known several shops away by its smell, a mixture of chip fat and melted cheese. The place's name was not familiar but its style was. A waitress glanced up as Hodge opened the door, letting in cold, and bustled behind him irritably while he paused just inside, the butt of his cigarette flattened between his fingers like a section of tapeworm.

"Tea," he ordered curtly, squashing the butt into an ashtray on the nearest table, "and a salami sandwich." He had not bothered to inspect the menu, half a dozen previous post-release adventures having taught him to know at a glance a place that would do a salami sandwich. Moving further from the door he settled at a corner table. Behind him the waitress's hand shot out, swiping the soiled ashtray away.

The street was barely visible through the café's steamy

windows but Hodge could sense the drizzle turn to rain. He had always liked rain, the way it began with careless stipple and then smudged the greyness of a moment into a dull pleasance of hours in which he would do nothing but sit by a window – any window – and smoke. When the sandwich came he ate quickly, the business of eating of no interest to him. Margarine streaked the long cleft of his chin and when he had finished, discarding the last crust with the dismissive gesture of one who does not drain the lees, he wiped his mouth and fingers on a slippery paper napkin. The waitress pushed a scrawled bill under the ashtray as he began to roll a cigarette. At ease in their tacit hostility, they did not bother to nod or smile.

Two cigarettes later, Hodge left the café and walked through the rain, now easing to a drizzle again, until he came to a bridge over the river. A few boats were moored alongside the towpath and from one came the sound of a hammer ringing on metal. A cold wind on the bridge and the harsh ring of the hammer struck uninvitingly at Hodge and he turned round, heading back towards The Chalet and the gas fire in his room he would now be able to light. Damp lay on his dark head like a cobweb and the rubber sole of one of his plimsoles was starting to come away from the upper, adding an extra half beat to the soft flap-flap of his stride.

Daley

After a few moments the hammering on the boat stopped and into the sudden quiet came a sigh. Daley's heavy body, arched up towards a metal pipe above the bunk, subsided like a slowly deflating tyre. Under him tools laid out on the bunk – screwdrivers, sockets, a pair of pliers – pressed through the limp resistance of clothes and flesh to dig uncomfortably into his spine. He closed his eyes and sighed again, louder.

It was eleven thirty a.m., too late for a second teabreak, too early for lunch. And Julie had teased him once too often about skiving off to the pub. The river was quiet and there was little traffic on the bridge. Daley gave in to his weariness and dozed, hammer still in hand, the tools beneath him digging in. Twenty minutes later his eyes reopened and stared uncomprehendingly at a bumpy sphere swinging around outside the porthole opposite his bunk. The sphere grinned and spoke.

"Boo!"

Daley eased himself off the tools and lay on his side, head propped on one hand. It gave him a pleasant feeling to be reclining like this and looking into Julie's face, albeit upside-down, outside and several feet away. Her fringe hung straight down, making her face look round and childlike and the dark plaits pinned loosely to the top of her head trembled appealingly.

"Hello, darlin'," he grinned, "I'm having a bit of trouble with this bend."

The bend he referred to was a curve of piping joining two lengths, part of a crude central heating system. He had been careless measuring one of the lengths and the bend, supposed to fit snugly above the bunk, stuck out like an awkward elbow. There were dents in it where he had struck it with the hammer.

Julie's head bobbed understandingly.

"I've finished painting in the other cabin. Shall I give you a hand?"

Daley liked the idea of Julie working close to him in the small cabin but he did not want her to see in detail the mess he had made of the pipe.

"No, love. Let's take an early lunch."

"Don't we always!"

Julie's face disappeared, replaced by the drizzle and the quiet river scene. For a few moments Daley lingered, senses gently bludgeoned by the thump of her young feet above him on the deck. Then he heaved himself up and went to fetch his sandwiches from the van. He always left them there on purpose to give him an opportunity to urinate without Julie seeing. He had not yet got round to fixing the tiny toilet on the boat. Head down, shoulders slumped, he trickled lengthily over a back tyre. When he opened the van door he sighed explosively. He had left a window open and the paper bag containing his sandwiches was sodden.

In the wheelhouse, half sheltered by a tarpaulin, Julie had spread newspaper over one of the slatted wooden seats as a tablecloth. She was opening a pot of yoghurt, licking the foil lid. Her cheeks were still pink from hanging upsidedown.

"Aren't you freezing?" she asked as they began to eat. Several buttons had burst off Daley's shirt and between the gaping halves of a homemade cardigan a slack two-tiered expanse of belly showed. He looked down and balanced a damp sandwich on the top tier, shaking his head. He did not feel the cold.

"Disgusting, isn't it?" He poked at his own flesh.

Julie gestured with her yoghurt pot towards the sandwich.

"Shouldn't eat so much white stodge."

"That's what Esther's always telling me. But I like it." He took a large bite and spoke through it defiantly. "And doughnuts. And pork-pies."

Julie ran a finger round the clotted yoghurt at the top of the pot and licked it.

"A little bit of what you fancy doesn't always do you good."

Daley stared straight ahead, took another bite and said vaguely: "Yeah." His paunch moved as he chewed and he felt Julie looking at it.

"You're hopeless," she said with a smile.

"I know."

He threw the wettest of the sandwiches into the river and they watched it float for a moment, gliding in a slow circle on the brown surface. It sank suddenly, without leaving bubbles or crumbs.

"Everything's hopeless," said Daley, the words as mechanical as the movement of his jaw. Julie gave a fidget and snorted.

"Oh balls!"

Daley grinned. He liked it when Julie came out with occasional rudenesses. The ugly words somehow made her more accessible, giving them laughter to share. At home there was no swearing and the only time Esther smacked Leonie was when she blasphemed in imitation of him. When the child had come to him crying after one such episode he had rested his hand on her burrowing head and said: "But Mum's right, darlin', and Dada's just a silly old thing." And that is what he believed. He respected, envied even, the codes of others; a welter of secret guilts being all that offered him one of his own.

Julie was eating an apple now, straight white teeth crunching into it, juice on her lips. The roundness of the apple made him think of breasts and the soft, mobile lips of other things. He sighed and took a sip of the tea made on a camping Gaz ring. Friday, when Julie worked elsewhere, and the two formless days of the weekend chasmed ahead. He had a vision of Leonie dancing round his knees and shouting, "Let's *do* something, Dada, let's *do* something." He never knew what to do. Swilling the tea round in his mug he looked up as if he had just remembered something.

"By the way, Esther says would you like to come over on Sunday – have lunch, maybe go to the park with the kids. Go on, they'd love to see you."

It was an invitation he issued on average once a fortnight, seemingly impervious to Julie's repeated refusals. Once or twice in the early days she had agreed to come and this was what made him believe she would again. He had never forgotten the new dimension her presence had added to the family's Sunday routine.

"Busy on Sunday, I'm afraid – going to visit an old lady."

Daley blew gloomily over his tea and took a long slurp.

"Old lady, eh? I bet you're going on the razzle with one of your boyfriends."

He said this with what was meant to be a sleazy look, then blushed. Every weekend he fantasised about what Julie might be doing with a man.

"Dirty-minded sod!"

He winced but she did not notice. She reminded him that a few weeks ago she had joined an organisation called the Treetops Club, which existed to encourage contact between the young and able-bodied and the disabled, as well as being a general penfriend club for the elderly. Daley had teased her at the time, saying she was just looking for a rich old sugar daddy. Now, unsmiling, she drew a letter from the pocket of her boilersuit. The handwriting was messy, full of little trailing threads.

October 20th

Dear Miss Barton,

Thank you for your letter. It was very nice to hear from you. I have been living in Pemberly for three years now. I used to live in a flat in Dean. I was there for thirty-five years but they moved me because they said I needed warden care. It is nice here and there is central heating and special facilities. I have to go in a wheelchair over any distance but here in the flat I have a zimmer and sticks. (I have M.S.) Also my hands are dicky sometimes but only bad when I am tired.

The warden is always in a hurry because she has so much to do. She comes in the morning to see that everything is all right and sometimes a nurse comes later in the day and the meals-on-wheels people. I go out every Thursday to the Thursday Club. We have lunch and there is sometimes bingo. In the summer they have Outings. Sometimes I get taken to a coffee morning or sale.

It must be very cold on those boats. It is cold here but I am lucky because there is central heating. I have a goldfish called Freddy. In the evenings I look at the television. I did enjoy your letter and it would be lovely if you could come to tea. Please say what day would suit and I will get some things in.

Yours sincerely,
Ann Evans (Miss)

Julie folded the letter and returned it to her pocket.

"Don't you think that sounds incredibly lonely?"

Daley finished his tea and wiped damp crumbs off his belly on to his thighs.

"Everybody's lonely."

Julie dismissed the implication that he was.

"Come on, it's relative, isn't it? Most people have got someone – wife, husband, children, friends – but what's this old lady got? A goldfish and a television. There's no comparison."

Daley closed his eyes, thinking of breasts, belly, thighs and deep warm rivers in between.

"You can still be lonely even when you've got a family."

Julie crumpled her yoghurt pot impatiently and folded it away with apple core and sandwich bag in the newspaper tablecloth. She repeated what she had said earlier, what had become a half-serious, half-joking theme running through most of their conversations.

"Oh you, you're just hopeless."

Daley grinned miserably.

"I know."

Julie

It was embarrassing the way Daley was always asking me over at weekends. It was probably a mistake to go a couple of times in the early days. When he told me about his wife and children I built up a picture of his home which, as it turned out, was entirely wrong. Somehow I had imagined that his own apathy and depression would have permeated everything in his existence so that his house, his wife and his children would fit round him like a drab stage set. I had little experience of young families and found it quite startling to be faced with the freshness of those children and the cluttered brightness, despite the breadline modesty of their home.

When I arrived that first Sunday the whole family was standing in the narrow front doorway. They must have been watching for me down the road. Daley, in the same grubby clothes he used for work, was resting either hand on the heads of the children, a girl of about four or five and a very small, plump-faced boy. His wife Esther, small and scrubbed, was drying her hands on an apron. (That fitted into my former picture.) I put down my bag to shake hands and immediately the little boy detached himself from Daley, squatted down, and started rummaging in it.

"Ooh Jonathan, you leave that alone," cried Esther, swooping down past my hand. She smiled shyly as she straightened up, the child in her arms. "He's going through ever such a naughty stage."

I knew, from having listened to dozens of exchanges during my supermarket and bus-stop 'socialising', that there is a special jargon that goes with small children. I dug into my repertoire.

"It's only natural. He'll be into everything at this age."

"That's right . . ." said Esther and continued to chat about the children, apologising for the clutter of broken toys in the hall, as she led the way in. Daley followed quietly, a heavy, though not dampening presence. It was clear that any 'hosting' would be left to his wife.

In fact, for the first hour or so, Daley behaved almost as if he were not there. He slumped into a worn old chair in the little front room and simply watched what was going on, hardly contributing at all. The children romped over him as if he were a piece of furniture but it was clear they adored him. When Leonie scalded her mouth stealing a sip of hot coffee, it was to her father she ran, sobbing into his paunch and dribbling the cooling milk Esther offered her down the back of his chair.

"It's all right, darlin'," he said distantly, while his hand, with chipped and dirty fingernails, rubbed her back. "Dada's here." He caught my eye then for a moment and added, with his sad grin: "God help her, God help us all."

Esther was embarrassed by this but not, it seemed, because of the conspiratorial glance.

"Don't take his name," I heard her whisper agitatedly as she brushed past him to fetch a cloth for the dribbled milk. He had told me she was 'religious'.

We had lunch early, or so I thought, for a Sunday. Living alone I tended to ascribe rules of convention to other people which were sometimes wide of the mark. So many Sundays I had wandered around streets like the one Daley lived in imagining all the Mums indoors basting roasts, Dads down the pub, kids playing noisy games. There were properly set tables and exhortations to good manners in my imagination. Nothing like the scene in Daley's front room where the only table was almost invisible under a large piece of mirror clouded with Windolene. Scattered on top were rags, comics, plastic ducks and pieces of jigsaw. As she brought in bowls of tinned tomato soup, Esther explained that before Daley had started installing central heating systems on boats he had worked at home, making decorative mirrors. 'Fancy' she called them.

"Trouble was, the materials were quite expensive and we couldn't always be sure the mirrors would sell."

Daley roused himself and gave another of his grins.

"The place I got the materials from is always on the phone about what I owe." He jerked his head towards Esther. "She's started putting on funny voices and saying they've got the wrong number."

Esther flushed.

"Shush! Julie will think we're dishonest."

His grin remained.

"Only when we have to be."

Esther shared her soup with Jonathan and Daley shared his, in a bigger bowl, with Leonie. My chair, opposite the four of them, was beside the television and I had the impression that, unconsciously, they were watching me instead of it. When the soup was finished Leonie fetched a large plate of brown bread from the kitchen, stuffing a piece into her mouth as she came. Esther brought in a round of tuna fish decorated with cucumber and tomatoes like the serving suggestion picture on the tin.

"I hope this is all right for you," she said, dividing it up and giving me a good third, "we don't eat a lot of meat."

Foolishly, I thought this might mean they were bringing the children up as vegetarians, but Daley, folding a piece of margarined bread into his cheek said, "Can't afford it," and then, to Esther, grimacing at the chewy wholemeal, "Isn't there any white?"

"No. *Shush* . . ." A gentle reprimand.

Throughout the meal – which ended with banana custard – both children stared at me without saying anything. Fearing to upset them, or get no response at all, by trying to make friends, I more or less ignored them. Then, when I was about to get up and help Esther clear away, Jonathan came and stood with both hands planted firmly on my knees.

"He likes you," drawled Daley, watching as I smiled cautiously at the little boy, "because you are beautiful."

I was embarrassed that Daley should say this in front of Esther and surprised that he should say it at all. He had never commented on my appearance before. I think I understand now why he did it. It was his way of being daring within safe boundaries and Esther's presence was essential. That afternoon in the park when I took Jonathan on my lap down the slide and my skirt blew up, Daley said loudly: "Gorgeous legs." It made me very uncomfortable.

Some of the regulars at the sauna behave in a similar way. They do not attempt to chat me up when they are on their own but if they come in with a group of friends it is amazing how bold they become. And I play along simply because it is easier than behaving honestly. And because it can, in a shallow way, be amusing.

I did not play along with Daley – not at that stage, anyway – but I did go back one Sunday, a month or so later, because Esther telephoned me herself. I had given them the number of the coinbox on the landing near my bedsit. I was the only tenant who ever seemed to use it, and then rarely.

"Please come," she said shyly and added something which makes me realise now how sensitive she was to his moods – and how caring. "You mustn't mind him, it's just his way – and he's so much happier when you're there."

The whole thing was odd but I was curious and, Daley's behaviour apart, felt drawn to the warmth of their funny little ménage. I had long ago ceased to look for warmth from my own family.

But that second time was worse. At one point, when I was about to come downstairs from the toilet, I met Daley on the narrow landing – I'm sure he had placed himself there deliberately – and was forced to brush closely against him. He said "Sorry, Julie" in a studiedly casual way but took a long time getting by. Esther was at the bottom of the stairs waiting to bring the children up. Later, in the kitchen, she murmured: "Take no notice. He's just a bit mixed up in himself."

I risked being open with her. Perhaps I wanted to reassure her as well.

"He's never like this on the boat."

"Oh no," she said, "he wouldn't be."

Whatever it was about, I did not want to get involved and it was a relief when, after months of polite evasion, the relationship with Ann began, giving me a genuine excuse not to accept their invitations at weekends. Dishonesty is only sometimes easier.

Ann

Ann lowered herself on to the specially designed seat with a groan. This was the third time she had had to 'pay a call' since the beginning of the afternoon play and each trip took at least ten minutes. It would almost be worth having a second radio in the bathroom. When *The Archers* was on she sometimes carried the set with her so as not to miss the most exciting part of the episode but it was difficult with her handbag and the zimmer to cope with as well.

She panted as she sat. It had been a rush to get there in time and although it was only a few yards along the corridor she felt as though she had struggled miles, the zimmer banging into the wall, handbag knocking against her belly and worst of all the wee-wee inside her bursting to get out. Wee-wee: a babyish word for someone of seventy-eight but somehow the smell she so dreaded clung worse to the word urine. Dear God, she prayed at night after Our Father, please don't make me incontinent.

It was awkward reaching round for the toilet roll; awkward reaching down for her knickers. The mirror on the bathroom cabinet, fixed at a special low-for-disabled height, showed her all bent forward in a tangle of knickers and toilet roll and handbag handles. She opened the bag to find her compact while she was there. Things fell out: used tissues, a fluff-covered biscuit, Julie's most recent letter.

"Oh no . . ."

The music at the end of the afternoon play reached her and as it faded the doorbell rang. Ann scrabbled at the things on the floor, hands refusing to obey her. The biscuit skittered behind the toilet seat and her glasses bounced maddeningly from a string round her neck.

"Just a minute, dear . . ."

Abandoning the effort to repack the bag she kicked the tissues behind a hanging towel and began the long process of standing up. Every few seconds as she struggled with her clothes, with her glasses, with the hair that kept falling over her eyes, she called out.

"I'm coming, dear, just a minute . . ."

When at last she reached the front door she was out of breath. She heard a light step outside and a throat self-consciously cleared. She tussled with the keys. The warden had her own key and Ann was advised to keep the door locked after meals-on-wheels time, except when a nurse was due.

"It's Julie, Miss Evans."

"Yes, dear."

The keys fell from Ann's hand as the door opened and the first sight she had of Julie was the top of her head as, quick as a flash – the phrase went through her mind – the girl bent down. But the keys had not fallen to the floor. They had merely clattered against the zimmer and now swung safely from a string round Ann's middle. Realising this, Julie looked up and laughed.

"Silly me!"

She stood up easily and Ann's eyes travelled with her. Most people seemed tall to her and quick in their movements but Julie seemed taller and quicker than most. Fumbling with bag and zimmer Ann freed a hand to shake the one offered – a small, strong, long-fingered hand in which her own seemed to squat for a moment, formless as a toad. The girl's dark hair was done in two plaits fastened on top of her head. It was an unusual, rather old fashioned style and Ann had to stop herself staring. Inwardly she admired Julie's thick sheepskin jacket and warm-looking boots.

"Come in, dear. I'm so glad you could come."

Beginning her slow passage down the corridor to the sitting-room Ann was conscious of the girl's buoyant presence behind: light, quick breathing as though she had been walking fast outside and the peeling off of the jacket as if she were very warm.

"I've got some things for tea but I'm afraid it isn't quite ready yet. I'm a bit slow . . ."

She had meant to have it ready; had begun getting in bits

and pieces towards it as soon as the second letter from Julie
had come saying that any Sunday would be good for her.
Sunday was not the best day for Ann, because if, as sometimes
happened, she was taken to church in the morning, she was
always very tired in the afternoon. But she was not going to
say that. She had replied saying what about the first Sunday
in November and here it was and here was the girl and the
tea was not ready. After church she had had to have a little
sit down, which had turned into a doze. Then there was her
lunch to get – no meals-on-wheels on Sunday – then the
gardening programme she always listened to even though she
did not have a garden and then that endless wee-wee business
during the afternoon play. She had been trying to make a start
then but had got no further than unwrapping the sliced bread,
ordered specially on Friday and kept in the fridge to stay fresh.
At last they reached the sitting-room and Ann stopped and
turned round, looking up into Julie's young face, a flush of
warmth over the high cheekbones.

"Do you like ham, dear? Or there's bloater paste . . ."

That was when Julie said, gently but, Ann could sense, with
determination: "I like both. But look, why don't I do it? You
rest and I'll get the tea."

And she had, very efficiently. She had even brought a cream
sponge as a contribution and seemed to know instinctively
where to find sugar, teaspoons, jug for the milk. Ann watched
from where she had been encouraged to sit in a comfortable
chair facing the kitchen. Her head was craned forward, the
hastily polished lenses of her longer distance glasses following
every movement.

"I think there's a tomato . . . cake in a tin . . ."

Crumbs fluttered down in a shower as Julie, finding several
old ends of cake in the tin as well as a new one, emptied it out
and wiped it clean.

"We'll have to make you a bird table," she said, smiling as
she held the breadbin upsidedown over the dustbin and shook
it. Ann could not recall the last time the breadbin had been
cleaned. Blinking, she said: "There are some napkins . . ."

When, finally, Julie stood back from the table and asked:
"Is that all right?" Ann noticed that her face – a pretty, sharply
defined little face – was anxious.

She had used the wrong sideplates and the tea cosy was what Ann called the kitchen one but the food looked beautiful: dainty sandwiches, fruitcake with a few slices neatly cut, chocolate biscuits and the cream sponge.

"Very nice, dear."

"Oh, I almost forgot," cried Julie, springing up a second after she had sat down and running to the front door. She came back holding a slender bunch of pink and white carnations.

"Where shall I put them?"

Ann was smiling, a hand at her throat, delighted but tired, the girl and the flowers seeming to blur for a moment as the television screen did sometimes when she was sleepy.

"There's a vase . . ."

"I know – next to Freddy. Give him something to look at."

Ann was almost more impressed that Julie had remembered the goldfish's name than by the flowers. Overwhelmed, she nodded. Freddy, fins a flutter, gaped incuriously through the murky glass of his bowl.

"And after tea," Julie went on, sitting down once more, "perhaps we might change his water."

Again Ann nodded. She felt, silently watching Julie pour, her freshness, energy and youth brilliant against the dull background of the flat, that her own 'water' had been changed; that the restricted element in which age and disability forced her to live, had been refreshed. Two sandwiches on, à propos of nothing but her own thoughts – and perhaps some memories – she said: "You'll make a lovely wife for some man, dear. Don't leave it too long."

The girl had laughed, tossing her head with its pretty coil of plaits, and helped herself to another sandwich.

Hodge

It was a week before Hodge left his room for anything other than a brief repetition of his first venture out to the corner shop and café. There was a small residents' bar in The Chalet where he could buy peanuts and crisps as well as the cans of Sweetheart stout that, away from immediate access to tea and salami sandwiches, were his main source of sustenance. He took the cans up to his room, shunning the studied inattention of the barman-cum-manager and the lugubrious curiosity of other residents. Breakfast was served in the dining-room between seven and eight thirty a.m. but Hodge never went down.

Soon rows of Sweetheart cans stood along the windowsill and the mantelpiece above the gas fire. The cold, damp weather continued and Hodge felt cocooned, the fire on all day, in his smoke-filled, can-lined room. He lay on the bed in his trenchcoat, bony ankles crossed, Golden Virginia tin beside him as an ashtray, and looked through half-closed eyes towards the window. Visions, mostly of women, rose for him in the damp glass. He dozed, dreamed, smoked.

On the seventh day a telephone call came for him. The barman-manager came thumping up the stairs to let him know, thumping down again after he had yelled twice. Hodge creaked his legs off the bed and re-lit his current cigarette. It would be the woman from PACS, the Prison Aftercare Service. To ignore her would only mean more attention.

It was cold in the hallway and Hodge hunched stiffly over the telephone. He answered the woman's questions minimally, ear wincing away from her bright, professionally friendly tone. Was his accommodation all right? Had he been to the Jobcentre yet? Did he need any help with his DHSS forms?

"Yes. Yes. No – no thank you."

She asked if there was anything he did need. More warm clothes would be useful and she would know where the nearest Lame Duck Pond was, where there would be free tea, jumble sales and more eager women dispensing advice. Lame Duck Pond was Hodge's own term for any project that catered for the elderly, the lonely and/or those who, like himself, were supposed to be undergoing rehabilitation after a spell in an institution of one sort or another. He had occasionally found them useful in the past.

When he had hung up, Hodge returned to his room, its fug welcome after the cold of the hallway, and stripped down to his trousers to shave. He stood in front of the basin with long legs braced, a black plastic belt holding the trousers just below his navel. The thin skin on his belly bunched with the movement of splashing face and neck, and two long hollows dipped from under his ribs towards his groin. His shoulder blades peaked and flattened and a white bicep, tight against his side to steady the razor hand, creased.

Chin up, mouth pulled to one side to stretch the planes of cheek and jaw, Hodge's eyes followed the razor's tracks and backtracks through the watery soap foam but did not observe his face as a whole. A mirror reflected no more to him than the windows through which he frequently stared, seeing not sky, not streets, not rain but images created in his own mind. He dipped his head in a fresh basin of water after the shave, using the same soap as shampoo and finally rubbing neck, face and hair roughly dry with one of his shirts. He smoked as he dressed again, then sat on the bed slowly finishing a can of Sweetheart before going out.

As he passed through the reception area, the barman-manager popped up like a glove puppet from behind the front desk.

"Oh, Mr Hodge, you'll let me know if you're staying next week, won't you?"

That would mean payment in advance at the end of the week. Another detail of everyday living Hodge had not had to think about for a while.

"Yes. Not decided yet."

Gupta was busy arranging an icecream sign outside his shop as Hodge's plimsoles flapped into earshot.

"'morning, sir!" he cried brightly, "cold again today." He seemed unaware of the incongruity of an icecream sign in November. "I hope your head is quite recovered now."

Hodge had forgotten about his encounter with the copying machine, although his fingers did sometimes pause, puzzled, on the packet of hairgrips still in his pocket. He nodded distantly and stepped into the shop to buy tobacco. It was this distant, gentlemanly manner that pleased Gupta – correct behaviour for a customer – and he responded enthusiastically when Hodge asked where he might catch a bus to the Green. He not only gave him detailed instructions how to get there but presented him – "free and without charge to a regular customer" – with a comprehensive bus timetable. He seemed reluctant to let Hodge go.

"So you are not a local gentleman, sir?"

"Not for a while."

"Coming from a long way?"

Hodge was nearly at the door now. He uttered a stock post-release phrase.

"Been abroad a while."

Gupta was excited by this information and followed Hodge outside.

"Really, sir? I myself come from abroad, you know." He giggled. "And now that you are back home, will you be starting up in business?" No one had used the copying machine yet. "I myself am in business as you see and –" waving vaguely in the direction of the icecream sign "– expanding all the time."

"Not decided yet," muttered Hodge, now stepping on his way. Gupta's cheery voice followed him down the road.

"Quite right, sir. You must take your time. Such important decisions . . . Good morning . . ."

On the bus, Hodge lit up absently on the lower deck. Instantly, he was reprimanded by the conductor.

"Smoking on top only, mate."

People turned round and stared, some disapprovingly. Hodge gazed, unperturbed, through the window. Not since early childhood had the opinions of others mattered to him. Looks, words, gestures, hostile or friendly, passed by him as though occurring in a realm separate from his own existence. A seemingly automatic valve only caused him to respond if the gestures could be useful to him. But, no deliberate rebel, he stubbed out the cigarette. He did not scorn other people's rules; they were simply irrelevant to him, unless he was directly confronted by them. Although he was capable, on occasion, of using them too.

The Elmgrove Project was housed in a converted crypt. A ramp had been made to allow wheelchairs access and inside there were trestles which doubled as stall counters and a small, sparsely equipped kitchen. It was mid-morning when Hodge arrived and piles of clothes and crockery were being arranged on the trestles. A jumble sale was about to begin.

"We're just waiting for the Thursday Club lot," said a fat woman, unasked, as Hodge paused in the doorway. Men and women stood singly and in clusters around the walls of the crypt. Some of the women had their eyes fixed impatiently on the loaded trestles, cigarettes gripped, bodies tilted forward as though waiting for a starting gun. But most of the faces were slack, the bodies sagging. There was a smell of old age.

Hodge edged in a little way and, leaning against a pillar, took out the butt left over from the bus. He felt weak from lack of food but it was a feeling he was used to and he knew there would be tea soon, possibly biscuits as well. Even in prison he had rarely eaten full meals, nibbling on bits of bread and cold meat or puddings, eating only when his body said it must.

"At last!"

The fat woman by the door said this as a man in ambulance driver's uniform trotted down the ramp, clearing the way for wheelchairs.

"Stand back, ladies, please."

Hodge, included in this general order, moved further round his pillar as large wheelchairs carrying large bodies began to trundle into the crypt. Picking something to focus on in the muddled flow, his eyes followed one old woman in a huge knitted jacket of lavender wool. Her enormous breasts sat in her lap like babies, limp and bundled, and her powdered face quested forward blindly like some creature from under the ground. An old man, abandoned now by the volunteer who had pushed him down the ramp, grasped his own wheels and guided himself alongside her.

"Awright, Eth?"

From close range she blew him a raspberrylike kiss and their heads went together like old fruit bumping in a bowl.

The jumble sale began as soon as all the members of the Thursday Club were safely down the ramp. Those in wheel-chairs had an advantage over the rest as, once wedged in front of the display they wanted, it was impossible for anyone to get past. However, it was hard for them to see beyond the heads crowding all around to the goods on other trestles, so the volunteers pushing them had to act as guides, calling out what was where. Voices filled the crypt in a blur of noise, driving Hodge to the furthest pillar from the trestles. From there he watched, smoking and rolling, knowing from experience that there would still be plenty left for him to choose from when the first excitement died down.

Hodge's vantage point gave him a view into the kitchen at the back of the crypt and as soon as steam began rising from an urn, he moved in that direction. A youngish volunteer, breasts bustling under a loose sweater, gave him a bright, busy smile as she lined up jugs of milk.

"Don't think I've seen your face before. This your first time?"

"Yes." He leaned his long, thin frame against the doorjamb. The woman turned away to draw water from the urn and Hodge looked at her bottom, eyes lasering through the thick material of her skirt.

"Any chance of a quick cup before the rush begins?"

The woman glanced back quickly at the odd, flat intimacy of his tone and was met by the intensity of his stare. This was only her third time as a volunteer.

"OK – only don't let anyone see."

He took the cup she offered and stirred in sugar with a dessertspoon, eyes on her mouth now. One of her hands went up to brush back a loose strand of hair, damp from the steam of the urn, and immediately Hodge's eyes went to her waist. She thrust a plate of biscuits towards him; a defensive, drawing-room gesture. He took a plain one, nibbling it quickly, and continued to stare. He could see her backed up against the urn, her body arching away from its heat towards him, his hand between her legs, dark hair tumbling.

"Oh dear, look what we've started now," she cried, looking past him to a short queue at the door.

"Tea up, is it?" asked a woman at the front.

The volunteer stammered.

"N-not quite. I was just . . ."

"But *he's* got one. Come on, dear, we're parched."

In the bustle that followed, Hodge edged out and went back to his pillar. An old man, tongue lolling out in a thick bulge, was unstacking chairs and arranging them around tables. As soon as they were out the chairs were occupied, rheumaticky legs bending, broad bottoms landing down hard. A few wheelchairs were making their way over, too, some pushed, others under their own steam. One anxious-looking old woman was wheeling herself towards the tables, packs of Christmas cards and a large piece of pink silky material on her lap. The material slipped off just as she was passing Hodge and she stopped and looked up at him, eyes appealing behind glasses looped on with string.

"Oh dear. I'm so clumsy."

Hodge was in the middle of rolling a cigarette and he did not stop. The pink material, feminine and crumpled, lay at his feet and the old woman, bending dangerously out of her chair, waved helplessly towards it with disobedient hands.

"Oh dear . . ."

At that moment the tea-making volunteer, who had been watching, rushed forward and swooped down to pick up the material. Her flushed face, as she handed it back to the old woman with kindly words, was directed briefly, furiously, at Hodge. He completed his cigarette unhurriedly, plucking off an excess thread of tobacco before lighting up.

"Thank you, dear," the wheelchair woman was saying, "it's a gift, you see, for a young friend of mine. I thought she might like it for a slip . . ."

The old face craned round curiously to look once more at Hodge and in particular at his RAF trenchcoat, as if it reminded her of something. The volunteer went on wheeling her towards a place at the tables, buttocks clenched tight with anger. Hodge mentally stuck his hand high up her skirt, and kept it there.

Daley

On Wednesdays and Fridays, when Julie was busy with her domestic jobs, Daley only attempted to work in the mornings, returning home soon after lunch and dozing away the afternoons. He would arrive at the riverside at roughly the usual time but instead of getting straight on to the boat, remain sitting in the van, staring through the windscreen at a fence. He parked with the river behind him and somehow turning round to face the hours ahead with only its sluggish flow for company required an enormous effort. If his sandwiches were on the front seat he sometimes opened them at this point, even though he had only had breakfast half an hour ago, and slowly, without enjoyment, ate one. If anyone passed by on the towpath he would watch them through the driving mirror, interest flaring dimly in his eyes if it was a girl. Sitting there chewing his sandwich and 'spying' through the mirror, he often had what he called dirty thoughts. It had crossed his mind to unzip himself but, fearful of being caught, he never did.

On this Wednesday, the first in December, he felt more than usually low. Leonie had been full of chatter about Christmas before she went off to school and Esther had been talking about it too. Last year they had had a chicken but this year she wanted to order a turkey.

"They're old enough to understand, now," she said, meaning Leonie really, "and we don't want them to feel they're the only ones not getting a proper Christmas meal."

Daley dreaded the day they were old enough to understand other things. Like the fact that their father was no good at anything, could not make any money; even that he had a dirty mind.

A girl in trousers walked along the towpath and Daley

thought of Julie in the boilersuit she wore for work. It had a zip at the front that went right from collar to crotch. Sometimes, when it was stuffy in the cabin where she was working, she would emerge through the hatch with the zip down to between her breasts. She was always wearing a T-shirt underneath but what Daley could not see of the soft shapes moving behind the hard metal zip, he could imagine. And sometimes she wore those black half fingered gloves, like legs in stockings.

Slowly, effortfully, he made the move from van to boat. He took what was left of the sandwiches with him as, when Julie was not there, he did not need an excuse to go back and urinate.

The heating system on this boat was almost complete and all that was left was the painting of the aluminium pipes and sealing of all the joins. An Aladdin heater minus its housing stood in the saloon covered by an upturned swab bucket with a hole cut in its bottom. From this broad pipes would spread the heat all around. Students, using the boats as cheap accommodation, alternately roasted and froze but, enjoying the kudos won by the eccentricity of their digs, rarely complained. Daley did not even bother these days to disguise the swab buckets and his painting was full of blobs and runs. Julie's varnishing showed up in sharp contrast, smooth and painstakingly clean.

By ten thirty a.m. Daley had got no further than opening and stirring a pot of silver paint. The river, matt brown, moved thickly outside the portholes and the sky, just within his vision, looked bloated with unspilled rain. He gazed around the cabin, clumsily draped with newspapers, carelessly strewn with tools and put the lid back on the paint. Slowly, effortfully, he made his way back to the van.

Using the towpath, it was only ten minutes' walk to the nearest shop, but Daley drove. He had only begun going there recently, and Esther discouraged the visits because the supermarket was cheaper. He told himself it was useful for small treats for the children, shying away from the real reason he was drawn.

Gupta looked up eagerly as Daley entered, then looked down again, with a little frown. He did not like the way 'this common chap', as he mentally referred to him, always came in with his bootlaces undone and sometimes did not buy anything.

"What can I do for you this morning – sir."

Gupta's dilatory use of the word 'sir' was lost on Daley, who stuck his hands in his trouser pockets and jingled change.

"Just looking," he said.

He sidled past a stack of soft drink cans towards the magazine rack, big body awkward in the restricted space.

"Take your time," said Gupta with a wave of the hand and, adjusting the mechanism on a price gun, began contemptuously stamping chocolate bars.

From the top section of the magazine rack two young women stared down at Daley. One, with a lot of black round her eyes, looked past her own rump at him, the white, moonlike sphere of flesh split shockingly by a whip thin fillet of black silk. The other, on whom his eyes rested longer, pouted at him with a mouth glistening like a lacquered cherry, ringed fingers just covering the nipples of huge, thrust forward breasts. Beside her, large letters proclaimed: *Inside Peggy Reveals All!* Daley wanted terribly to look inside, to see Peggy smiling at him from another pose, those great breasts completely uncovered as though inviting him to touch . . .

The soft tick-smack of Gupta's price gun came closer and Daley dragged his eyes from Peggy down to the middle section of the rack, stocked with weeklies on sport and cars. He reached for the thinnest of these, *Autoace*, and went to stand with it by the counter. Gupta was kneeling by the soft drinks stack, firing yellow labels on to the cans. He got up irritably as Daley pulled out a handful of change, leaving the magazine and a packet of gum balanced carelessly on top of the copying machine.

"Will that be all?" Gupta removed the gum and *Autoace* and made dusting motions over the machine. Following a mumbled request, he shook coloured sweets into a paper bag and dumped it on a scale.

"Twenty-seven pence," he said, taking out a sweet and twisting up the neck of the bag. "That is ninety-five in all."

Reluctantly, Daley abandoned his change counting and handed over a pound note. Back in the van he shoved *Autoace* into a side pocket and drove quickly to the river.

On the boat he sat in the saloon for some minutes crunching boiled sweets. He stared unseeingly out of the porthole while his fingers returned again and again to the bag, scooping up handfuls and shovelling them in anyhow. Then, as the picture of the big breasted girl came back to him and he saw once more the ringed, concealing fingers and the glistening cherry mouth, he stopped crunching and selected a single round, red sweet from the bag. This he held in his mouth as he went through the boat making sure that all portholes were fastened, both hatches battened down and the wheelhouse door closed. Satisfied at last that no one could find him out, he locked himself in the tiny, non-functioning toilet and took his penis in his hands.

Julie

Why was I so drawn to Ann? Was it that I was looking for a Granny figure, someone cosy and 'ordinary' in contrast to my own absent or problematic relatives? Certainly I encouraged the way my visits to her fell into a safe, predictable pattern. It was comforting to spend time in the aura of a life with unquestioned standards and rules – definitions – unlike my own which seemed so nebulous.

I made efforts all the time to counteract that nebulous quality, imposing quite a rigid structure on my days. I would get up half an hour earlier than necessary for work either with Daley or charring and run round the block. Not jog neatly but run, legs stiff from sleep, fringe in my eyes until my flailing arms had scooped past, with the suburban air, the transition from dreams to day. Then I would lie on my back in that small, creaking bedsit and raise my legs thirty times in the air while a bowl of sugarless muesli soaked in skimmed milk by my side. I did not imagine that either of these activities would preserve my health or improve my figure. I did them because I felt I *had* to; because I had told myself I would; because if I did not go through that small performance every day I feared that discipline in all other areas of my life would fail as well. It was part of a suburban survival routine and a way of combating an old enemy of mine: Private Nothing.

These days, the walk to and from the sauna is the only exercise I get but the ritual of the muesli is back in place after its, and everything else's disruption by Hodge. It is alarming to see that I was right. As one small discipline was abandoned, everything else, internally at least, went with it. Although celibacy, perhaps, is not such a small discipline. I wonder how much my little scar inhibits me now.

Ann survived by rituals too, although I think her reasons

for this were more solid, more founded in something she genuinely believed in than my own. I may be wrong. Fear of chaos or nothingness may have been her motivation as well. But there was no 'real' reason why she got up at seven every morning and went through the laborious business of getting herself down the corridor to the toilet, sorting out her wardrobe for the day and struggling with her wayward hands to pin up her hair, make breakfast and do her own washing up. She could have stayed in bed until nine, used the bedroom commode and waited for the warden or a homehelp to help her dress and make her a cup of tea. But that would have meant accepting that she was no longer capable of managing for herself. It would have meant giving in. And if she did that, what of her own life, her own will, her*self* would be left? I thought I understood.

The first time I visited her, when I bustled around so efficiently making tea, I could not help wondering if in fact she would have preferred me to stand back and let her struggle in her own way. But the seemingly endless trek just from front door to sitting-room was enough to decide me. I hovered behind her as, almost unbearably slowly, she propelled herself forward, the zimmer clomping down unevenly along the lino-leumed corridor and her swollen feet, ugly in too tight shoes, following at a shuffle. A piece of string looping on her glasses was knotted messily at the back of her neck, and her skirt was rucked up. There was a smell in the flat, a mixture of Airwick and underclothes and, already warm from walking fast outside, I felt stifled. I dreaded having to sit still, watching and waiting for God knows how long in that atmosphere, so I made Ann sit instead, being selfish but appearing kind. This established the pattern for later visits – except on Christmas day.

By the beginning of December I had been to her flat half a dozen times and it seemed natural that we should include each other in our Christmas plans. Having had my fill of post-divorce Christmases with family, I had for the past three years done nothing. Or at least done what I imagine thousands of other non-Christmas-loving people do – mooched around with a false air of scorn and independence while secretly feeling bitter and alone. That year was to be different. The sulky child in me was to be banished and replaced by a busy young woman

visiting friends and helping to bring a bit of cheer to an old
lady far lonelier than I felt entitled to be.

I planned the whole day weeks in advance. In the morning –
after an extra long running and exercise session – I would walk
to Daley's, a good hour along the river, and play with the children. I could not refuse Esther's invitation on this occasion.
Then, having somehow avoided staying to lunch, the idea was
to continue walking all the way to Ann's. Somewhere along
the way I would find a telephone box and make the necessary
Christmas noises to family. Every hour was accounted for; there
would be no lolling around the bedsit getting miserable. *Was
my whole relationship with Ann just another antidote to that?*

When I knew there was going to be more than a week
between visits, I would write to her. (Another ritual blown
apart by Hodge.) I am shocked when I look at those letters
now to see how cleverly I built up a picture of my life that,
although not actually untrue, was nevertheless false. I had
thought that would end when I started to see her face to face
but it did not. In fact, the more I saw of her the worse it got.
I began to understand – or imagine – the sort of person she
wanted me to be and for the short periods I was with her, or
writing to her, I almost seemed to become that person. I found
myself telling her about things that happened in my everyday
life with a sort of cosy righteousness quite alien to my nature.
This letter is an example.

Dear Ann,

    It was so nice seeing you again last week. I do enjoy our teas
together and look forward to many more. That Perkins & Day
fruit cake was delicious, wasn't it? *Almost* as good as homemade.

    Poor Mr Daley has been a bit down in the mouth lately so I
have been trying to cheer him up. Yesterday he accidentally
dropped a bag of tools overboard and it took nearly an hour
for us to get it back. Luckily, it caught on a mooring rope,
otherwise it would have sunk. I was quite proud when I
managed to retrieve it and we celebrated in the saloon with
mugs of lovely steamy cocoa. We worked doubly hard in the
afternoon to make up for the lost time . . .

Daley did drop a bag of tools overboard and I did retrieve

it, but the atmosphere on the boat was nothing like that implied – if only by omission – in the letter. What sticks in my mind from that particular episode has nothing to do with comradely teamwork and 'lovely steamy cocoa'. No, what sticks is the way I deliberately used my femininity to jerk Daley out of his depressed mood. Perhaps femininity is too subtle an expression; perhaps I just mean the power of sex.

It was not deliberate at first but it soon became so. I was leaning out from the dinghy towards the trapped bag of tools when I first realised that Daley was not concentrating on keeping the dinghy in the right place. Instead he was looking at the way my breasts, albeit encased in bra, T-shirt and boilersuit, were angled towards him and straining as I tussled with the mooring rope. With a look I let him know I knew what he was staring at and yelled: "Oy, concentrate on the work in hand!"

For a moment he looked away, clearly uncomfortable, then he giggled. And it was a very sweet giggle. After that we never went back to quite the same easy working relationship. Daley did not – thank God – start behaving in the embarrassing way he had done when I visited his home, but there was a new shyness in his behaviour towards me far more intimate than any of the bantering jokiness that had been between us before. And I noticed that he stopped referring to my current 'boy-friends', who had only ever existed in his imagination anyway, and when he addressed me as 'darlin'' it was in a strange, lingering tone.

I should have ignored it all, or left, or said something but I did not. I watched him furtively watching me and I admit I enjoyed it. Back in my room, when I stripped off the boilersuit ready for a bath, I even thought, once or twice, with amuse-ment that was not very far from pleasure, of how Daley's eyes would pop if he saw me like that. Yet I had no intention – not the slightest – of ever letting him.

Looking back, it is easy to say that towards the end of those three long bedsit years I was plain frustrated but I did not think of it like that at the time. One does not. When I moved in I broke off the last of a series of 'affairs'. Looking at the sexless period that followed, one might imagine that those 'affairs' had been serious or damaging. Certainly they were not

serious. For the seven previous years – sixteen to twenty-three –
I had more or less gone to bed with whom I wanted and when,
following whims. Whims that for a young girl with a warm
body in a world of hungry men are not very difficult to follow.
Things were, on the surface, uncomplicated. Under the surface
was – chaos and nothingness. Promiscuity was just another
way of combating or avoiding them. But it did not always
work.

I never wore boilersuits in those days but made a point of
emphasising all the sex appeal I had. Having done that –
presented an overtly desirable exterior to the world – I then
grumbled inwardly when all that seemed to be desired was
that exterior. At least it was the first thing that was desired
and therefore one must assume, in the eyes of the man, the
most important. I could never forgive them for that.

But, God, the absurdity of it all. I would spend hours
dressing up in see-through blouses, plunge bras, split skirts
and four-inch heels and later lie in bed beside some spent and
snoring figure fuming or crying silently because all I wanted
was a man who said: "I don't care what you look like. I love
you and even if you put on six stone and all your hair drops
out I'll never leave you." Instead they kept saying I was
gorgeous, the fools. Yet I was the one to keep things on that
level, making sure that strangers remained strangers. Because
only strangers excited me.

So, moving into the bedsit was the turning point at which
I meant to take a break from all that, as if just by not
participating in the hurly-burly of 'casual relationships' my
confusion would somehow cure itself. I read, I walked – I did
not lie to Ann when I told her I did those things instead of
'going out on the tiles' – but eventually the body, nature,
instinct, call it what you will, spoke louder than the caution
of the mind.

In the evenings, when I was not reading or writing to Ann,
I found myself looking at my work-roughened hands and
adding things like bubble bath and hand cream to my shopping
list for the next day. And after the bubble baths I found
myself doing pushing-up-sleeve movements of a kind that are
supposed to keep the bust firm and putting on nail hardener.
I even experimented with a curl in my fringe. The room, too,

received more attention. I had always kept it tidy but now I started adding odd decorative touches: attractively shaped winter twigs in a vase; a dark, bowl-shaped piece of wood filled with fruit. And I changed my sheets frequently.

But *would* I have suddenly – on a whim – invited some man into that so intimate domain; allowed some bulky masculine figure to dent the solitude that had by then become a habit, to dent those sheets, to dent me? Because of Hodge, initially uninvited, I will never know.

Hodge

Hodge told the manager of The Chalet he would be staying on there for a while. He announced this a few days after the Elmgrove Project jumble sale when he appeared briefly in the residents' bar at lunchtime. He bought crisps, peanuts and eight cans of Sweetheart and immediately disappeared up to his room again. The barman-manager raised his eyebrows to himself in the bar mirror and blew damply on the rim of the glass he was polishing. What the residents did in the privacy of their rooms was up to them, so long as they paid their rent on time and made no trouble.

Upstairs, Hodge stood with his back against the door staring at something on the bed. It was a life-sized drawing of a woman whose hair, body and clothes resembled those of the tea-making volunteer at the Elmgrove Project but whose face was a blank. The drawing was done on two six-foot strips of wallpaper sellotaped together and because the paper had tended to slip around as he was working on it, the body was in parts disproportionately wide or long. One thigh, for instance, heavily accentuated under the skirt, was at least six inches longer than the other and the breasts, one on each piece of wallpaper, were oddly far apart. This did not concern Hodge, for whom general feeling, at this stage, was more important than precision.

Along the windowsill, in addition to the row, now double, of Sweetheart cans, were a number of jars and cracked plates purchased at the jumble sale. These would be used as brush holders and palates when Hodge began to paint. The paints themselves, a carrier bag full of oils, were in the wardrobe alongside some shirts which Hodge had discarded as rags, having picked up several 'new' ones at the sale. The oils, at nearly a pound per tube – more for the larger ones – had eaten up all the remainder of his leaving prison grant and he had had to go through the process of claiming his DHSS money in order to have enough to cover rent, the rolls of wallpaper, some pieces of hardboard and two far too small canvases.

Hodge had been painting, on and off, for twelve years. He had begun when he was already over thirty, responding at first with only token interest to the urgings of a young art therapist during a spell in open prison. He had never talked much and, before the painting began, never evinced a need to express himself other than through the art of burglary. But painting behind bars, combining as it did for him a degree of premeditated exactitude with elements of risk and luck, soon became an obsession. At first he followed the therapist's suggestions, painting a variety of things from bowls of fruit to dockland scenes copied from photographs, but gradually his interest in subjects narrowed down to one: the female nude.

His most recent spell in prison had been his longest, a sentence of two years. During the twenty months he served, Hodge's obsession grew. The moment he came off work detail he took out a bulging folder of sketches and spread them all over his cell. Fellow inmates would wink and whistle at the nudes and Hodge made himself popular by doing small bedside pin-ups on request. But what he was after in his larger works was far more complex than a mere pin-up. Going over, day after day, the same limb or twist of a torso, he was struggling to capture the volume, heat and very feelability of the flesh; to make it pulse with blood unseen but sensed below the skin; to make it breathe. And to pin it down.

His repertoire of shapes and poses was based both on memory and current desire. The women all tended to be tall, dark haired and long boned and the pubic area was often exaggeratedly large. He sketched and painted them standing, sitting and sprawling but what came across repeatedly, whatever the pose, was an impression of accessibility. Thighs were never tightly closed and mouths – the only facial feature regularly included – were always a little open. Occasionally he would outline some object, invariably phallic in shape, hovering near vulva or lips as though to emphasise their purpose. One picture, of a woman seen through a mirror, one arm raised and legs parted as she applied talcum powder to herself from a long, cylindrical dispenser, was repeated over fifty times.

Now, in his room at The Chalet, Hodge was recreating the companions of his cell. He had brought a few sketches out with him but given most away. He no longer needed reminders of all those bodies he had imagined when it was possible to base his work on a real model. The volunteer at the Elmgrove Project had the kind of figure he was drawn to, long and supple but – until painted – distant and withheld. After he had sketched her with her clothes on he outlined the same pose and simply left off skirt and sweater. The blank above the neck became suddenly voluptuous with a wide mouth and hint of tumbled hair but otherwise the face was still a nothing.

He gave himself short breaks between sketches during which he smoked and dozed. While working, he took small, frequent sips from a can of Sweetheart but paused rarely to relight or roll a cigarette, a dead butt sometimes held absently in the corner of his mouth. He pinned pairs of sellotaped wallpaper strips to wardrobe and walls and spread one pair on the floor as well. Soon he was surrounded by mouths, hips, breasts and large, jungly pubic areas. He brushed against them as he went out of the door to use the toilet, trod on them as he stepped out of bed; they flapped at him as he opened and closed the wardrobe and curled over him as he sat dozing in a chair.

At the end of ten days – days in which Hodge's already gaunt features became gryphon sharp, his eyes bagged and red veined – he was ready to start on the first canvas. But his rent was due again and, in order to keep the manager out of his room, he knew he must pay it soon. Rolling up the sketches and stowing them roughly under his bed, he shaved off stubble which at times like this he allowed to grow until it itched, then went out once more for his dole.

More wobbly from lack of food than from the one can of Sweetheart he had had for breakfast, Hodge flapped erratically down the road. He approached the corner shop with head down, wasted profile almost hidden beneath a lank wing of hair. His hands, even deep in pockets, shook a little in the cold and his shoulders swayed. But to Gupta, grinning and waving behind a jolly display of Christmas cards, Hodge still looked like an interesting and distinguished gentleman. The interesting and distinguished gentleman raised a mauve, claw-like hand briefly as he passed and Gupta bounced up and down on his heels. Just that morning he had received a whole sheaf of airmail letters from his family and he was happy.

After collecting his money, Hodge went and sat in the High Street café. He had been there several times now and the same waitress always served him, hostile and unappealing as on the first occasion. To Hodge, an unpaintable woman was not a woman at all and his red-veined gaze went right through her, resting, as he gave his order, on some inner vision projected into the air.

"A cup of tea and a salami sandwich."

"Salami sandwich," she echoed flatly and her thick, un-paintable body moved away.

As usual, the windows of the café were steamed up and there was a smell of grease and melted cheese. This scene, recurring with only slight variations whenever Hodge was spending time in the world outside prison, was so familiar it was like a replay from a film. Instead of now it could have been '67 when he had just come out of Bryford, '71 after Rosewell or '75 after he had done his stint on Gibbs Island. Cafés, except when converted to fast food outlets, never changed. And neither did the people who used them. Hodge gazed into the steamy mirror of the window, watching the dimly reflected scene within.

There were two other tables occupied, one by a man reading a newspaper, the other by three middle-aged women smoking and eating Chelsea buns. Their conversation could be heard clearly.

"They say it were quite quick," announced one, a green scarf tied gipsy-fashion over rollers.

"Yer," agreed her friend, "all over within the hour, poor soul."

"Better that way, though, isn't it?" contributed the third. "Better than goin' on for days an' days."

There were nods.

"Makes you think, don' it?" said the green scarf and there were more nods and silence for a moment while they thought, sipping tea and tapping ash, nibbling at the sugar on their buns.

Hodge's sandwich came and the waitress's noisy movements

blocked out the women's next sentences. He sprinkled five teaspoonfuls of sugar into his tea, then, against a background of steady stirring heard: "What'll become of the house, then?"

"Yer. Beautiful house, Gormley Gardens, the best. No family was there?"

The green scarf looked knowing, took a long drag from her cigarette and blew out smoke through her nostrils. Hodge finished stirring and bit into the first quarter of sandwich.

"I heard," the woman said, "they're shuttin' up the house 'til the New Year. I also heard there's a nephew in New Zealand, *Harry* Wainwright. He'll be comin' for whatever he can get, you betcha. Never bothered with her when she were alive."

"It's money money all the way with the young ones these days, isn't it?"

"Yer. Vultures."

There was a pause.

Hodge took the second quarter of sandwich in one mouthful. The women pushed their crumbs around and offered each other fresh cigarettes.

"Mind you," said the green scarf slowly, "she must have left a pile. You ever been in that house? I did for her three years and I've never seen stuff like what's in there."

Hodge was on the third quarter now.

"Lot of fancy stuff, was there?"

"Rugs alone must be worth a fortune and *hundreds* of ornaments – gold, porcelain, you name it. And the silver, there was no end to polishin' that silver . . ."

Heads looked up as the café door opened and another woman came in. Cries of welcome, change of subject. Hodge left the last crust of sandwich, drank his tea and took tobacco and papers from his pocket.

As he sat smoking, still gazing into the steamy windows but no longer watching or listening to what was going on inside the café, he mentally traced a six foot long thigh on the glass. A rivulet of condensation dribbled down, adding to the image.

Hodge's next stop was a pub called The Threshers, a large, anonymous-looking place set back from a main road. He sat in there from one until closing time, soaking up the warmth and several cans of Sweetheart. Around him, people were talking about Christmas and eating pie and mash. At about two o'clock, Hodge, making up for days on peanuts and crisps, ate half a cornish pasty, wrapping the rest in a paper napkin and pushing it into his trenchcoat pocket for later. He took a roundabout route back to The Chalet, passing a number of shops with strident Christmas displays in the windows. He paused in front of a large card depicting Madonna and Child. The Madonna was dark haired and long limbed. Mentally, he stripped her robes away, along with Child, halo and face, and replaced them with phallic fruit and a full, hovering mouth. The pose was altered subtly to give a clear view of the inner thighs.

He stopped for a few moments in a telephone box after this, going through the Ws in the local directory but not making any calls. Back in The Chalet he made a note on the corner of one of his sketches: *Wainwright, Miss, deceased. 36, Gormley Gardens. New Year?*

Some days later a woman's foot, completing the sketch, smudged the word Gardens, making it look shorter, so that it might have been Ave. or Rd.

Two

Ann

The fridge was so full it would not shut properly and a pool of water was collecting on the floor. Ann, unable to kneel, pushed a wad of newspaper underneath with her foot, hoping it would soak up the worst. As she reached in for a dish of trifle base – still unset – a carton of cream bounced out, spewing a white stream from a corner it had earlier taken her ten minutes to cut. She thought a wicked word, hand groping for a clear space to lean on among the cluttered surfaces and a wooden spoon laid out specially to stir the custard fell to the floor, followed by a tub of glacé cherries and a fork.

"Oh dear! . . ."

Eventually she found support in the only unoccupied gas ring on the cooker and stood clutching it, feet braced wide for balance, until she felt steady enough to move again. There was not enough room in the kitchen for her zimmer. At least she had not upset the trifle base which now slopped about like a lumpy sea in its bowl, half in and half out of the fridge. She gave it a little shake, saw the first signs of setting, and smiled.

In one of the saucepans on the cooker were potatoes intended for a salad to go with the cold turkey and ham tomorrow. Ann had fought with them half the morning, scraping her own flesh almost as much as their skins. Another pan held the tipped out contents of her meals-on-wheels carton which, being too tired to eat at midday, she had let go cold and meant to have for supper. The third pan was full of milk, ready for the custard. Humming to music on the radio, she started to make that now.

As she worked, Ann tried to remember the last time she had prepared a meal for anyone other than herself. She had half hoped, in the spring, that an old friend might make contact in

59

time to be invited to her birthday tea and, with considerable difficulty, had baked a cake in anticipation. But the friend, silent for the last three years, had remained silent and the cake, eroded slowly by Ann, with only a little help from Freddy, had eventually gone stale. It gave her pleasure to know that this custard would be tasted by Julie tomorrow and anxious that it should be perfect, she stirred and stirred, ignoring the grating of the metal spoon. From time to time she shook the trifle base, reassuring herself that it was going to set and after pouring the custard into a bowl to cool, she made a search of her cupboards for something to use as decoration in place of the fallen glacé cherries.

Among the stacks of cans – a few so old the labels had faded to blurs – she came upon a packet of desiccated coconut. Dim, dim nostalgia nudged at her as she lifted it down, the dusty pink and white picture on the front taking her back decades to another kitchen and the vision of Mother's comfortable behind jigging under apron strings as she toasted coconut to decorate a pudding. Ann's brother, Alec, used to run into the kitchen demanding a taste before anything was ready and Mother's good natured grumblings were as steady and predictable as the sound of the trains that used to trundle by on the railway line across the field. But she always found him something. The cupboard was never bare.

Ann's cupboards, like her fridge, were always full to overflowing at this time of year. All day long, for weeks, the radio and television had reminded her that Christmas was 'just around the corner' and that it was time to stock up. The women's magazines brought by one of the meals-on-wheels ladies all spoke of 'getting ahead with the catering' and 'beating the rush'. Ann had no Christmas hordes to cater for but still she had been caught up in the festive mood projected by the media. The shopping lists she made out once a week for the supermarket that delivered locally had been growing longer and longer since as far back as mid-November. She had ordered packets of dried fruit, sugar and flour for a cake; extra butter, eggs and even, extravagantly, a bottle of ginger wine. But she need hardly have bothered struggling over her mixing bowl because not only the Thursday Club but also a local school having a Help the Elderly drive, had handed out free Perkins

& Day Christmas cakes. And there was still a pudding left over from last year.

The excess perplexed Ann and, although thrift made her hoard them carefully, she faintly, guiltily, resented the free gifts. Why was it always assumed that because of her age and disabilities she must always be a receiver, that she had nothing herself to give? Just that morning a box labelled Special Surprise Mini Hamper had arrived from the Friends of the Treetops Club and she had found herself going through the contents almost irritably. A tin of ham identical to one she had bought for herself joined its twin on a crowded shelf, as did a jar of cranberry jelly and a packet of chestnut stuffing mix. The Special Surprise was – another Perkins & Day Christmas cake. The woman who delivered it had not had time to stop for a cup of coffee, let alone share some of the food. But there was Julie. Julie would make all the difference this year.

When at last the washing up was done, surfaces tidied and trifle finished but for the custard which she would pour on shortly, Ann brought a cup of tea through to the sitting-room and sank into a chair, lifting each leg in turn to rest her feet on a stool. There were Christmas carols on the radio now and it was not long before they lulled her into a doze. Freddy, weighed down by quantities of crumbs left over from the trifle base, swam languidly near the bottom of his bowl. He was the only one awake to hear the radio's next offering: 'a thrilling tale of murder and suspense for Christmas Eve'.

In the chair opposite Ann's, the one Julie used, was a large, pink-striped paper bag. Ann had wanted to make a proper parcel but the sellotape had curled and twisted in her fingers and the string unravelled in kinks from its ball. She had sent off a card last week, a nice one with ponies and a sleigh bought at the Elmgrove Project sale. She had bought two assorted packs there but only found use for one, even when she had given a card to two of the people on the meals-on-wheels roster and several members of the Thursday Club she did not particularly like. One had come from Julie two days ago. It was huge, merry with cut-outs of berries and greenery and the warden had remarked on it when she whirled in on her customary morning visit.

"What an unusual card, Miss Evans. Did somebody make it for you?"

Ann had nodded proudly.

"Yes, my friend Julie. Here's her photograph."

The warden had glanced perfunctorily at a snapshot of a smiling girl with plaits wound on top of her head.

"Very nice, dear – pretty."

When she had gone, Ann replaced the photograph carefully beside the card. Julie had said she would bring her camera on Christmas Day so soon there might be another one.

In previous years, Ann had joined in the Christmas activities organised by the Thursday Club. These included special shopping trips, lifts to church and a big lunch on the last Thursday before Christmas. Ann had quite enjoyed the lunches but found the 'knees up' afterwards exhausting. Some of the old people had become rather loud after a glass of sherry and on one occasion a red faced old man in a paper hat had 'made advances' to her (and several others) and had had to be removed. The others had laughed about it but Ann had been upset. It had been nice this year to be able to say: "I've made my own arrangements" and skip the lunch. But she would be going to church.

It was a thought about church, cutting into a dream, that jerked Ann awake. There were still her clothes to lay out for the morning, her shoes to polish and things to be transferred into her best bag. And there was the custard. Tired but still cheerful, she grasped the zimmer and pulled herself up.

"Mum's got such a lot to do," she told Freddy in the special voice she only used when they were alone. She made her way over for a little chat.

"Auntie Julie's coming tomorrow. We're going to have a lovely tea."

Gently she tapped the glass to catch his attention and Freddy swam up obligingly to return her gaze.

"Yes, and lots of crumbs for you, too."

Then, as she turned away to get on with all her jobs, her right hand gave a sudden, involuntary jerk and Freddy's bowl crashed to the floor.

"Oh no, no . . ."

It was eleven thirty before she got to bed that night and her last thought before sleeping was one of sadness. There would be no one, not even Freddy, to say Happy Christmas to first thing in the morning. And the warden was bound to be put out over the broken glass.

"Our Father which art in Heaven . . ." she murmured. The prayers were automatic, a ritual, but in her heart, Ann was put out with God.

Daley

It was cold on Christmas morning and Esther had wrapped the children in double layers of socks, vests and woolies beneath their coats. Their small bodies moved stiffly along the pavement, the bobbles on their knitted hats nodding and each shiny-buckled foot planted and picked up with care. They walked in double file, Esther in front holding Jonathan's hand and Daley behind with Leonie, who was counting lamp posts out loud.

"Eighteen, nineteen, twenty – what's next Dada?"

Daley shifted his gaze from the top of Esther's round, old fashioned hat to his own slowly moving feet. The laces of his workboots were done up for once and they felt tight.

"Don't know. Hundred and nine."

Leonie danced up and down pulling at his hand.

"'s'not! 's'not!"

"Snot to you," said Daley, swinging her hand, "but that's how old I feel."

Esther glanced round, worry and warmth in equal quantities on her face.

"Could you carry Jonathan? We might be late."

"Yeah, suppose so." They stopped for a moment while he lifted Jonathan up and carefully wiped away a dribble from his nose with a thumb.

"Use a hanky," admonished Esther, but with a smile.

"Too late now," said Daley and wiped the thumb on his trousers.

"Oh you!"

"Oh me."

They both smiled.

In church, Daley went back to looking at Esther's hat. There was what the vicar called 'a good turn out' and Daley, who did not like sticking out on the end of a pew, found a place behind his wife and children. Beside him was a blind woman with a white stick who gave him a big smile when he helped her locate her hassock. Esther's hat began to sway in time to the music as the first hymn began.

Daley traced down the lines in his hymn book with a grubby forefinger, listening to the way the voices around him swelled and ebbed. Above – within – the even mass of sound he could hear his wife's soft humming tone and the quavery flutings of the blind woman. Somewhere behind him a man sang strongly in perfect tune; somewhere to the left a woman swallowed the end of every line. No sound came from Daley's throat but from time to time his lips formed words.

Halfway through the Christmas story, read out in turn by children from a local school, Jonathan became restless. Hemmed in by adults on all sides he could see nothing but legs and the dusty back of a pew. Daley could sense Esther's distress as she whispered to the little boy to shush.

"Not long now, darling. Be a good boy for Mummy."

But Jonathan would not shush.

"Dada!" he called out clearly, "Dadadadadada!" And then began to cry.

The small voice bounced into the hushed atmosphere, a bright, distracting ball of sound. People turned their heads and coughed. Esther, flushed under her hat, bent right down to speak to the child and the blind woman beside Daley inclined her head and whispered.

"Poor little soul. He's bored."

The Christmas story had got as far as the shepherds watching their flocks when there was a break for the appropriate hymn. Under cover of the rustling of pages and clearing of throats Esther turned to Daley and spoke.

"His trainers are ever so wet. I think I'll have to take him out."

In his mind's eye Daley saw Esther, small and red-faced, trying to creep unnoticed from the church with the crying child in her arms.

"Give him here, love. I'll go. Got spare pants?"

Esther's look was grateful.

"Yeah, here."

She fished a folded pair of trainer pants out of her bag and handed them over with the little boy. 'While shepherds watched' was rising to full swing but the clatter Daley made as he tried to negotiate the blind woman's stick still drew attention. Jonathan stopped crying and Daley quite enjoyed making his exit down the aisle. Looking at all those solemnly mouthing faces and returning knowing parental smiles made him feel comfortingly normal; a father caring for his child on Christmas Day in church. No one knew what he was like inside.

He changed Jonathan's pants on a bench in the graveyard. The novelty of this made the child giggle and squirm and Daley had a job to hold him still as he dressed him again, tucking in everything firmly so he would not catch cold. Then, balancing Jonathan, still giggling, on his shoulders, Daley began to walk.

The singing in the church faded behind him; there seemed to be no cars around and soon the only sounds were his own footsteps and the croonings of the child. Lights were on in people's front rooms and he caught glimpses of sparkling Christmas trees, women at kitchen windows, children running around, old people in easy chairs. He thought of his own cluttered front room, their own tiny Christmas tree and Esther earlier that morning laying bacon strips over the turkey, a cat's tab of tongue poked out in concentration. He thought of her last night, eyes shut and lips trembling as he tried, and failed, to enter her. He had stopped trying when he saw the wetness seeping from the corners of her eyes. Below, as always since Jonathan's birth, she was totally dry. It was not something they could discuss.

The icecream sign outside Gupta's shop had fallen down and its bright colours looked tawdry against the grey pavement. The front of the shop was dark, just a few strips of randomly placed tinsel making a dull glitter here and there. Daley peered in, Jonathan quiet on his shoulders now, and his eyes went automatically to the magazine rack. Usually there were several girlies on display, but today there was only one. The cover, its gloss diminished by the unlit window, showed a girl leaning against the belled and ribboned front of a sleigh. She wore a Father Christmas hat, furry boots and in between, a tinselled suspender belt and a smile. The tassel of her hat hung down over one nipple and the other was just hidden by a sprig of holly held up coyly in her hand. But her thighs, with nothing but a pole from the sleigh in front of them, were wide apart. Daley drank her in, groaning inwardly; a lonely man in an empty street on Christmas Day staring into the window of a closed shop. Not so normal now.

But it was only the front of the shop that was closed, for Gupta, in the storeroom at the back, had been going through his stock since seven thirty a.m. It was just after eleven now and he was having a cup of tea, pleased with his own industry. Yesterday, Christmas Eve, business had been slacker than he had anticipated and, tied to the front of the shop, he had become bored. So bored, in fact, that towards evening he had done something he had never permitted himself before. He had taken a selection from the 'top of the rack' magazines behind the counter and read them from cover to cover. Normally he would have reread his weekly packet of airmail letters at such a time but, what with the Christmas post, they had not come. Never mind, he told himself, better to just keep busy. That was why he was going through his stock this morning. Sipping tea and indulging himself in a KitKat bar, Gupta remembered that the magazines were still behind the counter and, mind firmly on business now, decided to return them to the rack.

It was just as he was about to switch on the lights behind the counter that he noticed the figure at the window. Perhaps he should have stayed open after all? But no, it was that man again – and with a child. What on earth could he be wanting here on Christmas Day? Then Gupta saw the direction of his stare and a knot of indignation gathered in his chest. Angrily, he pressed four switches at once, snapping on all the shop lights. The figure moved away immediately. Gupta, striding forward, glared after it.

"Disgusting," he said to himself and the word echoed in his mind as he went to fetch the magazines. Fussily, with pursed lips, he replaced them on the rack.

"And him a family man, too, with no excuse!"

Daley preferred to think that he had not been seen but he hurried all the same. Jonathan, enjoying the movement transmitted to his father's shoulders by the new speed, clutched at the lowered head and kicked out with his shiny shoes.

"Hey monkey!" cried Daley, catching a foot. "You're hurting your old Dad. Poor old Dad. Mad Dad. Mad Dad."

He repeated the words over and over in rhythm with his hurrying feet. The Christmas trees in windows flashed by and a family, all dressed up and carrying parcels, trooped down a garden path.

By the time they got back to the church the service was over and Daley's sense of guilt doubled. There was Esther, a lost-looking figure in her old hat and coat, peering round anxiously for him, Leonie tugging at one hand.

"Oh, there you are!"

Her eyes scanned his down-turned face.

"I was getting worried."

She kept looking at him, aware that something had upset him. In silence he set Jonathan down on the ground.

"Are you all right, love?"

Daley straightened slowly and, still not looking at her, said: "'course I am."

The children, excluded from this quiet exchange, began clamouring and the blind woman, who had just come tapping down the church steps with the vicar holding one arm, turned towards the sound of their voices.

"It's that little boy who wanted his Dada, isn't it?"

She approached and felt the presence of the parents close by.

"Merry Christmas!"

"Merry Christmas!" responded Esther, giving Daley's arm a squeeze.

"Mer' Christmas." He avoided the vicar's smile.

The vicar chatted to Esther for a moment, patting the children's heads, the blind woman smiling at his side.

"And how are things with you, Mr Daley? Nice to see you here even if it is only once a year!"

Daley managed a slight smile but said nothing.

"He's fine," Esther answered for him, still holding on to his arm.

Suddenly Daley shook himself free, picked up Jonathan and started walking fast in the direction of home.

"Yeah," he said loudly, addressing the pavements and the lamp posts and the sky, "he's fine. Everything's bloody fine! Merry bloody Christmas to the world!"

The vicar touched Esther's shoulder sympathetically before, grabbing Leonie's hand, she hurried, blushing, after her husband.

The blind woman, no longer smiling, stared uncomprehendingly at sounds.

Julie

I got to Daley's at about ten to twelve on Christmas morning.
They had been to church and the children's cheeks were
still pink from the cold, hair tousled from being trapped under
hats. I thought they looked beautiful and said so. Esther
touched them proudly. Daley's greeting was dreamy and
blank.

I had taken some trouble to dress up for Christmas, mostly,
I suppose, to please Ann but the children seemed to appreciate
my efforts too, especially Leonie, who came and sat beside me,
fiddling with my bracelets and stroking my dress. I had even
twisted a piece of tinsel around a brooch on my chest and once
or twice I caught Daley looking at it in a peculiarly intense
way. Esther, all quick smiles and bustle, wore an apron over
a 'best' skirt and jumper. Daley's workboots, I noticed, were
done up for once although they did not stay that way for long.
There was a Christmas tree.

The mirror that had been on the table when I came before,
was still there, although now partly covered by a paper cloth.
Esther placed a pudding bowl full of crisps on it, saying:
"Please help yourself, Julie. I've just got a few things to do
towards lunch."

I knew then that I was not going to be able to escape.
Daley's face broke into a sloppy grin.

"Have a drop of wine, Julie. It's Christmas."

I smiled, twirling a bracelet for Leonie.

"I'd love some."

Daley did not get up but groped around under his chair,
hands emerging, after some clinking, with a mug and a giant
bottle of cut-price Moselle.

"Got this," he said, pouring lavishly, "specially for you."
He shrugged towards the kitchen. "She doesn't drink. And I

70

haven't got any friends" – the sloppy grin broadened – "except you."

I wondered how much he had had before I came.

Jonathan, trainer pants bulging over the waist of girlish red trousers – handmedowns, I guessed, from Leonie – clutched the neck of the open bottle still on Daley's lap. Wine splashed over his small fingers and he shook them, droplets dancing in the air. Esther came in with a jug of squash and swept him up before he could make any more mess.

"There's orange if you'd prefer," she said to me and then, seeing the dripping mug held out in Daley's hand: "Oh, get her a proper glass, love!"

But Daley did not move, only patted his knee for Esther to put Jonathan there.

"Na, our Julie doesn't need a glass. You should see her on the boat. Slurps her yoghurt straight out the pot."

I took a sip from the mug.

"Really, it's OK." Esther wrinkled her nose at me sweetly and disappeared again.

I had made gifts for the children. The crackly paper attracted their attention immediately and Jonathan bounced on Daley's knee, stretching out his arms.

"Chuck his over," said Daley, "we'll open it together. Leonie can manage on her own." He yelled for Esther to come back. "Here, look what Julie's gone and done – presents."

They were glove puppets, with toilet roll centres as necks and yellow wool for hair. One was a boy and one was a girl. At first Jonathan was more interested in the paper but when Daley started making the puppets play a crazy game, popping up and scaring each other over the arms of the chair, he squealed and clapped his hands. Esther stood in the doorway laughing.

"You shouldn't have, Julie, love, you really shouldn't."

Sometimes people said and did exactly what I imagined they would do and say. "Got a tiny thing for Mum and Dad, too." I held out a box of homemade fudge. Hours in the bedsit stirring and testing. I liked that sort of thing, sometimes.

"Thank you ever so much." She put it quickly on a high shelf out of the children's reach. "We'll have some after." There was a box of Milk Tray for me.

I tried to imagine, as we sat later with plates of turkey and overcooked vegetables spilling gravy on to our knees, what their Christmas would have been like if I had not been there. A long time afterwards, when he was in St Brides, Esther told me that the year before, Daley had drunk several mugs of wine in the morning then fallen asleep halfway through Christmas lunch and snored for the rest of the afternoon. She had made the pudding flame alone for the children, Jonathan just a baby, and later, leaving a mess of food and games round the sleeping figure, taken them alone to the park.

"I knew there was something wrong even then," she said, "but I didn't know how bad it was."

Daley did not stir from his chair all the time I was there. Things came and went off his lap – food, children, toys – but he remained rooted, something dreamlike in the automatic actions of his hands and in his words. Even when he played a rude game with the puppets, making the children laugh and Esther blush at the undulating movements of the two felt bodies pressed belly to belly in the air, he did it gently, dreamily. To stop him staring at my tinselled brooch I took it off and gave it to Leonie, but she gave it to him. He sat there, tossing it up and down in his hand as though it had special significance. I took refuge behind the sofa, playing peep-bo with Jonathan while Esther cleared the dishes. We filled the gaps in adult conversation by pressing chocolates into our mouths.

I left as soon as I could, explaining that I had promised to be at Ann's before three thirty and that it would take a good while to walk there. Daley said he could give me a lift in the van but I was firm.

"She doesn't want to be alone with me," he said and I thought: no, I don't. We said goodbye on the doorstep, the children round our legs and Esther said: "Come more often." I said I would, not meaning it, and spent a long time thanking her for the meal and apologising for not helping with the washing up.

"Oh don't worry about that, he'll give me a hand later. He's ever so good that way." She paused for a moment, unspoken thoughts in her eyes, "He's a good man."

That simple statement kept echoing lamely in my mind.

Somehow the way she said it, coupled with the vision I had of Daley's permanently slumped figure and sad, sloppy grin, made 'a good man' seem a very lonely thing to be.

I have two photographs to remind me of Christmas afternoon at Ann's. She took one and I took the other. The one of me is blurred because she jogged the camera trying to balance it on the back of a chair and pressing the shutter with her palm. Her hands were always worse when she was tired. But you can still see what I was wearing, my expression and the funny stiffness of an arm raised in a 'cheers' gesture with a glass of ginger wine. In front of me, distorted by the wide-angle lens, stretches an expanse of red tablecloth with one oversized cake crumb on it and the edge of the trifle bowl. I had two helpings of that trifle, even though I was still full from lunch, and the custard, evidently heaped on after it had gone cold, was rubbery. Ann explained that this was because of Freddy. He had been floating, dead, in a teapot when I arrived. She said it had taken her ages to get him up off the floor and, although he had stopped gasping when she had finally managed it, she had not wanted to give up hope.

"I should have been seeing to the custard then, dear." She blinked behind her glasses, "But I couldn't leave him."

We had a little ceremony, involving flushing him down the toilet, which we called burial at sea.

The photograph of Ann is lovely. In it her head is held a little on one side, so that her smile seems almost coy and there is a girlishness about her old figure, frail boned but at the same time heavy with unmuscled flesh, that makes me realise that this person I tended to see as just 'an old lady' had once been young and perhaps, inside, still was. Take the grey from the hair, smooth away the lines, cut out the wheelchair, the zimmer and the smell of leaked on underclothes and there is a young woman, timid, eager to please and – wasted. Because (I suppose I believe) a woman is only half a being without a man. And here I am . . .

We exchanged gifts. I gave her a funny homemade bird table which we set up straight away outside Freddy's old place at the window and she gave me a pink half-slip, very long, with a strip of lace sewn round the hem. She had had it made up specially for me out of a piece of material she had bought at a sale. I put it on under my dress and minced about the room showing off the fancy hem, making her laugh.

We listened to a repeat of the Queen's speech and I made a second and then a third pot of tea. I kept imagining her on her own before I had come, struggling with pots and pans and potatoes and rubbery custard. I admired her so much, envied the seeming certainty of her values and even her faith in God. But at the same time I pitied her and thought: Oh God, if you are there (which I don't believe), please don't let me end up like this.

After most of the clearing away was done she asked me to open the ginger wine. I described to her what fun I had had with Daley's children earlier and she kept nodding and asking for more details. "Yes and what were they wearing and what was the little boy's name?" Then she said: "You'll get married and have children one day, too, won't you?" I thought of the way I fed her visions of me in the letters I wrote and found myself doing it again.

"It's what I want more than anything else in the world."

Was I drunk? I could not believe the words coming out of my mouth. In the odd, peripheral, game-playing world I inhabited they seemed far too simple to be true.

I made moves to go at about eight when Ann was beginning to nod off in front of the television. There was a plate of turkey sandwiches at her elbow in case she got peckish later on and she insisted I pack some to take with me too. Just as I was putting on my jacket she started murmuring something about a brother, or perhaps it was a friend. I was too tired to start talking again so I carried on buttoning, kissed her on her soft cheek and left. I regret that now. She so seldom gave me any solid information on which to base my visions of her past. The vision building worked both ways. I needed her to fill a space in my life and imaginings as much as she needed me.

It was freezing outside, a white film of frost on the pavement making my footprints stand out sharply for a moment and then fade. I kept away from the river to begin with, tracking through a maze of residential streets looking for a telephone box. Curtains were drawn over the Christmas evening scenes in the homes I passed and I imagined all the televisions on, a canned and carbonated version of reality keeping the big bad world at bay. And yet how real or unreal was the little world I built around myself, the visions I wove around other people?

The first telephone box I came to had been vandalised; the second looked all right but did not work. I would not risk using the coin-box at the bedsit in case shouting was involved. Marriage and children? No, even Private Nothing was better than shouting and schisms. Although not necessarily, I was beginning to feel, better than strangers and whims. Guilty and relieved, I left my family unphoned on Christmas Day and took the river route home.

The towpath was transformed by lamplight and frost. Earlier it had been grey, cold, drab, something to be hurried along, a route taken for exercise. But now, with the willows drooping their thin, spangled arms and crushed leaves, pieces of mud, stones shining like jewels it was – fore-echo of the dawn walk back from the sauna – like another planet. I sat on a bench for a while, the cold creeping swiftly through jacket, dress and Ann's Christmas gift worn with three folds at the waist to make it the right length. My body beneath responded to the cold by holding itself stiffly, secretively. I felt my nipples pinch up inside my bra.

Walking on, I listened to the way my footsteps rang beside the still river, sending echoes like pebbles thrown on to the other side. I stopped again, standing with body gripped and secret close to the edge, looking for movement in the black water and finding the sway of a reflected light. Silence made the cold seem deeper, harder. I hugged it to me almost as though hugging some grim, hard man. When I moved on again slower, longer strides broke from my thighs and I forced myself to accept the cold, open to it. I imagined the air freezing, expanding, filling all my empty spaces, and there was pleasure in the way my body was braced but yielding under my clothes.

Right then, I would have liked to drink a whole bottle of ginger wine striding under the stars and finally loll senseless with my head pillowed against some frozen, arm shaped root. But all I had in my pockets were Ann's turkey sandwiches. Too much cosy comfort and none.

Hodge

The painting began to go badly on Christmas Eve, the Madonna's body, with the hips of the Elmgrove Project volunteer, spreading again and again off the edges of a canvas and pieces of hardboard which were far too small. Hodge took refuge in Sweetheart. Twice during the evening he left his room, closing the door on all those smudged and clamouring bodies – two of the largest sketches were now fixed to the ceiling, one stretched on the bed – and stood shaking for a few moments on the landing before flapping his way down grimly to the bar.

The explosion of sound as he opened the bar door hit him like a wind. The barman-manager had a number of relatives staying and there seemed to be a continuous party going on both in front of and behind the bar. The second time Hodge went down an attempt was made to include him in the goodwill-to-all-men atmosphere growing ever thicker as more empties piled up and plates of mince pies were passed round.

"Sure you won't join us, Mr H.? Go on, come down for some turkey tomorrow. Have a drink on the house. 's Christmas."

Hodge's long, bony fingers plucked at a foursome of Sweetheart and his dry lips twitched in what might have been interpreted as a smile. He came out with a statement he was not aware of planning.

"Thank you, but I'm going to my brother's for Christmas."

The gap in bar noise that had opened when Hodge entered and closed over as he made his purchases, opened again. A small woman with a face like Barbara Windsor's gave him a sherryish grin from under the manager's arm.

"That's nice, going to yer fam'ly."

"Christmas," said someone else, "that's what it's all about, isn't it, *fam'lies*?"

When Hodge had flapped his way out of the bar again the manager said to no one in particular: "Funny, a bloke like that. It's hard to imagine him having any kin, isn't it? Goes round like he was born on the moon. No trouble, though. Wish they was all like that!"

There was laughter, a punched shoulder, slopped beer.

Upstairs, Hodge was perched on the edge of one of his sketches emptying out a carrier bag to find the most recent communication from his brother, last year's Christmas card, postmarked Dean. It was addressed to D. Hodge, 19004, H.M.P. Colinton. The message read:

Merry Christmas from Geoff and Bea! One of these years when you are footloose and fancy free again you must come and spend it with us. Cheers and all the rest of it! Geoff.

Hodge smoothed out the card and reread the message several times. Then he stretched out on the bed and smoked, narrow back cradled by the crackling torso of the woman there. The light in his room stayed on until five a.m. and through the hours he did not close his eyes but stared at and beyond the woman above him on the ceiling. Now and again an arm reached out for a can or he turned on to his side to roll a cigarette. The last time he did this he accidentally tore the paper under him, making a slit near the woman's knee. Briefly then, the light went out and he stuck his hand into the slit.

At six thirty on Christmas morning he got up, shaved, ate half a squashed *Kaboom!* bar discovered in his trenchcoat pocket and set out for Dean.

Two hours later, it was Bea who opened the front door. She was still in rollers but her make-up was on. Her freshly lipsticked mouth gaped.

"Donald!"

"Merry Christmas," said Hodge.

He stood quietly, hands deep in pockets, only his jaw, sharp as crossed knife handles, moving a little. Bea turned and called shrilly into the house.

"Geoff!"

Footsteps clomped down a staircase into the hall and a voice grumbled.

"Good God woman, no need to yell like that. Whatever is it?"

Plump fingers knotting a pink tie over a pink shirt stopped working. Round, pink lips under a neatly brushed moustache formed an O.

"Good God, I mean I say . . . Donald . . ."

"Merry Christmas," said Hodge.

They sat him in the front room beside an unlit Kosi-hearth fire. Geoff, uttering Christmas greetings repeatedly to cover his initial shock, touched a switch so that an artistically asymmetrical pile of logs began to glow. Steam rose unexpectedly and in the doorway, Bea waved fat hands.

"It can't go on yet. I've just been over it with a damp cloth." She turned to Hodge. "Sorry, we'll bring in the fan heater for you until the central heating comes on. We've got guests coming . . ."

The sentence trailed off as her meticulously planned Christmas day, neat as a menu, crumpled before the figure hunched in her best chair. Broken plimsoles poked from under the trailing hem of an ancient trenchcoat, ugly as rubbish dumped on her white rug. Clawlike hands began to roll a cigarette.

"I'll get you an ashtray."

In the kitchen Bea stood with fingers gripping the edge of the sink, breathing deeply. Geoff came after her and she made frantic eye movements for him to shut the door.

From behind the calm, upward trickle of smoke from his cigarette, Hodge took in what was immediately before him in the room: smoked glass coffee table; white leather sofa scattered with Christmas parcels; fluffy white rug on the floor. Dimly, he heard a whispered exchange.

"I don't think I can stand it, Geoff. You know he's always impossible."

"Give him a chance. We haven't seen him for years."

A pause then an explosive hiss.

"But what about the Fields? Drinks? Lunch? *What are we going to do with him?*"

Geoff's answer was indistinct but its tone was chivvying and firm. Bea's response was grim.

"I may never forgive you for this."

Smiling, they reappeared and Geoff told Hodge of their

plans. The idea was that they should drive over for drinks with one set of friends, then pick up the Fields around noon and bring them back for more drinks and lunch.

"But we thought you'd be more comfortable staying here. Holding the fort, so to speak."

Hodge was welcome to join them for a 'slap up' Christmas lunch. There would be a walk on the common in the afternoon; a video and light supper at the end of the day. How did that suit? As brothers, they had few memories of past Christmases to share. Only their mother's blood was common to them both and she had not kept them together.

Hodge nodded and inhaled smoke deeply. Bea stared at the lengthening cylinder of ash and willed it not to fall on the white rug. In the kitchen, while preparing the turkey for the oven, she drank a large gin and when Geoff asked her to fix his tie-pin at the right angle, she deliberately nicked his skin.

While she was upstairs doing her hair, Geoff sat with Hodge. A small electric heater murmured evenly between them.

"So how's it going?"

Hodge muttered something and lifted a butt to his lips for a final pull. Geoff noticed that he held it downwards, between finger and thumb, like prisoners in films.

"You're not *just* out, are you? I mean that would be a bit thick, wouldn't it, sent out into the wide world on Christmas Day . . ."

Hodge shook his head.

"Working."

"That *is* good news. Straight and narrow from now on, is it? Marvellous."

Geoff was unsure of his ground. Even as a small child he had always been ill at ease in the presence of his older brother whom he saw rarely. And whom his own father had once described, in anger, as 'that mistake'. The fire murmured and Bea could be heard moving about upstairs. Hodge made a small gesture upwards.

"Matures well."

There was a hint of a query in the phrase and Geoff let out a brief, over hearty guffaw.

"Well, can't complain. Kept her figure and all that. You got any . . . ?"

Hodge shook his head and said again: "Working" as if it made everything clear.

He started to roll another cigarette then drew a scroll of paper from his pocket and passed it to Geoff.

Geoff opened it out, went pink and put his hand over his mouth as though to suppress another guffaw.

"Phwaugh! Hot stuff!"

Hodge's lips twitched.

"Better put it away before she sees."

Geoff was pouring large whiskies when Bea came in ten minutes later with a tray of coffee and toast.

"Sorry to have been so long. You can't have had any breakfast . . ."

She saw the whisky and glared.

"Come on, Bea, love, it *is* Christmas," said Geoff. "I'm sure Donald would love a slice of toast, though."

Bea sat on the edge of the white leather sofa, hands and knees pressed together and watched Hodge completely cover a slice of toast with marmalade. He chased each bite down with whisky. Amber jelly glistened in the cleft of his chin.

"I'll get you a napkin," she said and, in the kitchen, gulped gin. She was flushed by the time they were ready to leave and had agreed to let Hodge peel the potatoes. As they left Geoff kept saying: "Make yourself at home, Donald. Make yourself at home."

Afterwards, he wished he had not used those particular words.

Hodge followed the passage of the BMW out of the garage and into the road. Vapour from the exhaust blew into the cold air and behind the shiny windscreen Bea's head moved energetically as she spoke. Geoff had on a preoccupied, man-at-the-wheel expression but he turned, just before accelerating away, and searched out Hodge's face at the window. They waved, Bea automatic and girlish, Geoff with an attempt at man-to-man. Hodge's right hand came up slowly and hovered palm outwards and fingers pointing straight up, just above his shoulder. It stayed there for several seconds after the car had gone.

The house was quiet, double glazed and Axminstered, but there was a constant muffled babble of gadgetry. The deep freeze boosted itself; the tumble drier thrummed and some-where upstairs a digital clock or watch went meep-meep-meep on every hour. Geoff had explained that he had altered the time switch on the central heating so that the house would be warm for lunch. Precisely on the ten a.m. meep-meep-meep there was a soft report from somewhere beyond the kitchen and a rumbling in all the radiators. Hodge, as instructed, turned off the fan heater when the front room began to warm up but did not take off his coat. The whisky had gone down by six of its seventeen years before he was ready to do that.

It was a long time since Hodge had drunk anything stronger than Sweetheart and the effect was considerable. His limbs, usually stiff and erratic in their movements, began to relax. One arm even floated briefly in the air when he switched on the television and there was music. His eyes remained expressionless, intent on something inner, but there was a temporary smoothing of the deepest vertical furrow in his brow. He remembered that Bea had said something about potatoes.

He stood in the kitchen, blank for a moment, surveying shining pans, crockery and bottles. There were dozens of small jars of herbs on racks; coffee beans and spaghetti decorative behind glass. Tendons worked in Hodge's neck and he warbled: ". . . a partridge in a pear tree."

Then the idea of potatoes came back and with it, thoughts of Bea. He conjured up a vision of her naked. She would have big, possibly dimpled buttocks, big, gelatinous breasts. She would only be paintable elongated, perhaps stretched out on the white rug, mouth only in lieu of face and somebody else's hair. The warble starting up in his throat again, he lined up fifteen potatoes on the draining board and sliced them neatly into chips.

Returning to the front room for more whisky and a cigarette, Hodge creased himself into a corner of the sofa. Threads of Golden Virginia fluttered from his knees and his plimsoles, grey against its whiteness, wrinkled the white rug. Beside him the wrapped parcels crackled, reminding him of the sketch he had torn at The Chalet. He was disturbed, beneath his superficially light mood, about how badly the painting was going.

The coffee tray was still on the table. Hodge reached out for a slice of toast and broke it, keeping only the soft middle section which he dipped in the marmalade before bringing it to his lips. Bright gouts of Old Fashioned Thick Cut decorated the sofa's arm. The remote control for the television was beside the tray and he picked it up, pressing buttons. Singing mouths on the screen were replaced by lines and blurs and then a sudden, crystal clear image of a woman dressed in a spangled leotard swinging upsidedown from a trapeze. Her body was large, tightly packed into silver. Muscles bulged as boldly as breasts beside armpits a little carelessly shaved. Hodge concentrated on her brightly pronounced, pleasantly swinging crotch, and remembered the turkey.

The telephone began to ring as Hodge was lifting the bird from the oven and, because there was no space on the table, he lowered it on to the mock-marble linoleum floor before going to answer. Sizzling and spitting followed him into the hall.

"Hullo? That you Donald? Geoff here. Look, Bea's in a state because she forgot to put the pudding on. Wondered if you could do it. Hullo?"

Hodge murmured "Of course" into the mouthpiece.

"Marvellous." It came out as 'barvellous'. Geoff was evidently enjoying himself. "Says it's in the larder – little room off the kitchen – middle shelf. Says make sure it doesn't boil dry. Everything OK? Got a drink?"

"Everything fine," said Hodge, "giving the turkey a poke."

Geoff guffawed, said 'barvellous' again and hung up.

Hodge poured more whisky into his glass.

The turkey, he discovered, after sitting through a performance of ponies and poodles and a girl with ham-sized thighs, had left an angry brown mark on the floor and he could not seem to find the pudding. The little room off the kitchen he looked in was full of brooms and the only thing on the middle shelf was a plastic bucket containing, not a pudding, but a bottle of gin. Hodge slipped this under his arm. The whisky would soon be down to its final years.

Finding the pudding became a major project and Hodge left no stone – or bowl, or saucepan, or cloth – unturned in his search. He lowered his thin frame down in front of cupboards and emptied them out like a child, long fingers working slowly, thin black locks flopping solemnly about his face. At last, in the dining-room, he was rewarded and leaving napkins, cutlery, stamp albums and a mass of loose family snapshots spewing from sideboard and cupboards, he made his way back to the kitchen, the rich-smelling foil-wrapped object held carefully in his arms. It seemed too large for the steamer waiting on the electric hob so he fitted it, by squeezing and pressing down hard, into the biggest colander he could find and set it above a pan of boiling water. Soon steam and the smell of moist, hot fruit filled the kitchen and Hodge returned, duty done, to the front room. It was warm enough in there now to remove another layer of c'othing.

It was as his head emerged from the long tunnel of an insideout Elmgrove Project sweater that his eye fell on Bea's token collection of art books. They were the editor's choice range from a bookclub – Picasso, Chagall, David Hockney and Ukiyo-E. Discarding the sweater over an arrangement of dried flowers, Hodge spread all the books out on the floor and revolved around them on his knees, turning pages rapidly. He was familiar with most of the pictures in the Picasso and soon pushed it to one side with the Hockney, concentrating on a crucifixion in the Chagall and a bathing geisha in the Ukiyo-E. There was a pastel stub in his trouser pocket and using the blank pages at the back of the books, Hodge began to sketch. He was drinking gin now at the rate he usually downed Sweetheart while working, sucking it in in small but frequent sips. Space and pastel ran out and he had to improvise, searching all over the house for materials. He had just about got the Christ and the bathing geisha coupling in mauve lipstick on June 10th of Bea's bridge club diary when the chimes at the front door tinkled and a key turned in the lock.

Geoff's face was first round the door of the front room but Marjory Field's came close behind. Both, one above the other, stayed quite still for a moment and Hodge, preoccupied with the angle of the geisha's thighs, did not look up until a sound, half giggle, half gasp, broke from Marjory Field. Geoff, the joviality etched into his features by the morning's festive rounds fading, said: "I say, bit of a mess in here . . ."

There was a shriek from the kitchen and Roger Field's voice rose nobly above its tipsiness to sound in control.

"Now Bea, love, stay calm. Damn vandals – drug addicts probably. I'll call the police."

Loud, animal sounds were coming from Bea.

"Merry Christmas," murmured Hodge to Marjory Field and quickly sketched in her mouth near Christ's right ear.

Moves were made. Marjory escorted Bea upstairs (more shrieks as they discovered her plundered make-up, eye-pencils blunted, shades of lipsticks tried out on the lace runner) and the men, Roger now in the picture, held a council in the hall.

"Point is," said Geoff, who had not yet seen his scattered stamp collection, "it doesn't look as if there's any *serious* damage done. It's all just superficial."

Roger raised his eyes upwards to the sobs coming from the bedroom. Geoff looked unhappy, nodded. Just audibly Roger mouthed: "He'll have to go."

It was about one thirty p.m. when the front door closed behind Hodge. Crumpled sketches were stuffed anyhow into his trenchcoat pockets, among them four five-pound notes pressed into his hand at the last minute by Geoff. He stood swaying in the cold, staring at the wintry skeletons of Bea's well pruned rose bushes, each in its own neat circle of earth between the patio stones. He wanted to urinate and began to open his clothes but suddenly a door slammed at the back of the house and something like a whirlwind rushed at him. It was Bea, hair on end, heels clattering and she was brandishing a parcel – not one of the ones off the sofa – and yelling. White stuff dripped from a silver wrapping, steam rose and Hodge staggered as a blob of molten icing hit him on the ankle. His hands closed automatically round the parcel as it was thrust at his belly and let go again immediately as the heat stung his palms. Bea's face before him was a streaked, senseless, yelling thing and he turned his gaze upwards and looked beyond it to the clouds.

Finally the yelling stopped and the clattering heels died away. A door slammed again and Hodge was left alone beside the stubby angles of the rose bushes and the boiled Christmas cake splattered on the patio stones. His eyes came slowly down from the clouds and he watched the steam rise around his feet

until most of it was gone. Then, stooping carefully so as not
to fall, he gathered up a large handful of the earthy, fruity
mess and moulded it into a ball. Wrapping this in a layer of
torn foil and a sketch, he pushed it deep into one pocket where
it bulged thickly and nudged his thigh as he began to walk.

Behind him a five-pound note fluttered on the ground
pinioned by a blob of icing and in the house Bea, discovering
as the last straw the loss of her secret gin, was about to tear
up a snapshot of a thin, serious little boy with long legs posed
on a park bench beside his chubby, smiling younger brother.
In the background of the picture Geoff's father, with an
impatient expression on his face, leaned smoking against the
bonnet of a handsome car. There was a smudge in one corner;
a strand of long, dark hair blown across the camera lens. Their
mother's hair.

When he had walked to within a mile of The Chalet, Hodge
stopped in a park by the river and lay down on a bench. The
alcohol in his veins had warmed and spurred him while he
was on the move and now that he was still, cocooned him in
a soporific haze. He kept his eyes open at first, enjoying the
phenomenon of his inner visions parading unconjured above
him in the sky, but soon he plunged through clouds and visions
into sleep, chin pointing upwards, ankles, one with a blob of
white on it, flopped apart.

The park, empty for the rest of the afternoon, came alive
towards dusk when a small woman with two children appeared. Hodge slept on and his figure on the bench was such
a quiet, flat, drab-coloured thing that for some time it went
unnoticed. The children, faces excited in the half dark, ran
from swings to slide to roundabout and back again, the little
boy following his older sister and the mother always close
behind, lifting them on to things, lifting them off, pushing
them up and down, round and round. After a while the little
boy got tired and the mother sat quietly with him on the still
roundabout while the girl raced around and tried to climb up
the slippery part of the slide. It was when she reached the top
that she began to giggle and point.

"Mum, look. There's a man!"

Esther called "Shush" and "Be careful" but her eyes followed the dancing, pointing hands and her breathing faltered when she saw the figure on the bench. Light from a street lamp on the road caught only a pair of feet in plimsoles; the rest was a long, indistinct shape but she could just make out a pointed chin. There had been recent headlines about stabbings in a park and the identikit picture in the paper showed a man with long hair and a pointed chin. Tightening her arms around Jonathan she called softly to Leonie.

"Come down now, darlin'. We're going home."

But Leonie was not ready to go home. She sat defiantly at the top of the slide shouting questions.

"Who's that man, Mum? Why's he there?"

Esther walked to the bottom of the slide and stood there with Jonathan, sleepy and a little tearful, in her arms.

"I expect he's tired, darlin', having a rest. Come down now."

"Tired like Dada?"

"Yes, darlin'. Come on now. We're going home."

"Don't want to."

Esther's eyes kept swerving away from Leonie to the figure on the bench. She saw one of the ankles twitch and, horrible visions in her mind, heart jumping, she pulled her skirt above her knees and started to climb the steps to the slide. Leonie wriggled and yelled, thought it was a game. Jonathan sat quietly now on his mother's hip, looking down at the dark tarmac getting further and further away. All three of them were at the top of the slide when Hodge sat up.

He was cold and his fingers shook as he emptied out his pockets looking for tobacco. Bits of paper and a glittering round object appeared on the bench beside him. He crossed one narrow knee over the other and a plimsoled foot swung up and down, up and down, trying to get the circulation going. As soon as it was ready he drew deeply on the cigarette and flung back his head, hair wild about his face. Madly, his foot swung and light from the street lamp fell on hollow cheeks and staring eyes. Esther, in silhouette at the top of the slide, gathered her children close to her and prayed.

"What are we waiting for, Mum?"

Hodge's head turned slowly, like an old owl's. He took in

the little group without surprise and, drawing again on his cigarette, began stuffing the paper back into his pockets. There was movement among the small, silhouetted figures and whispered instructions to "Hold tight". Then, as if in slow motion because the slide was damp, all three, clutched together, came down. When they reached the bottom Hodge, whose bench was not far away, said: "Merry Christmas," and began unwrapping the silver thing at his side.

Esther swallowed, trying to right her skirt without letting go of Jonathan.

"Merry Christmas," she whispered and turning, dragging Leonie, ran.

Hodge continued unwrapping the cake and, crossed legs still now, pushed pellets of it into his mouth. He was trying to remember whether it was Gormley Gardens or Gormley Road where Miss Wainwright's (deceased) silver would be shut up until the New Year.

Julie

In the bath, relaxed by the warm water and soft light of the candle, I found myself thinking again about Ann. At one point in the afternoon – annoyingly because the tea was just ready to pour and I was afraid it would get stewed – she disappeared for a long time into the bathroom. When she came out her nose was freshly powdered and there was a smell of floral talc mingling with the usual taints of old age. I wanted to offer to pin up a long strand of hair that had worked itself out of her bun but did not want her to know I had noticed, so said nothing. All through Christmas tea that long strand trailed around at the back of her head, sometimes coming over one shoulder as perhaps all of it had once, washed and shining when she was young.

I knelt up in the bath to wash between my legs and caught myself wondering if Ann, although almost certainly a virgin, had ever experienced the sort of feelings and fantasies I had then. What I imagined was that my hands, gently soaping, were not my hands but those of a man. The man did not have a face but there was hair involved, maybe chest hair warm against my back, and resilience of muscle, heat of flesh. Most important there was the imagined odour of man, pungent as hot wine, which made me take extravagant gulps of the bath's steam, breathing out slowly as, in my mind, his fingers found my second tongue and made it speak.

Sensation and fantasy displaced thoughts of Ann but, as usual, did not get very far and I flopped back after a moment, moody and splashing. When the splashing stopped and I was relaxed once more, I thought I heard a bird land on the roof.

I gazed up through the candlelit steam at the blackness of the skylight and made kissy bird noises with my lips. In the spring a quartet of pigeons had been regular visitors and I had tried to lure them down off the roof on to the windowsill of my bedsit. But someone had made a fuss about bird dirt so I gave up. I often thought that I would like some kind of pet. I still think about it. Maybe I will end my days trying to revive a dead goldfish in a teapot, like Ann.

If it was a bird, I mused, it was a large one. There was a movement and something skittered down the tiles. I waited for the sound of it landing on the roof of the garden shed four storeys below but there was nothing. Then there was another movement and a sound like something scraping round the edge of the skylight and I knew suddenly that it was not a bird.

Momentarily paralysed in mind, I lay as still as it is possible to lie in a deep bath where limbs float involuntarily. The candlelight and steam continued to weave slow patterns in the air and warm water eddied gently round my toes. I had just begun to understand that I must move, and fast, and my hands were on the sides of the bath lifting me up when the crash came.

It was not a violent crash but it was prolonged. I froze (sweating) in a crouched position as glass tinkled into the room. The candle guttered and, panicking at the thought of total dark, I leapt up – a foot sliding on soap, great splashes of water hitting the floor – and scrabbled for the light switch. The naked bulb, milky with steam, lit up a leg in the air. I had a view of a flailing plimsole and a thick coat somehow hooked under a twisting groin and then the whole body came through, muddled up with more glass, and crashed to the floor where it lay spread-eagled, head half-hidden under a cork-topped bathroom stool. Cold air flooded through the skylight, clearing the steam.

I do not know if he was knocked out briefly by the fall but I do know that the seconds before he moved seemed endless. It is the memory of those endless seconds that disturbs me now. I had plenty of time to scream, even to dash from the room, but I did neither; just stood there dripping, back against the towel rail with the long metal soap holder from the bath clutched diagonally across my body, and stared.

I had never seen such a thin man. His legs, flung apart with one knee slightly raised, were as wasted as a cripple's, with white ankles like tapers visible between the frayed ends of blue, once formal trousers and not quite matching socks. The plimsoles on the ends of those legs seemed huge, like clown's feet and one hip bone under his rucked up coat stuck out so sharply it looked as though he had a stick in his trouser pocket. His hands, the nails yellow and long, reminded me of the stilled claws of a run over bird.

Into the silence that followed the crash he breathed a short and at first meaningless phrase.

"Merry Christmas."

His lips, moving stiffly, were dry and pale. They continued to work, without forming words, as the rest of his face emerged from under the stool. His body slid a few inches towards me as his head came up and I dropped one end of the soap holder and groped for a towel without taking my eyes off him. My hands found Ann's Christmas gift instead, the pink slip, and I held it bunched against my front. Hodge stared at the slip and a deep vertical line appeared in his brow. He was half sitting up now, elbows propping him, the back of his head against the stool.

"I want to paint you," he said suddenly and as he did so his eyes glittered for a second as though backlit. He sat up further and pulled at his coat, looking for pockets. He took out tobacco and cigarette papers and I saw that his hands were shaking.

"Paint . . . ?" I echoed, voice mystified, strange to my own ears, and began to shiver. I let go of the soap holder and it clattered into the bath. Recklessly, I tugged at the towel behind me, spilling clothes on to Hodge's feet. He did not seem to notice and I wrapped the towel tightly round me as he went on rolling his cigarette, tobacco jumping around in his shaking hands. When at last it was complete he lit it with two matches struck together from a squashed box. He drew in smoke deeply, twice, and waved towards the skylight.

"It shouldn't happen to a dog," he said, voice low, slow and emphatic, "let alone a cat burglar."

There was a pause, then I said:

"Merry Christmas."

And giggled.

Three

Daley

Daley stopped working on the boats in the New Year. Something had happened to Julie and she said she was no longer able to help him. He could not stand the hours alone on the boat. He could not stand half an hour. And something was happening to him.

Esther went with him to the Jobcentre, in search of some occupation he could stand. He slumped as deeply as possible into a school-like chair, legs apart, head down, while she perched forward, both hands gripping her handbag, nodding and smiling at the man behind the desk.

"And you say you'd be willing to do more or less anything?"

"Yeah."

One of Daley's undone workboots kicked at the worn linoleum under the desk.

"Sweep your office for you if you like."

The man, instead of smiling, made a note on a form.

"Call in again before the end of the week and we'll let you know if anything's come up."

He also suggested looking in newspapers and checking the advertisements in the Jobcentre window.

Esther said thank you several times as they left. Daley formed his lips into a nonchalant whistling shape but no sound came out.

For four days he slumped in his chair in the front room, only moving to go to the toilet or to bed. Esther went shopping or to the Social Security office in the mornings and bought him his favourite pork-pies and white bread. Crusts and blobs of aspic fell round his feet and every evening she swept them up, crawling about with a dustpan and brush and feeling his gaze, gentle and bitter, on the back of her neck.

"You could go in tomorrow and ask," she suggested on Thursday.

"What's the point. Three million unemployed."

"You might be lucky."

"I'm never lucky."

"You mustn't give up."

On Friday Esther got up early and brought Daley a cup of tea in bed. She popped her head round the door again to wish him luck before taking Leonie to school. The children scuffled in their outdoor clothes, peering past her legs at Daley.

"We'll be thinking of you."

Daley took a swallow of the tea he had allowed to go cold, nodded and sank down for another twenty minutes' snooze. Sometimes he thought he would like to go to sleep for ever.

When Esther came home from shopping at the end of the morning Daley was slumped in his chair, several empty beer cans by his side. She could tell by the look in his eyes that this was consolation, not celebration.

"Didn't they have anything for you, love?"

He shook his head.

"Never mind. I'll make us a nice cup of tea. Are you hungry?"

Daley said no and then, as she stood up, "Oh all right."

She made him a big plate of fried bread with an egg on top and sat watching him eat it, nursing her tea. She had brought in a newspaper.

"There's an advert here for a carpet salesman. Looks like quite good money."

"I'd be useless. They'd never have me."

"You don't know until you've tried."

Daley balanced egg yolk on a corner of bread, added a dollop of tomato sauce and bit into it carelessly so that red and yellow smeared the sides of his mouth. He wiped it with a wrist then sat staring at the red stain on his skin.

"Carpet salesman slashes wrists."

Esther winced.

"Why don't I phone for you. It's worth a try, isn't it?"

She leaned forward, touching his arm as she took his empty plate.

"You're so unhappy doing nothing."

"I'm always unhappy."

Esther telephoned and came back triumphant. They would interview him that afternoon and if he got the job he could start next week. It was on a commission basis but training was given free.

"I'll never get it."

"Go on, you never know."

Daley did not get that job, nor others that Esther pursued on his behalf the following week. Before each interview she bustled around checking his clothes and dabbing antiseptic on cuts he had given himself shaving. When the interview was for a doorman, the ideal applicant described as 'of smart appearance', she even persuaded him to have a bath.

"I'll look a mess anyway, I always do."

"No you won't, love." Esther spoke through a mouthful of pins as she altered an old jacket. "Anyway, I bet they give you a lovely uniform."

To save hot water, Daley had his bath after the children had had theirs. He sat in it heavily with the door open, pushing a rubber duck around.

"Come in and scrub my back," he called to Esther, touching himself as she passed on the landing. He knew she would not.

"I'm just going to get the supper on."

He nodded to himself and idly prodded the duck.

"Doorman spins himself to death in revolving door," he said softly and sat on, eyes shut, until the bath water was cold. He did not get the job.

Four weeks into his unemployment Daley telephoned Julie. He used the excuse of asking if she could come back and work on the boats but in fact all he wanted was to hear her voice and to conjure a picture of her on the other end of the telephone. She sounded pleased to hear from him, asked after Esther and the children but said she was still busy.

"Busy doing what?" he asked, and when she replied, "A bit of modelling, actually, as well as the old domestic jobs," he got a prickling feeling in his lower belly. In his mind's eye he saw her taking off and putting on clothes at great speed; a lot of zips; panties and bras. He wanted to go on talking, to hear her say more about it but his throat had gone dry.

"Take care, then," she said brightly.

"Yeah. Take care."

February came and with it snow, bills, a dozen more failed interviews and Leonie's birthday. Daley had meant to make her a doll's house, had constructed it at least six times in his mind, but when the day came he had nothing to show. Esther, anticipating this, had made a doll's wigwam herself out of a pillowcase and long knitting needles. She had painted it in bright colours and arranged doll-sized heaps of sweets inside. Both children played with it for half an hour and then there were tears because Jonathan kept knocking the spindly frame askew.

"Outside, the pair of you," said Esther, mock-angry. She shot Daley a hopeful look. "Dada will make you a snowman."

Daley stood in the tiny front garden watching the snow gather in his open boots. The children, mittened and hatted, jumped up and down on either side of him.

"Make a great big one, Dada," shouted Leonie. She waved her arms around pointing to snowmen of varying sizes up and down the road.

"Bigger'n all of them."

Daley was about to say there was not enough snow when, glancing down, he caught the look of anticipation on Leonie's face. She believed he could do it.

"OK – we'll make the biggest one of all."

He sat down where he was and began heaping snow over his legs and chest. "Come on. Give us a hand."

The children understood immediately and Esther, torn between pleasure and concern, watched from the front room as, to hoots and giggles, Daley gradually disappeared. Her anxiety grew as Leonie started working on the head, piling snow on as thickly as she could and leaving no breathing holes. Quickly, Esther joined the group outside.

"Good gracious, where's Dada gone?"

This was for the children. To the white, shapeless blob in front of her she whispered: "Are you all right, love?"

"Mmmmmmn."

The long outbreath sent a miniature avalanche down the ski-slope torso and revealed part of Daley's face, pinched under its white helmet. His eyes, the lids pink and vulnerable, opened slowly and focused on Esther with difficulty, as though from far away.

"I was nearly asleep."

Esther had read somewhere about sheep getting buried in snow and falling asleep never to wake up.

"I think we'd better go indoors now, love. Tea's nearly ready anyway."

Objections from the children were silenced with promises of cake. Daley worried Esther further by saying as he drank his tea: "I liked it under there. It felt – I don't know – safe."

Another time, after the snow had thawed, Esther persuaded Daley to take the children to the park so that she could clean the house in peace. She had just started with the carpet sweeper in the hall when there came a frantic banging on the front door and Leonie's voice yelling: "Mum! Mum! Dada's gone to sleep and he won't wake up."

Esther stared at the excited little face, trying to keep herself calm.

"Where's Jonathan?"

"With Dada. He's sleeping too."

Still wearing her apron, Esther hurried to the park holding Leonie's hand. She was not used to running and her house slippers slopped around, threatening to trip her up.

"Show me where they are," she panted.

"There! There!"

The scene that met Esther's eyes was peaceful. Daley was slumped on a bench, mouth open, snoring softly. His jacket was across his lap and from its folds, under a loosely sheltering arm, peeped Jonathan, also sleepy but grinning a little Daley-like grin. Esther gently shook Daley's arm until he woke.

"Come on, love. Time to go."

Daley nodded, rubbing his eyes and allowed himself, like a third child, to be led home by the hand. When asked if he felt poorly he said no, he was just tired. Tired of everything.

In March the man from the Jobcentre told Esther, who had dropped in while shopping, that he might have something for her husband.

"Easy shiftwork. Starts six a.m., knock off at two." He paused and took in her anxious, listening face. Hope dawned there slowly. "Only thing is, he needs a reference, preferably employer's. He hasn't got one, has he?"

Esther began to shake her head, hope fading, then stopped. Her cheeks went red as a not-quite-honest thought crossed her mind. The man was busy fiddling with forms. Boldly she said: "I think I know someone who could give him one, who he used to work with – *for*." The lying word came out with unnatural emphasis.

"In that case I can arrange an interview for tomorrow."

Back on the High Street Esther hesitated. She had meant to go straight home and speak to Daley about asking Julie for a reference but she remembered that after the last time he had contacted Julie he had seemed unhappier than ever. Perhaps it would be better if she did it all herself.

She rang from a telephone box, perching Jonathan on the directories and struggling to find the easiest way to frame her request. Julie interrupted her half way through saying: "Of course!" but could they collect the reference as she was getting ready to go out and would not have time to drop it round before tomorrow. Esther said she would come as soon as she had fetched Leonie from school. Did Julie mind her bringing the children?

"Don't be daft. I'd love to see them!"

It was the first time Esther had been to Julie's and although she had known it was a bedsit, she was taken aback by how small it was. Julie, who had come out and waved to them over the banister as they climbed the long stairs, seemed much too lively and long-limbed to live in such a confined space. There was violin music coming from a tape recorder balanced on the wash hand basin and a kettle and typewriter were stowed under a chair. Most of the space was taken up by a bed, one half of it invisible under suitcases which seemed to serve as drawers. Clothes were hung from nails banged high into the walls. There did not seem to be a wardrobe or any ordinary cupboards.

"This is ever so kind of you," said Esther, meaning the reference, and Julie standing straight and tall, wisps from hastily done hair floating over eyes smudged with make-up, laughed, voice loud in the little room. The children gazed up at her admiringly.

"I've done three versions. Take whichever suits you best. They should do for any job."

The references were neatly typed with Julie's signature, extravagant and underlined, at the bottom. They all seemed suitable to Esther, to the point but generous with impressive phrases as well. She took one which included the words: 'trustworthy and reliable' and thanked Julie warmly.

"The only thing is, they might ring up and check."

"That's all right," said Julie, "I'll cope." And it sounded as if she could.

There was only one easy chair in the room and it took some persuading to make Esther sit in it for a few moments. The children, who had gobbled their way through half a packet of cakes – the only food Julie appeared to keep in the room – were now sitting on the bed playing with cheap earrings and a necklace brought out for their amusement. It seemed to Esther that Julie had changed since her visit at Christmas but she could not define in what way. She was asking after Daley now.

"Oh, he's all right. Been a bit down over the last couple of months but he'll cheer up now this job's come along."

Neither of them mentioned the boats.

"And how have you been keeping? We all miss you, you know."

Julie gave Leonie another bracelet to try on. Gaily, evasively she said: "I'm fine! Just been busy, you know."

Esther nodded, wishing she found it easier to talk. There was an odour in the room that was oddly familiar and she kept wondering what it was. A pair of very brief panties and a lacy bra hung over pipes by the wash hand basin and cigarette ash overflowed a scallop shell beside the bed. Julie did not smoke.

"I wish you'd come and see us sometimes – see him, really."

The words came out in a blurt. Julie's eyes stayed down, watching a necklace coil like a snake into her palm.

"Of course I will."

There was a little silence before Esther stood up, the ticking away of the moment in which she might have begun to confide.

"Come along, darlin's."

The reference safely tucked in her handbag, she started down the stairs carrying Jonathan as well as her shopping.

When they were half way down and struggling, Julie's door reopened and she came rushing out to help. She insisted on carrying the shopping all the way to the bus stop, holding Leonie's hand.

"I'm sorry, I just didn't think before."

Her mouth, fuller, it seemed to Esther, than it had been at Christmas, quirked to one side. "I'm so scatterbrained these days!"

She stood waving for a long time when the bus came.

Somehow, Daley got through the interview. There was a medical form to fill in and it seemed to him that he wrote 'no' about a hundred times in answer to all the questions. To the questions asked aloud by the interviewer he kept answering 'yes', trying not to make it a lazy 'yeah' for once. Yes, he wanted a permanent job; yes, he was interested in the company pension scheme; yes, he could maybe work his way up from Feeder Grade IV to Operator Grade III; yes, he could start on Monday.

The premises of Perkins & Day ('Bakers to the Brits') were several miles away and Daley decided to take the van which, as an economy, he had not used for a while. Esther was worried that it might not start and got him to run the engine on Sunday afternoon. The children played by the front door, making vroom vroom noises as the van spluttered in the road, Daley banging about inside it with the head of an old broom.

For the first time in a long time he felt stirrings of optimism. Once, on his birthday, Esther had given him a little pamphlet of encouraging quotations. He had dismissed them at the time as 'all just words' but now, clearing out *Autoace* and a stash of old page threes from the van's side pockets, he remembered something about 'Hope beyond the shadow of a dream'. Passing the interview had surprised him. He had, in however small a way, achieved something real and that was what he wanted to go on doing. He crumpled up the page three lovelies before the children could see them. Perhaps he could even take the family away somewhere in the summer now that he had a proper job.

For once, he did not go to bed at nine on Sunday evening

but sat up with Esther watching a film on television. She woke him at five on Monday morning with tea and a big smile.

Daley's optimism lasted until he was through the factory gates. He parked the van where he saw other workers pulling up and sat in it for several minutes, wishing the river was behind him instead of that great corrugated iron façade with double doors in it like huge black teeth and crowds of people bustling in and out. Two tall silos rose palely to the sky on one side of the main building, half lit by white outside lights protected by metal grilles. There were metal grilles, he discovered, on the wall lights inside too, and over all the windows. It gave him an uncomfortable feeling to be surrounded by so many busy little bars and the noise, which hit him as soon as he was through the nearest of the double doors, made his head spin.

He was taken by a man with a badge through several sets of swing doors to a narrow room stacked with laundry. There he was handed white trousers, a tunic and a cap, by a woman with a gold tooth wearing a white hair net. She pointed along a corridor to the changing room. For a few seconds, young, teasing laughter fluted above the din of machinery as two workers going off night shift fooled around, and the bright sound seemed to Daley all muddled up with the white glare of striplights in the corridor before it was closed off by the swish of the changing room doors.

He stood blinking under other lights, feet in socks cold on a stone floor. A man striding past knocked his shoulder and did not say anything. Other workers were wearing white boots or plimsoles and Daley felt self-conscious lacing up his workboots. But no one looked at him; no one said anything. There was a long, numb wait until another man with a badge – this one wearing glasses – stuck his head round the door and nodded for Daley to follow him.

They walked through grey linoleumed corridors and green swing doors until they came to a vast hall with squares of corrugated plastic dotted among the sheets of iron on the triangular roof. Something like dawn light filtered through the plastic squares, soft and secretive compared to the chain-hung strips lighting the work area from half way down the building.

Metal and wooden trolleys divided into shelves clattered past Daley, frightening as trains on a level crossing and his eyes kept floating up involuntarily to that large, triangular space of filtered outside light, something soothing in its church-like quality. There was a powdery, chemical smell and a sense of fine dust sniffed in with every breath. The noise was constant and shattering.

The man with glasses stopped for a moment to run his finger down a metal clip-sheet and tapped a biro inaudibly against his teeth. He said something and Daley shook his head to indicate he could not hear.

"Panbread," the man shouted, thick glasses thrusting close, "you'll be on tinning up."

It was like a foreign language. Daley did not understand but nodded. The man walked on.

They passed machines that wrapped and sliced and the men who fed them. Wrappers and slices littered the floor and the men's white shod feet moved carelessly among them, their hands, grey-white and naked-looking, working absently. Daley, gaping as he passed, noticed the peculiar uniformity of their complexions; faces pale and soft as maggots but grey, the faintest shadow of stubble showing up like scratches on a baby's skin. The noise and the lights and the immensity of the machines seemed to bounce at him and the floor did not seem quite still. He was relieved when they stopped again.

"Roll oven!" yelled the man and waved an arm at what looked like a huge wheel-less caravan, all yellow and silver with levers and glass dials on the side. There was a dirty metal slit at the front which opened to admit the baking trays. Steam belched out of presses nearby. They moved on.

"Cooler!"

A seven-inch thick door was flung open and a blast of chilled air came out. Vapour on the wrapped rolls inside showed how cold it was in there. Daley nodded. His hands, holding nothing but his feelings, were beginning to feel like paws and the blasting, juddering noise of the cooler close up made him want to cover both ears and eyes. A little way away they stopped again and did not move on.

"Panbread!" shouted the man for the second time.

They stood close together beside what looked like a truncated silo and the man pointed slowly from this to another machine a short conveyor belt away.

"Dough mixed in there," he instructed, still shouting, "goes into divider."

The divider made a sharp, regular noise, rhythmic above the blast of the cooler. Round blobs of dough came out of it and were spun lightly, like icecream in a cone, before vanishing along another short length of belt into a prover. A weight-checker stared blankly at Daley and, without looking, took a lump of dough out of the prover and dumped it on a scale. Briefly, his eyes registered the weight and the dough was tossed back again. An arm of conveyor belt carried the lumps of dough, swollen from proving, into a moulder from which they emerged bomb-nosed and were passed under a roller dripping with vegetable emulsion.

At this point the man with glasses nudged Daley's elbow and they moved round to the great, square mouth of a second prover. A belt running at just below waist level took a continuous stream of dough pieces past that great mouth and the job of the man in front of it was to pick up the pieces, two at a time, and stack them into the tins in which they were to be baked. This was called tinning up. This was to be Daley's job.

For ten minutes he watched the worker whose place he was to take and was then allowed a turn. A few yards behind him hot bread was being taken from an oven by a youth with his hair tied back in a ponytail, but facing his conveyor belt, Daley could see no one. Pieces of dough, shiny with emulsion, came at him in clusters and he tried to imitate the casual, floppy action of the wrists of the worker who had been doing the job before. Awkwardly, he grabbed the dough and its warmth and stickiness felt repugnant to his palms. But he managed to get two pieces into two tins and looked round for approval. The man with glasses was chatting in a bawling way to the weight-checker but he waved for Daley to carry on. The next cluster of pieces was almost upon him now and he had to take a step sideways to stop them falling off the end of the belt. Clumsily, he threw them at the tins revolving in the mouth of the prover and reached for more. After five minutes the first worker shouldered him to one side and demonstrated again. Daley, greasy hands open by his sides, watched and nodded. The man with glasses watched and nodded at him.

All morning he took turns with the other worker and by mealbreak he was beginning to get the hang of it. Still the action of his hands tended to lack rhythm and several pieces of dough had rolled off the end of the belt into a waste bin, but most were landing squarely in the tins now and he had learned how not to tear them as he picked them up.

After the break he was left to carry on alone for a while and it was then that he began to feel the strange, loud isolation of the job. All around him was grinding noise and sometimes shouts without sense but he could see nothing except the conveyor belt and the clusters of dough coming endlessly towards him. All small sounds obliterated by the general din, he watched his own hands lift the dough and drop it silently into the tins. The feeling of it was no longer repugnant and now, whenever there was a short break for machinery to be cleaned, his hands felt uncomfortably redundant. The vegetable emulsion left a thick film of grease on his skin and clogged under his nails. Standing slack-armed and silent during those breaks he felt an odd intensity in the waiting and moved like an automaton to his place as soon as the conveyor belt began rolling again.

When he got home that afternoon and Esther asked how the day had gone he shrugged and said: "All right."

But she was worried by his glazed look and commented on his pallor.

"They're all like that," he said and waved a hand, dredging up a grin for the children, "doughmen. Dada's a doughman now."

Leonie giggled.

"Snowman! Doorman! Doughman!"

Ann

The short winter days were long for Ann; the nights like years. In the mornings as she struggled through the awkward business of washing and dressing and pouring, with jerking hand, the milk on to her cereal, she would sometimes find angry words exploding on an outbreath.

"Bother!"

In the past she had managed to keep her irritation in her head but it seemed to be more difficult now. And the words were becoming stronger.

"Blast it!" as toilet paper slipped from her fingers and lay in an ugly, unreachable scrumple on the floor; "Damn!" as a thickened nail caught on the one stocking she wore on the leg with the less painful vein; once even: "Oh God!" as, getting up hurriedly to switch channels when there was violence on television, she knocked over her meals-on-wheels lunch and a grey mess of fish and potatoes, dotted with green, slopped like vomit on the carpet and all down her bandaged shin. The worst thing about that was that it took her a long time to reach the television and she could not help seeing some of the violence. Roars of prompted laughter and funny hats on the other channel failed to drown it out of her mind and she went to bed that night knowing she was going to have one of her four a.m. sessions.

Ann tended to wake early all year round but in the spring and summer it did not matter. It was pleasant to lie in a light doze, warm from sleep, and wait for the first bird sounds, the gentle arrival of dawn light through the curtains and the comforting sotto voce buzz of an early milk van on its rounds. It was so different when she woke at three or four a.m. with winter darkness locked around her like a clamp, her hot water bottle gone tepid and her hands too afraid to grope for the light switch; too afraid not to. Visions came to her then of things she had heard on the news or read about in the papers: muggings, stabbings, murders, rapes; 'Woman of eighty strangled in her bed'; 'Pensioner smothered'.

For perhaps an hour she would lie without moving at all, eyes open on blackness, a pain in her throat she did not like to think about, fear in every limb. Then, like a clumsy, sightless animal, one hand would fumble out of the blankets and try to land softly on the light switch. Usually she missed and the floating arm would catch other things on the bedside table – a glass of water, her old clock, a medicine spoon. Any noise she made alarmed her, as though she suspected someone was hidden in the room and just waiting for a sign of life to spring. When at last the light was on she would half sit up, reach for her glasses and shake several pain killers from a bottle into her palm, nibbling them down with difficulty and afterwards holding the water glass to her lips with both shaking hands. The visions would go on.

She had no idea how muggers and stranglers got into places that were locked up but she was sure they could. Once, on television, she had seen the profile of a man with expressionless eyes filing silently at a window. The face and the cleverly working hands kept coming back to her and she imagined the eyes remaining expressionless as he lifted a pillow to smother her. She dreaded the length of time it might take to die.

At the Thursday Club one day, when some of the others were discussing a recent murder, she made an attempt to talk about her fears.

"Yes," everyone agreed, "it's terrible. Nobody's safe these days. And by the time the police come, it's too late."

They were all afraid, yet they seemed to delight in telling each other horror stories and this Ann could not stand. She was in her wheelchair at the time and desperate to escape the terrifying phrases – 'bashed her face in with a flash-light'; 'gagged with a bandage' – she caught hold of her own wheels and pushed frantically backwards, almost knocking over a table of tea things. The faces of the others turned curiously upon her with the unnerving openness of the old and she smiled apologetically, ducking her already bent head.

It had been no more soothing the one time she had tried to discuss it with Julie.

"I don't like it when the days draw in, do you, dear? I get nervous at night – imagine things."

Julie had responded at once in her explosive way.

"I know what you mean. In fact – I know it sounds daft – but I keep a hammer by my bed."

She had looked as though she meant to go on but, glancing at Ann's face, had checked herself.

"But you shouldn't have to worry here. After all, the warden is always on the premises. It's not as if you were completely alone."

Ann had said: "I'm sure you're right, dear, and I'm just being silly," but in her heart she knew the warden was no protection. What about that time Mrs Winton in flat fourteen had broken her hip and lain for hours pressing her buzzer before help came? She had a vision of herself doing that, pressing and pressing the little button with no answer coming while some creature in a mask stood over her, something heavy in his hand. Julie had begun to talk about the punishments that should be meted out to such people and what caused them to do what they did. But Ann could not think about it that distantly – sociologically, as Julie put it – and she had just nodded and murmured in reply. Fear was a very private thing.

Christmas had been a distraction – a happy one this year with Julie around – but there was the usual flat period after-wards when there seemed to be nothing to look forward to besides programmes on the radio and television; nothing to break up the days. Ann had hoped she might see Julie again over New Year but there was no word.

In the daytime, between favourite programmes, she pulled her chair close to a radiator and let her eyelids droop. In that half waking, half sleeping state her own dead dreams of the past and dreams she might live vicariously through Julie in the future seemed to interweave. From time to time one of her hands would reach out and pat underwear airing on the radiator, thick, shapeless garments designed never to be seen. In her mind was a slender young woman with long hair wearing a pretty cotton frock. She was standing in a field with buttercups brushing her shins and waving to a young man.

Ann had stood waving like that once, although not in a field. Her hair had been long, but her figure more 'well-upholstered' than slender. Not that her brother Alec Graham. She had never been sure, that last time she had seen them off at the station, who her final wave – a kiss carried on the fingertips – had been for. Both looked so handsome, laughing and joking in their smart uniforms – heavy blue trenchcoats worn lightly on young shoulders – and the delicious embarrassment she had felt when Graham looked into her eyes was only just beginning. It had never had a chance to develop into anything other than a sensation of something missed but never experienced. Over the years it had become muddled up with things she had seen on television, other people's imagined feelings witnessed and then cherished as her own. But although the buttercups may have only existed in her mind and the pretty kiss was borrowed from some film, the young men had lived and died and the frock, the only solid thing left from the memory, was real. She still had it somewhere, wrapped in tissue.

January brought thirty-one endless nights, dark days filled with domestic struggles, television and dreams and one letter from Julie. In February there was a hurried – although significant – visit and then, one day in March when Ann had just settled down in her chair with an after lunch coffee, another letter came.

Dear Ann,

Again I must apologise for not coming to see you lately. The new job I mentioned is taking up a lot of time and I find I get so tired I haven't much energy left even to write. But that does not mean I don't think about you and wonder how you are getting on. We must certainly get together for your birthday next month. Will you be inviting Miss Abbot and the friend you mentioned? It would be nice to make up a little party for tea.

The gentleman I spoke of last time we met has continued to be, as they say, *very attentive*.

Here Ann paused in her reading and smiled, any resentment she had felt at Julie's recent neglect wiped away. She had

Ann

suspected that the sudden infrequency of visits and letters had more to do with this gentleman friend than any job. It had given her a strange little rush of pleasure when, at tea in February, Julie had said, not looking quite straight at her: "I've got something to tell you. It's rather exciting."

Ann had leaned forward, the hand that jerked most uncontrollably held carefully away from the china, and said: "Wait, dear. Let me guess."

Julie had looked at her then, surprised.

"I think you've been seeing a gentleman. Have I got it right?"

Julie's mouth had quirked at the word 'gentleman' and she had flushed.

"You clever thing! Shall I tell you about him?"

Ann's response had been keen.

"Well, to begin with his name is H . . ." Here Julie had cleared her throat and sat up straighter. ". . . Mr Donald Hodge."

She had not in fact said a great deal about Mr Hodge other than that they went for long, wintry walks together and he sometimes took her out to lunch. Eager to learn more, Ann read on.

. . . We have been out to lunch quite a few more times and sometimes we have a glass of wine together too. Did I tell you he is rather a lot older than me? I don't think that matters though. It is nice to be with someone who has more experience of the world than I have.

His hair is black and probably longer than you would approve of (!) but I think it suits him and he has lovely long artistic hands. I have lost weight since we started going out (must be the excitement!) but I keep telling him he should put some on. Although his thinness is really quite distinguished-looking. He has recently gone on to working at nights so if we meet it is usually for tea now as he has to go to bed during the day. Sometimes he brings me presents of delicious little cakes or meringues. I must bring some to you next time I come.

By the way, I'm already planning to make you a specially good birthday cake. You must let me know if you would prefer fruit or sponge . . .

III

The rest of Julie's letter was about a leak in her bathroom and a skirt she had recently bought. After skimming through it quickly Ann went back to the paragraph about Mr Hodge. She wondered how much older than Julie he was. It would not be so nice if he had been married before, although perhaps it would not matter. There was so much of that sort of thing around nowadays. She heard about it on the radio, saw it on the television. Thinking about the radio made her look at the time. Not long before *The Archers*. To make sure she did not doze off completely she switched the radio on low, knowing she would 'come to' when the theme music began. Then, eyelids drooping again, she gave herself up to another ten minutes of dreams.

She liked the description of Mr Hodge's hands as 'artistic' but she hoped he was sensible, too, not flighty as she understood some artistic types to be. It would be lovely if Julie would bring him to tea some time. A picture of the table popped into Ann's mind: salmon sandwiches; chocolate biscuits; swiss roll. The only thing that jarred was the image of Mr Hodge's long hair. But perhaps that, like his thinness, was 'distinguished-looking' too. At least it was not grey. An old saying ran through her head, making her smile: 'Better to be an old man's fancy than a young man's slave.' She must remember to include that (with an exclamation mark) in her next letter to Julie. She was still smiling to herself when *The Archers* began.

She listened to the programme with eyes open, one hand holding Julie's letter in her lap, the other resting on the arm of the chair but moving occasionally to touch the glasses on her chest. Her gaze was directed towards the window and, whenever a robin landed on the homemade bird table outside, her eyes focused for a moment and she made cheep-cheep noises but most of the time her look was distant and what she saw was inside her head. She had a mental picture of each one of the characters in the serial and saw them clearly going through all the actions indicated by their speech. When they met to gossip in the village shop Ann was there with them, a basket on her arm. When the farmers stamped their feet and said "brr" as they worked in their yards in the mornings, she shivered with them. Even when that good-for-nothing Grundy boy revealed the latest of his work-dodging schemes over a pint of Shires in the pub, Ann was somehow there.

Sometimes she dreamed about living in a village like Ambridge. She would have a little cottage and Granny Perkins and that kind Mrs Archer would drop in for tea. But it was nice to have something closer to home to dream about now: Mr Hodge asking Julie to marry him; the two of them coming to see her and take her out in the car he was bound to have; 'grandchildren'. This last was the sweetest dream of all. She would not be able to do any knitting for the babies now that her hands were so bad but she could always pick up little things for them at the Thursday Club or when there were sales on at the Elmgrove Project. Or she could cut out coupons from the magazines brought by one of the meals-on-wheels ladies and send off for things . . .

When the nurse came to change the support bandage on her leg that afternoon, Ann was asleep, the radio still on. Startled, she woke with the woman's face looming near.

"Julie, is that you?"

It was a disappointment to see the uniform but at least the nurse was one of her favourites, who gave five minutes of her time after she had done the bandage and chatted while she worked. Today she talked about her sister's family in Australia and Ann smiled as she listened, another, as yet non-existent family in her head. Just before leaving the nurse said: "And what about that pain you told me about last time, Miss Evans? Have you had any more of it?"

Ann's hand went involuntarily to the front of her cardigan and she touched her throat.

"No, dear," she lied. "I don't think it can have been anything very serious."

Hodge

Hodge left Julie's bedsit late on Christmas night and stood smoking by the dark river for a long time before walking back to The Chalet. It was freezing and his right hand, lifting a cigarette to his lips, went first mauve then orange-blotched with cold but he was too preoccupied to feel discomfort. When, in the early hours, he reached his room, he did what he had been thinking about ever since he had crashed through the skylight: unrolled all his sketches and half-finished paintings of naked women and, one by one, tore them up.

He knelt on the floor to do this, bending intently over the slowly severing paper flesh as the gap widened to yards between knees and navels, thighs parted for ever and breasts were separated, some landing beside each other in unmatching pairs. His right hand took some time to thaw so he made use of it as a weight on the paper while his left did the tearing. When the job was finished he nursed the hand between his knees and stared unseeingly for over an hour at the mound of ripped paper before him. He was looking beyond it to Julie's face.

The greatest shock of their encounter had been her face. Even as he had lain winded on the bathroom floor, the skylight above him like a jagged television screen on space, he had felt a jolt of recognition go through him far more powerful than the several physical jolts of his fall. And with that recognition he experienced a desire so complex – for it had to do with old wants buried so deep he no longer knew they were there – that it came out as a simple imperative: he had to paint that woman's body. Paint it, fuck it; fuck it, paint it. But he also had to paint her face and somehow make it and all that was behind it, as accessible to him as he would make the body. Nothing else and nothing less would do.

Hodge spent the next few days in his room, drinking little and leaving his paints untouched. He lay on the bed most of the time, visions of Julie projected above him on the ceiling and when, as happened at odd hours through the day and night, he turned on to his side to sleep, her face came and lay beside him so that it was the first thing he saw when he opened his eyes. It was so real to him that, stretching out a hand while still not fully awake he believed he could feel the texture of her cheeks and lips. When his eyes were closed his other hand released itself from the folds of his trenchcoat and he imagined finding her other lips and parting them again and again and again.

On New Year's Eve his supply of tobacco ran low and he ventured out to the corner shop. There he listened, no expression in his eyes, as Gupta enthused about a new line he was starting in frozen food.

"Look, sir." The lid of a bulky icecream freezer was thrown open. "Is this not a good idea? Not much sales for icecream in winter but oh-my-goodness how about nice handy fish fingers?"

Hodge, who had eaten nothing but a couple of pies and bags of peanuts since the last of Bea's boiled Christmas cake – pudding after Julie's turkey sandwiches – peered at the fan of packets in Gupta's hands and selected two. The freezing wrappers burned his fingers and, all diplomacy, Gupta took them back and went behind the counter to wrap them.

"And did you have a nice Christmas? I myself was very quiet here."

Hodge muttered non-committally and handed across a five-pound note.

"Well, Happy New Year to you, sir."

Gupta watched Hodge leave the shop and stop a few yards down the road to roll a cigarette. "Poor chap," he said to himself, going through to the back to heat up curry on a primus and look again at photographs sent with the airmail letters which had, at last, arrived, "I think he too is needing a wife!"

The next day Hodge, leaving a mess of thawed, uncooked but partially eaten food on his bed, went out again. This time he walked past Gupta's, raising a hand dismissively at the grinning figure in the window, and headed for the river. There was a telephone box by the bridge and he stepped into it for a moment, Julie's number, noted as he passed the coin-box on the landing outside her bedsit, on a scrap of paper in his hand. But he stepped out again without dialling. Her face was before him all the time, the hair pinned up roughly, the shocked and then curious eyes. Unable to bring himself to speak to that face over a wire, he walked to where the towpath, at a distance of several streets, gave on to the back of the house where she lived and stood there, as he had stood in the dark, staring at the river. He had not taken in much of what she had said — nervous chatter spilling from her as she found plates for the sandwiches, one hand holding up a towel — but he did recall something about running by the river. Something she did, she said, to keep herself sane. She had laughed when she said that so that her flesh had shaken a little under the towel.

At midday, when cold had stiffened his limbs, Hodge moved a short way along the towpath to a railway bridge and leaned against its damp concrete wall. From this position he could see along the path in both directions and also along an alley winding through allotments which led down to the river from the houses. A man with a dog came down the alley after a while, the dog snuffling and peeing along a row of neglected brussels sprouts; then a dog by itself. Then Julie.

She was running fast, dressed in a dark sweater, trousers with striped socks pulled over them to the knees and black plimsoles. A black woollen hat hid her hair and her hands were in fingerless mittens. Hodge drew back into the shadow of the bridge, tobacco fluttering on a cigarette paper in his palm. He watched as she came closer, breath jerking urgently from her mouth in white puffs. No sound and no visible breath came from him.

Julie's head was up and her eyes were half-closed. She was at the patch of sprouts where the dogs had peed now and Hodge could hear the way her plimsoles wafered the thin ice in the alley. Her panting was loud and the cold had made her skin very white so that eyes, mouth and nostrils seemed large and dark; chalk and charcoal in Hodge's mind. At the end of the alley she stopped abruptly, almost skidding and her panting slowed to irregular gasps as, eyes quite closed now, she stood with one mittened hand resting on the allotment fence.

When her eyes opened she looked first to the right along the towpath, the direction from which Hodge had come and then, slowly, taking in all that was and was not happening on the river, in the stripped trees and in the sky, to the left. Her gaze caught as though snagging on a bramble on the figure under the bridge.

"Hodge!" It was more a mouthing of the word between breaths than a sound.

"Happy New Year," he said and his fingers began to work again on the cigarette.

Julie came towards him but stopped before she was under the bridge. Blood flooded her cheeks, red on white, making her look very young.

"I fixed the polythene like you told me but it's not very satisfactory."

"I told you I'd get a pane of glass." They were talking about the skylight. No more words came for a moment and she studied him studying her.

"You look very cold."

"I am."

Slowly he came out from under the bridge and they began to walk along the towpath together. The sun was invisible but the cold made the scene around them sharp. Ice was splintered in puddles and frozen drips shone like snails' trails in the trees. Julie walked stiffly, head down, a tightness about her hips and her feet in the black plimsoles treading with care. Hodge's stride was longer, less controlled, but there was a tightness about him too. The torn away sole of his right plimsole flapped and the arm lifting his cigarette moved woodenly. Some way along the path Julie said, indicating the cigarette: "Can I have one of those?"

"Sure," said Hodge, the expression incongruous, as though borrowed from some other scene, and stood still to roll her one. There was a bench nearby and she sat on the arm of it, watching. His fingers worked deftly now, despite their colour, not shaking as they had in the bathroom and his tongue, wet and alive-looking between dry lips, swept delicately along the edge of the paper. She held out her hand and he placed the cigarette in her palm.

"Can I, then?" The vertical line in his brow deepened, becoming several as he noted the way her long, half mittened fingers turned the cigarette and brought it to her lips.

She did not answer at once and in the pause he struck a match for her in cupped hands, her hat touching the sleeve of his trenchcoat as she leaned forward. She sat back sharply, puffing out unswallowed smoke and waving it away.

"Can you what?"

"Paint you," he said and the backlit glitter was in his eyes again. "*Paint you, paint you, paint you.*"

Julie

I sometimes wonder if what I did was mad.

When I woke up on Boxing Day morning, I was aware at once that something major and possibly important to the rest of my life had happened the night before. Or not so much the event itself, as my reaction to it.

I got up, shivering, to light the paraffin stove and discovered that the matches were not in their usual place. I remembered where they were, though, beside the scallop shell I had offered Hodge as an ashtray. The ash was still in it with three short, squashed butts and there was – unheard of for me – a dirty plate left in the wash hand basin. I put it on the floor while I splashed my face, remembering how, having seen Hodge out after the turkey sandwiches and that extraordinary cake he produced, I was so tired and shaken I had collapsed straight into bed.

My good clothes from the Christmas visits of the day before lay in a heap on the floor, the pink slip Ann had given me on top. Slowly I shook them out and hung them from hooks on the wall. Hodge had kept looking at the slip as though it reminded him of something. Once he had bent forward from where he was sitting on my one easy chair and rubbed the material between his fingers. My eyes kept returning to those fingers which reminded me so much of claws but which had a bony beauty too.

Still in my nightie – I had put it on only after he had left, moving about awkwardly in a towel while he was there – I went up to the bathroom and examined the broken skylight. Hodge had said to knock out any remaining pieces of glass with a broom then tack on a bit of polythene until he came by with a pane. It made him sound for a moment like the most ordinary of handymen, not someone who had just crawled over the roofs of three houses with obvious intent to burgle. I did as he had advised, banging in drawing pins with the hammer I kept by my bed, which I had never thought of using on him.

Back in my room I stood irresolutely looking into the mirror, out of the window, at the furniture. I did not know what to do with myself. Next to the suitcase-drawers on the bed was a pile of books I had been saving up. The plan for Boxing Day had been to stay in most of the time and read. But now the last thing I felt like doing was reading. My pre-planned distractions had been displaced. Restless physically and mentally, I twitched about the room in a wound up, indecisive way until at last I pulled on my big sweater, long socks and woolly hat and marched myself out into the cold.

I walked fast, keeping warm and pushing the time by with action, in my head a constant stream of images rising from the night before. I did not go to the river that day, nor the next, covering street after street instead and when I was tired, hanging around a playground. The seats of the swings were sticky with frost and my bottom left a damp mark on each as, thinking persistently of Hodge, I shifted along the row. It was a shock to realise how badly I wanted to see him again and that wandering around like this, I was almost hoping our paths would cross.

On the day before New Year's Eve and on New Year's Eve itself, I worked. The arrangement had been made months before with one of the women for whom I charred and it was a relief to be earning and occupied. Even so, washing up, sweeping floors, making sausage rolls, I thought of Hodge. I conjured him like a phantom all over the house. There he was in the lounge where I was dusting, reclining on the Parker-Knoll with narrow knees drawn up and thin, thin profile half hidden by black, straggling hair; there he was on the stairs when I was hoovering the landing, perched six or seven steps above and staring into space with an urgent-but-distant expression, smoke from one of his hand-rolled cigarettes rising thinly beside the spiral of the banisters. And again in the bathroom when I was cleaning the toilet, this time balanced, cross-legged, on the side of the bath. In all the visions he did nothing but sit, smoke, stare. I wanted to fathom that unfathomable stare.

My employers held a party on New Year's Eve and I stayed late to help with the clearing up. Everyone was drunk by the time I was ready to go so I said I would walk rather than take up the offer of a lift. (I preferred the risks I took with my life to be more consciously voluntary.) The lady of the house plied me with leftover food. The man added five pounds to the agreed wage and planted a whiskyish kiss close to my mouth. Loud echoes of bonhomie bounded round the porch and followed me down the street. As it had been a relief to go there, it was a relief to get away.

The night air felt clean, its chill a welcome astringent after the heat of the party. Strolling in the cold, gazing alternately up at a black sky thickly dredged with stars and down at the familiar phenomenon of rubbish glittering like silver in the gutter, I munched my way through two sausage rolls and conjured another vision of Hodge. This time he was by my side, gaunt, wordless but somehow companionable. I looked to see how many sausage rolls were left: four. I would save them for a day or two, just in case he really did turn up with that pane.

I was late up on New Year's Day and it was ten before I thought of breakfast. This sort of irregularity in my 'survival' routine was always disruptive. Somehow, if I did not sit down to a bowl of muesli at seven thirty on the dot, the whole day was put out. Shrugging mentally – in other words, accepting in advance that discipline for that day was broken – I foraged in last night's bag and picked out two of the sausage rolls I had intended to save for Hodge. I ate them irritably, trying to read and then, with a cup of coffee I did not even bother to heat up properly, the other two. Sitting where he had sat, eyes fixed on the now clean scallop shell, I brooded self-critically. It had been absurd to imagine I would ever see him again. He was just a criminal – not even a very clever one – and by now, if he had any sense, he would be a long way away from the scene of his bungled crime. All that business about painting was nothing but flattering nonsense, probably meant to charm me into not calling the police.

How deftly we convince ourselves of one thing and then of

another. Now, I believe I was upset that morning because I had suddenly been faced once more with the essential emptiness of my busy little existence and how easily visions of a stranger could fill it. Is that why, when the unlikely reality presented itself I went on, at first, treating it almost like a vision, not at least to be cheated by reality?

Around midday, making a belated stab at discipline, I decided to go for a run. But no hanging around parks half hoping; this was exercise. And I thought about going to see Ann that afternoon. She would be lonely, the flat inadequately filled with radio and television voices, the cupboard laden mockingly with food. But I was reluctant. There would be the long ritual of tea to go through again: preparation, consumption, clutter and effortful cheer. I believe I would have gone, though (I *would* have, Ann) if it had not been for Hodge.

Will I ever forget that phantom appearing under the bridge? Who was it conjuring whom that time and how was it all suddenly real?

I suppose it must have been about twelve thirty when we met and it had been dark a long time when we parted. All that time we walked, sat on benches, walked again. He hardly spoke and I found myself chattering, not deliberately to fill the silence, which was full enough, but to expend some of the energy that seemed to be building up inside me. I asked him for a cigarette and he made me one. It kept going out and the smoke tasted bad in my mouth but somehow it was what I wanted, like taking a little piece of his world into me and experiencing it for myself. He was such a stranger. Was that what excited me most?

And then there was the business about painting. I think I knew what he meant when he said "Can I?" out of the blue but I wanted to hear him say it again. He almost spat the 'p' of "paint you" but at the same time there was something tremulously controlled about the repeated phrase. He threw down a just re-lit cigarette after he had said it and it lay glowing on the path, a focal point for both our gazes. When, after a minute or two, I said "Perhaps", he began to roll a new one.

We left the towpath towards the end of the afternoon and started walking around a run-down residential area I did not know well. Bags of rubbish, some spilled out, were piled high outside many of the houses, debris of New Year jamborees, and there was glass in the road. There were few cars about and no other pedestrians. Hodge seemed at home in the cold and the quiet and my voice, babbling about nothing, sounded loud and overbright but I could not stop it. We passed a corner shop with lights on and an Indian inside peered out at us, seemed about to wave, then grinned and did not. Hodge acknowledged him with a twitch of the lips that might have been a smile.

Outside a detached house with a sign on it saying 'The Chalet – Vacancies', Hodge stopped.

"This is where I live," he said and not wanting – that day – reality to mesh too closely with vision, I turned round and announced that it was time for me to go home. He came back with me in the dark all the way to the railway bridge where, saying only "see you", with no definition of how or when, I walked away from him up the allotment alley. The image of him standing under the bridge, smoking and staring into blackness, was still in my mind when, a long time later, I fell asleep. For the first time in three years I slept without a nightie on.

Almost a week went by with no contact, then a sketch came through the letter-box. It was barely larger than a postcard and the woman on it, blurred, long-bodied and long-limbed, seemed to be struggling to get off the edges of the paper. Where the head should have been were two words: 'Your face'. I looked up the telephone number of The Chalet.

Communicating on the telephone with Hodge was not easy. Most of the time he was silent and then the few grunts he did make sounded ambiguous but we did manage to arrange to meet for lunch and as soon as I had put the receiver down, I rushed upstairs to the still draughty bathroom and washed my hair.

I arrived early at the café and, not wanting to wait alone inside, positioned myself in the doorway of an antique shop, watching the direction from which Hodge would come. It was cold and soon my face, lightly, carefully made up, began to feel raw. At ten past the hour, more disappointed than annoyed, I entered the café, face at once further discomforted by grease and steam. But Hodge was there, sitting behind a mist of smoke at a table near the back and staring towards the door. He must have arrived even earlier than I had.

When I came in he looked away for a moment and then back, the muscles of his face and all his lines still. How could a face look so empty and at the same time so full? I went over, smiling, and said sorry I was late. He did not reply.

It seemed to take abnormally long to remove my jacket and unwind my scarf. I pulled back a chair and the noise it made on the floor was loud. All the time he sat silent and his clawlike hands, sticking out of his trenchcoat sleeves, looked both vulnerable and predatory. A waitress came and stood behind Hodge's chair, a hip bulged out to one side.

"Yes?"

I glanced at the little plastic covered menu propped between salt and ketchup. Combinations of sausages, pies, eggs and chips were listed in smudged biro.

"Could I just have a sandwich?"

The waitress shifted her weight on to the other leg and the other hip bulged.

"Cheese or 'am?" Her unfriendly glance swept over Hodge, "– or salami?"

I ordered cheese, Hodge salami and tea for us both. I thought of the sausage rolls I had almost kept for him, when he was just a vision. There had been salami left over from the party too.

The grease in the café's atmosphere made my newly washed fringe flop limply over my brow and I brushed it back with the tips of my fingers, conscious of the way Hodge's eyes traced the movement through my upper body, resting as easily on breasts as hands. Again, I found my voice attempting to break the tension. Words came out clumsily, tossed across the table half as offerings, half in self-defence.

"It was terribly cold coming . . . I waited for a bus then walked . . ."

The words trailed off as I saw his gaze alter, intensifying. It travelled from my brow to my chin, round the other way and back again. As our tea was put down he murmured, "Fleshtints." He did not speak again until after the food had come and we had eaten it.

When I began the first quarter of sandwich in that silence I thought I would never get through it. My jaw, under his scrutiny, felt stiff and the bread and cheese cleaved to my upper palate like gum. Alone in my room I would have finished the sandwich in a few gulps, washing its stickiness down with tea, but Hodge brought out another side of me. I took smaller bites after the first, dabbed up crumbs neatly with my fingers and licked them one by one. And I found that, with his eyes upon me, a smear of margarine on my lips felt curiously sensual. I thought I knew what was going to happen.

Hodge pushed his plate away when he had had enough and reached for tobacco and papers.

"I can pay you," he said, placing a cigarette on the table in front of me. "Got a job."

"Oh?" I was affronted, my budding fantasies mocked.

"Bakery," he continued, "confectionary section, dispatch."

I ignored the cigarette waiting to be picked up and, folding my arms on the table, challenged him.

"How much will you pay me and when do you want to start?"

"Three pounds an hour. Now."

I got one pound seventy-five an hour for domestic work, one pound fifty working for Daley. The price of my pride was high.

"Four pounds."

He agreed.

Hodge knelt in front of the gas fire in his room striking damp match after damp match. I was sitting behind him on the one narrow bed and I could see how thin his neck was where his hair, tucked into his collar, parted over the nape. When he had lit the fire he went to the wardrobe and rustled about in it for a long time. There seemed to be a lot of paper in there and he shoved some that fell out beneath with his plimsoled foot. It was torn. When he turned round there were two carrier bags in his hands. He emptied one on to the bed. Three packets of meringue shells.

"Thought you might like those," he said and emptied the contents of the other bag – dozens and dozens of tubes of paint – along the windowsill, which was already lined with beer cans.

I picked up one of the packets of meringue shells and examined it. He must have assumed I would come to his room. Did he always give presents to a paid model? "Thanks. Where do you want me to sit? Shall I take my jacket off?"

No reply.

It is when I think of what happened next that I wonder again about my state of mind. It can't just have been a matter of pride and it did not feel like any ordinary whim. (Although do they ever?) I stood up, went to where Hodge was sorting through his paints, and slid my arms round him from behind. My jacket was unbuttoned and I breathed in deeply, pressing my breasts against his spine, spiky even through the thick material of his trenchcoat. Round his arm I saw him put down the paints on the windowsill. But his hands had not been freed for me: they plunged deep into his pockets, searching for tobacco. I let go, unsure how rejected to feel and sat down on the bed facing the window. He sat down on the other side, facing the fire.

I don't know how long we sat there without speaking, the fire hissing softly and the three packets of meringue shells between us like swords. He rolled two cigarettes and smoked them without offering me one and I found in the furtively glimpsed vision of his narrow profile – head down with skeletal fingers rising again and again to his lips – the cigarette held so professionally, so nervously – something ineffably lonely. I wanted to warm him, to straighten his hunched shoulders and hear him sigh out his tension. But I also wanted to rekindle that strange backlit glitter in his eyes and to feel the urgency of his want for me. I wanted to cuddle him like a child but at the same time create in him an excitement that was fiercely adult, that would make him take hold of me and drive all calculation from my mind.

When he had finished his second cigarette Hodge rolled another but did not light it. Neither of us moved for another long time. Finally I said, an echo of our conversation on the towpath on New Year's Day: "Can I have one of those?"

I asked this because I wanted him to turn round, to force a change in our postures which were becoming frozen. Instead, without turning, he reached back and let the already rolled cigarette fall on the bed between us among the meringues. Automatically he began to roll a new one for himself but I did not wait until he had finished.

"Match," I said, leaning diagonally towards him across the bed. The first one he struck died straightaway and he threw it down and tried another. That died too, then a third. His fingers began to shake and I leaned closer. From this distance I could breathe in his smell – ashy, dry, not 'pungent as hot wine', but no less effective. He used two matches at a time now, striking a bright double flame and protecting it in his hands. I dipped the cigarette down and drew quickly. His own unfinished roll-up lay on his knee, tobacco in a ginger nest on the paper. It was the first thing to go when, without warning, he grabbed my shoulders and scrambled to a kneeling position on the bed.

The just lit cigarette was plucked from between my lips and flung away. Hodge's knees burst cellophane and crunched meringues as he moved closer, eyes without expression but wild. One hand remained gripped on my shoulder as the other began a rapid exploration of my face and neck. His teeth close up were yellow; the skin over his cheekbones brushing mine, unexpectedly soft.

My jacket was cumbersome and I longed to pull it off but sensed the importance of not interrupting Hodge. Or maybe I was afraid. He had let go of my shoulder now and both hands were on my face and hair. His mouth moved along my eyebrows and then to an ear, breaths coming loudly, jaggedly, against the distant continuing explosion of meringues.

Was this not what I had wanted – the being-taken-hold-of, calculation-driven-from-my-mind? Yes and no. It all happened with such rapidity that first time. Too much, too fast, then not enough. My body, held in suspense for so long, cried out for the sort of exploration he had given my face all over and at length. There was a sweet, drawing sting of anticipation in my breasts as he tongued an ear; an involuntary loosening of my thighs as his dry lips swept my throat, but he touched neither. Instead, releasing himself suddenly from his trousers, he tipped me back on the bed, pulled up my skirt and, grasping the back of my tights and knickers in one hand as he held my ankles in the other – there was extraordinary strength in that fleshless frame – pulled them to my calves in one movement where they bunched, holding me trussed as he bent me up towards him, thrust, missed once, twice, entered, came almost immediately and – immediately – came out.

I remained stunned for several long seconds in that ridiculous position as he sat up, groped for tobacco and papers and started to roll.

Then I began to tremble and, face burning, stood up, tights and knickers still below my knees and pigeon-stepped over to the window. My skirt righted itself, covering my white, absurdly hobbled legs and the sperm I could feel running down the inside of one thigh. I opened the window, knocking over a beer can and gazed blindly out. A dirty lace curtain billowed coldly against my cheek but I did not move. From where he was sitting smoking, facing the fire, Hodge said: "I'd like to buy you a drink."

It was after two thirty and the pubs were closed. If they had not been we might have left his room that afternoon and sat locked in private worlds in some drab local bar missing the chance of establishing the bed and painting routine – both irresistible and maddening – around which our lives would revolve (spin in my case) for the next few months.

Hodge went downstairs, caught the manager of The Chalet as he was locking up the residents' bar and bought four cans of Sweetheart stout and a bottle of ginger wine. I laughed when I saw the ginger wine but was touched. I had mentioned at some point in my chatterings along the river that I liked it. I had not thought he was listening.

"That's very extravagant."

Hodge, making no comment, opened the bottle and filled a handleless mug, reminding me of Daley, at Christmas, filling a mug with cheap wine. He opened a Sweetheart and took a pull straight from the can, brownish foam ridging on his upper lip. I sipped at the ginger wine, enjoying the way it seemed to stain the whole of the inside of my mouth with heat and sweetness. I had finally taken my jacket off while Hodge was out of the room and although my body still tingled, still wanted, no longer felt stung. I believed it was only a matter of time before our bodies met in a different way. I was right, but I had no idea then how deeply and permanently Hodge's past life had scarred him, or what 'different' would come to mean for me.

When he was down to the bottom of his second can and had smoked two cigarettes in silence he said: "I want to paint you."

The way he said it made it not just a repetition of a line I had now heard several times, but more an expression of something urgent but probably impossible. I shifted around on the bed, running a finger through the mess of broken meringues.

"You can."

He said – one of the rare occasions he answered something so directly and in a way that might have begun a conversation – "It's not as simple as that."

But there was no conversation. Hodge's lips closed, almost disappearing in a tense line before he put a cigarette between them, and he prepared for work. Foraging once more in the wardrobe, he brought out a roll of paper, a length of which he pinned to the door. He pinned another length over both doors of the wardrobe and another to the wall. He then stood restless and smoking by the window examining the tubes of oil paint individually before sweeping them all back into their carrier bag and producing in their place pencils, charcoal and a small, brutal-looking knife. He sharpened the pencils as I began to undress, cutting at one so ferociously it broke in half.

The room was no longer cold and the ginger wine was warming me inside but still I had gooseflesh all over. It was a long time since I had been naked in front of a man – not counting the skylight episode – and I felt at once reckless and shy. I slipped under the top cover of the bed but let it fall to my waist. The plastic head rest felt slippery against my back and I pulled a pillow up, making a show of getting comfortable but conscious all the time of my own body and the way Hodge's eyes followed every movement. He did not ask me to fall into any special pose but started sketching straight away, using the paper on the wardrobe first.

He worked standing up, kneeling down and crouching, swaying, on narrow hams. The hem of his trenchcoat got in the way at one point and without ceasing to work, he shrugged his right arm, holding the pencil, out of it, letting its whole weight droop for a full five minutes from the left. I had never seen anyone so absorbed. Under the coat he wore the same loose bottomed trousers that had flapped through the shattered skylight and on his top half the worn collars of two shirts fell like limp petals over a long, grey sweater. It seemed extraordinary that he had entered me wearing so many clothes. It seemed extraordinary that he had entered me at all.

At about five thirty – there were sounds of the bar downstairs being reopened – Hodge put down the charcoal he had been using and ran both hands over his hair, flattening it momentarily so that the shape of his skull showed, peaked and birdlike. I could make little of the life-sized scrawls now covering all three lengths of paper and thought it wiser not to comment. Instead I reached down beside the bed for a can of Sweetheart and opened it for him. He took it without a word and I poured more ginger wine into the handleless mug and sat nursing it between my breasts. The more I drank and the more I looked at Hodge's long, thin, distant seeming figure, the more I wanted to reach out and touch him. Eventually, I did.

"Hodge?" I said quietly and laid a hand on his woolly grey sleeve.

Once more, he sat on the bed, not facing me. He held up a cigarette.

"Want one?"

I said no. Gradually, as his cigarette grew shorter, I moved up until I was close enough to nuzzle my chin into his shoulder. Very slowly then – I almost expected to hear creaking – he let himself fall sideways until he was lying down, legs still drawn up in a sitting position. I fell with him and fitted myself closely against the bony angles of his legs and spine. His hands, empty now, were clasped loosely together in front of him and I inserted one of mine between them. I laid my cheek against his hair, savoured the thin smokiness of it, and pressed closer.

The next thing I knew was that my legs were opening with my eyes and Hodge was on top of me again. This time, because I was naked and sleepy, the assault seemed less crude, but it was no less remote. I saw his gaunt face above me, eyes open and intent but still somehow unseeing. He was cupping between my legs with his whole hand, pressing as though imprinting the shape on his palm. Then his fingers began to play, those long, clawlike hands behaving so unlike claws and I heard myself sighing, felt myself opening, wished he would look at me properly.

But he did not. Within seconds there was the brisk struggle with his trousers again and the urgent stab-miss-hit entry. He moved in me three or four times before spilling but, as before, came out straight away, sat up and rolled a cigarette. I saw him glance up quickly at the sketch on the wardrobe door and his eyes, running over that, seemed more focused than when he looked at me.

"Can't do it any more," he said.

I knew at once that he was talking about painting, not bed. Under the covers, my hand rested where his had.

"I believe you can," I said.

But I did not know what I believed.

Was it madness? I sit at my desk during the quiet periods of the night at the sauna and wonder. I suppose I adopted Hodge as the instrument of a major change I had been seeking towards the end of those three essentially solitary bedsit years. (Major Change as opposed to Private Nothing?) He – literally – fell into my life and, ignoring all negative signs, I not only accepted him but, to begin with at least, pursued him. When he asked, after that first painting session, when I could come again I said without hesitation: "Whenever you like. And you can come to me, too." An answer that was to turn my former existence, with all its protective little rituals, upsidedown.

The second half of that January, the whole of February and the beginning of March are moulded together in my memory as one long painting-stroke-fucking session. Looking back, I can see that new rituals did develop and there was a pattern to the days but it is very blurred.

Ditching Daley and the haphazard work on the boats completely, I clung – just – to my two domestic jobs. Hodge gave me money sometimes but my break through the paid model barrier had been successful and I did not want to rely on it. The quality of my charring suffered. Before, it had been an absolute rule with me never to be late. Now, I frequently turned up a good quarter of an hour after time, with no apology, and left as soon as the minimum work set was done. No longer did I attempt to please my employers with little unasked for extras. Makeup bottles with the tops off on a dressing table were left to clog; boots slung impatiently in the direction of a hall cupboard were cleaned around but left unpaired.

And my appearance must sometimes have been startling. Hodge painted me in The Chalet after his day shift had ended, then often accompanied me back to my room, staying until the early hours. I would get up as late as possible the next day, hungover, reeking of sperm and ash and stuff my hair, formerly so neatly plaited and pinned, into an old school beret which I kept on all the time I worked. Under it I wore a single curler in my fringe, ready for the evening painting session.

I took baths in the middle of the night, Hodge sometimes watching, sometimes waiting below in my room. If the women I worked for were out I swigged from their sherry or pinched squirts of their expensive perfume, things I would never have dreamed of before. I caught glimpses of myself in their mirrors and saw a quickly moving figure growing daily more angular and a white face with eyes so darkly circled they looked bruised. Running and seven-thirty-on-the-dot muesli were abandoned and I ate and slept erratically, one day gorging on Hodge's gifts from Perkins & Day and sleeping thickly for hours, the next eating nothing but apples and staying up until dawn. I was not healthy, I was not happy but I was thoroughly distracted; my days, my thoughts, my body completely occupied.

Odd moments of what might be seen as sanity emerge from that otherwise incoherent phase. I notice I wrote to Ann late in January, a stilted, apologetic piece of nonsense but which brought from her a reply so unconsciously lonely in tone I went to see her the following weekend.

As I waited outside her door, listening to the heavy shuffle-bump of her feet and zimmer struggling along the corridor, I was aware of the physical changes wrought in me by Hodge. I had plaited my hair in the old style but it felt odd, a throwback to another era and my hips and thighs, which before and after painting them, Hodge was by then touching – he was more than touching my whole body – felt constricted in the sensible skirt I wore. Greeting Ann, my smile was strained and as I spoke and began to go through the familiar dance steps of our old tea-together routine, it was almost as though I were acting in a play. Perhaps in an attempt to break the sense of imposture, I suddenly started talking about Hodge, knowing, even as his name slipped out of my mouth, that this was unwise. I could not paint her a true picture of him, so, without ever having intended to, I painted her a lie.

At first I did try to keep things under control by being deliberately vague. He was just a new person, a friend who had recently come into my life. But she used the term 'gentleman' and referred to him as 'Mr Hodge' so that he became, even in my own mind, temporarily, a being totally other than the disturbing, obsessive character I was just beginning to know.

But what I find so strange, so unforgivable, is that I did not, having seen my mistake, stop. I could have dropped the subject or dismissed it later in a letter but instead – I have the evidence before my eyes – I played along with what I saw were becoming her fantasies. I made Hodge into something he definitely was not and by doing that, gave a false picture of myself as well.

> . . . Did I tell you he is rather a lot older . . . ? . . . nice to be with someone who has more experience of the world . . . lovely long artistic hands . . .

And the reality was that madness of fucking and painting and drinking, behaviour that I knew would be incomprehensible to Ann. Silence on my part would have given us both more dignity. I wonder, though. Perhaps I underestimated Ann's ability to see through her own illusions. Perhaps she *chose* to see only what she wanted to see. Like selecting television programmes. The value of keeping strict tabs on reality in the mind is surely questionable when a body is as painfully rooted in it as hers was. And I wonder how much she knew, or wanted to know, about that, too.

Then Esther turned up a week or so after Hodge had gone on to night shift and a second topsy-turvy era had begun. She wanted a reference for Daley and guilt made me bend over backwards to help. When he had telephoned some time before, asking me to go back to work on the boats, I had fobbed him off with a misleading tale of modelling. It had given me sly pleasure to use that word, which was only partially an honest description of what I was doing, and make it mean something quite different to him. He had sounded lonely and sad but I had ignored his unspoken pleas, because his type of loneliness and sadness held no appeal for me.

It amused me that he was applying for a job in the same place as Hodge but at the same time I was relieved that, with one on day and one on night shift, it was unlikely they would meet. It would have given me a worrying sense of being out of control if I had thought they might discuss me. In retrospect guilt strikes a double blow: would I have given Daley a reference if he had been aiming to work the same hours as Hodge? Probably not.

Control, at that stage, was a vanishing commodity in my life but it was gradually being replaced by something just as rigid, just as dominating. I was becoming as obsessed with Hodge, and his changing treatment of my body, as he was with his painting. And that was frightening.

Daley

Daley, never varying the route he took from the changing room to his place in front of the prover, adjusted his little gauze-crowned Feeder Grade IV's cap at exactly the same place every day. The rhythm of his breathing altered as he entered the now familiar vast hall with the chinks of filtered sky above and he walked heavily, evenly as he passed the shining body of the roll oven and the loud, juddering cooler. Something about the cooler's seven-inch thick door and a story he had heard Esther tell Leonie made him think of the stone rolled in front of the cave where Jesus's body was laid when it was taken down from the cross. He imagined the corpse wrapped in vapour misted cellophane like the hundreds and hundreds of rolls and loaves he glimpsed when the door was opened. It made him want to giggle.

Once or twice during the month he had now been working at Perkins & Day, a fellow worker had tossed a greeting in his direction but usually he reached his place, walking behind, beside and in front of scores of other white clad figures, without any communication. Anxiety mingled with relief when he separated himself from the crowd and stood, back to the world, facing the mouth of the prover. He was anxious because he feared that overnight his hands might have unlearned their job and he would stand helpless while an endless stream of dough clusters fell off the end of the conveyor belt; he was relieved because, somehow, he had managed to get himself to the right place at the right time once again.

The moments before the conveyor belt started were tense and Daley's thoughts jerked about in a disjointed way. Words he had heard recently repeated themselves in his mind like advertising jingles and sometimes he wondered if he had spoken them aloud. The words were not obviously connected yet he seemed to want to link them, as though striving to find some meaning or message there. 'Legend' he thought, one of the children's storybooks coming before his inner eye, then 'ledge end', with a sense of vertigo and finally 'fall off', which might have had something to do with his fears for the dough. It was only when the belt started to move and his hands automatically plopped the first pieces into their pans that he began to relax.

For hours then, with legs apart and pelvis thrust forward so that all his weight centred on belly and groin, Daley performed his simple task with dedication. Every couplet of dough pieces nestled safely in their pans was a small achievement and these days the feeling of the dough, far from being repugnant to him, was almost sensual. Once, as his palms landed evenly on two perfectly matched pieces, he had the sensation that he was touching a pair of warm, pulpy breasts and it gave him pleasure to squeeze and lift them lightly. After this he always thought of the dough pieces as breasts. And the constantly gaping mouth of the prover began to seem like a huge, dark blow-up of what to him was the forbidden zone between a woman's thighs. Day after day, hour after hour, Daley unconsciously fucked his machine.

A company nurse making her monthly round of the workers commented to one of the overseers: "Got an earnest one there. Looks set for life!" Daley, mesmerised by his task, did not notice her presence.

He did not look forward to mealbreaks. In the first week he had not minded them, imagining that sooner or later he would 'fit in' with the other workers and sit in the metal and plastic canteen chatting easily, as it seemed to him they did, between gulps of weak tea. But he never had fitted in. It reminded him of school where he had been the fat boy, James Leslie Daley, standing in a corner staunching the wound of his shyness with bun after bun after bun. Nobody had come up and chatted to him then. Nobody did now.

He did however have one comrade of sorts. Not someone who talked to him but at least a familiar figure who, when their breaks coincided, would sit down next to Daley as though by preference. The two of them would chomp through their meals in silence, staring straight ahead but somehow in sympathy. This was the man whose job it was to feed the flour sifters. Like Daley, he worked alone. His workspace was a large, granary-like room filled with flour sacks and hour after hour he opened the sacks with a knife and poured their contents down funnels into the sifters below. His skin was always dredged with flour, his eyelashes white. The rest of the workers regarded them as a pair. Not very secretly, they were known as 'the wallies'.

At two thirty in the afternoon, when Daley's shift ended, he felt, along with the relief of resting his arms, a frightening emptiness. There was half an hour to kill before he picked up Leonie from school and he never knew what to do with himself in that time. On some days he would sit in the van and doze, hands flopped in front of a growing paunch, eyes flickering open occasionally to check his watch; on others he would drive to a row of shops near the school and wander slowly up and down past the windows, staring in but rarely entering. There was a small supermarket with special offer notices on hoardings outside. Daley watched the hoardings like television. *Mace tinned peas only 19p*. "Peas please Louise," he said to himself. He worked sluggishly on rhymes or connections between words. An advertisement for Jungle Juice led to 'Juicy Julie' and magazine cover images flashed through his mind: Julie, hair loose, unzipped to the navel; Julie balancing a carton of Jungle Juice on a naked thigh. His body, from the unconscious hours of congress with the prover was in a constant state of exhaustion but forever unsatisfied. His hands as he drifted past the shop windows rested deep in his pockets close to his penis. His eyes were glazed. Once, a woman in the sweetshop banged angrily on the window as he was staring blindly in. He did not understand why.

When the school bell rang – a sharp electronic whistle – his hands jerked out of his pockets and he strode, brisk for a moment, to a gap in the hedge some distance from the main gates. He positioned himself here because he could not bear to be near the other parents, listening as though from ten miles off to their airy exchanges and all the time afraid that one of them might address him. He was also afraid of being ignored. Leonie, in unwitting collusion with her father, treated her exit through the gap in the hedge as a game, popping out like a rabbit minutes after the bell rang with coat trailing and beret askew. She plastered herself briefly against his knees as though flung, and hand in hand, they walked to where he had parked the van. It did not matter to Leonie that Daley did not often respond in words to the bright stream of chatter flowing from her. He smiled when she giggled; squeezed her hand when she skipped.

On the way home they played a guessing game. Every day Daley brought a treat from the bakery. It might be a bag of soft rolls, a currant loaf or half a dozen iced buns, all of which he got at discount. Leonie's job was to guess which it was. Her small brow furrowed if, after she had gone through all her favourites, Daley still shook his head. She knew then that the treat was only a singed or misshapen loaf.

"But it was free!" she would cry, instead of complaining, because she knew that made him smile. Esther, waiting aproned on the doorstep, approved of plain loaves.

"Better for you," she would explain.

But she stopped making any comment when one day Daley muttered: "Not only free, but good for you – like sex."

Demonstrating her love in a way that came more easily to her, Esther scraped all the burnt bits from the loaf and spread margarine right to the edges.

The routine of tea, playtime and the children's baths kept her thoroughly occupied but even in the midst of the noise and mess Esther was disturbed by the vision of Daley slumped silently in his chair before a loud barrage of children's television. The glazed look she had noticed after his first day at work had become permanent and often when she spoke he either did not answer or mumbled something she could not understand. He took the children on to his knees when they came down in their pyjamas, glowing cheeked from the bath, but even his hands moving gently over them seemed to Esther to be behaving in a distant way, almost as though neither hands nor children belonged to him. Leonie and Jonathan thrust their storybooks under his eyes and his forefinger moved automatically over the pictures, but he did not speak, leaving them to do all the naming of monsters, counting of baby rabbits, tracing of shapes. Esther, drying a dish or pausing in her ironing, would come up behind them and lean over the back of the chair helping to tell the story. Daley's hair was flattened where his Feeder Grade IV's cap had sat for eight hours and the sight of it, grubby and innocent, brought out all her protective care.

"Bath tonight, love?"

No answer. A forefinger pausing on a panda bear.

"Shall I run you a bath, darlin'?"

"Naaaa . . ."

"Well, tomorrow night then, eh?"

"Panda bear . . . Mmmmn . . . panda-monium."

In bed, even when, as once or twice she had steeled herself to lately, she shut her eyes and reached for his hand, he always went straight to sleep these days.

The weekends were something Esther looked forward to now that Daley had a regular job and money worries were less acute, but time and again the little plans she made for family activities fell through or were spoiled and she began to long for Monday morning again.

Once, they went to the swimming baths on a Saturday afternoon. Esther changed the children into their costumes and all three ran giggling to the pool, feet slapping on the wet tiles.

"Where's Dada?" shouted Leonie above the splashing and excited shrieks at the shallow end.

"He'll be here in just a minute, love," said Esther, "I told him we'd be by the steps."

For the next ten minutes Leonie floated on her back, duck-dived and practised a thrashing dog paddle, arms awhirl in bright red wings. Jonathan, nervous of splashes, dipped a blue and white ring at the see-through waves and stayed close to his mother. Esther's eyes kept straying towards the men's changing rooms, looking out for Daley. Eventually she said to Leonie: "Be a good girl and stay here by the steps while Mummy goes to find Dada."

"Say 'hurry up'!" yelled Leonie and duck-dived again, her yellow costume blossoming like a flower over her small rump.

Holding Jonathan tightly by the hand, Esther hovered outside the men's changing rooms. A pair of teenaged boys came dashing out, callous seeming with their young rushing bodies and whooping cries; then a youth on his own who gave her a 'funny' look. An elderly man resting on a bench nearby saw her discomfort.

"Lost someone?"

Esther nodded, a short woman with sagging thighs in a washed-out blue swimming costume.

"My husband, yes. He seems to be taking ever such a long time."

The man offered to go in and find him.

"What does he look like?"

Esther struggled for words to match the picture in her mind.

"He's kind of plump, walks slow – hair's a bit messy . . ." She laughed. "Daft, isn't it? We've been married eight years."

The man smiled and disappeared. Jonathan pulled at his mother's arm and cried: "Dada!"

When the man came out again he looked embarrassed. Daley was not with him.

"Your husband wants you to go to him," he said. "I tried to get him to come out but he wouldn't. I'm so sorry." He smiled awkwardly as he moved away, saying: "Fourth cubicle on the left."

Esther had reddened.

"Thank you for trying, anyway," she said and, lifting Jonathan on to her hip, entered the men's changing rooms.

Blue plastic curtains on metal rings billowed and ripped aside in a narrow corridor. Heads, shoulders and feet twisted in and out of clothes and the sound of wet trunks hitting the floor mingled with shouts and laughter, seeming to slap at Esther from all sides. Graffiti rising up the back walls of the cubicles yelled at her whenever there was a small gap in actual sound and a man wearing a tight rubber cap stared at her expressionlessly over his curtain. Jonathan's fingers, still wet from the pool, raised red marks where they dug into her neck. Outside the fourth cubicle she stopped.

"Are you in there, love?"

A group of youngsters ran past dripping and flicking splashes from wet hair.

"Hey! This is the men's!"

Esther, eyes down, said again: "Are you in there?"

From inside the cubicle came a familiar giggle and Esther slid back the curtain. Daley, in his underpants, was sitting on the narrow wooden seat, head in his hands. His thighs, flabby and sparsely haired, shook. His shoulders heaved.

"What is it, love?"

One hand came away from his face and pointed to a neatly printed piece of graffiti on the wall.

"Look at that!" he gasped and collapsed into giggles again.

"Come on out, love. Leonie's waiting."

"Just listen!"

It seemed to Esther that the shouts and laughter echoing round the changing rooms died down. She was not the only one listening.

"*When the bottom is falling out of your world*," recited Daley, slowly, loudly, finger pointing. "*Take Andrews and . . .*" His eyes screwed up and he started to wheeze, ". . . *the world will fall out of your bottom!*"

Somebody blew a raspberry and there was stifled laughter nearby.

"Better put your clothes on again, love. Better go home."

Esther watched as, suddenly quiet, Daley pulled on a sock and set his foot on the damp floor.

"God," he said softly, head in hands but for a different reason now. She helped him to dress.

Another time, they went to a funfair and Daley, after filling himself with beer, hotdogs and candyfloss, became almost hysterically giggly on the big wheel and vomited, splashing Leonie's dress. The child, usually so unquestioningly loyal to her father, was very upset.

"I stink, Dada," she wailed. "I stink because of you!"

Daley, full of unnameable guilts, went white and silent for the whole of the rest of the day.

At the beginning of April, despite the fact that he seemed to be getting on all right at work, Esther made an appointment with the family doctor.

Four

Ann

Easter fell close to Ann's birthday so the cake Julie made in the end was a cross between birthday and simnel. They laughed together as Julie described how she had assembled the mixture in a plastic washing-up bowl in her bedsit then carried it round to bake in one of her employers' ovens while she worked.

"Let's hope it's cooked through."

She told Ann she had had to borrow a thick tea-towel to wrap it in and oven gloves to hold it on the way back.

"You should have seen the funny looks I got!"

Ann smiled.

"I'm looking forward very much to trying it, dear."

But she was worried that she would not be able to eat it. Eating, always a comfort in the past, had become a problem.

It was just past three and Julie was due to fetch Miss Abbot for the birthday tea at four. The friend Ann had mentioned previously would not be coming. Ann did not tell Julie that, remembering last year – the hopeful, hopeless waiting; the wasted cake – she had not even invited her. She did not know why she had mentioned her at all. Perhaps because the stark truth of her aloneness in the world embarrassed her. The friend was probably dead and distant cousins did not count.

Unlike at Christmas, Ann had done no private struggling in the kitchen towards this occasion. Julie had said: "It's your birthday so you must not lift a finger." Relieved, because she doubted she would have been able to anyway, she had agreed. She watched now as the girl flipped slices of buttered bread on to bases with exotic looking fillings and cut them into triangles. Julie was humming a jerky little tune as she worked and seemed preoccupied.

145

"What's that, dear?"

"Salmon delight à la Julie."

The humming resumed.

"Sounds delicious. Now tell me before Miss Abbot comes: how is your young man?"

A crust Julie was trimming skidded off the edge of the plate and the humming stopped. She popped the crust into her mouth and chewed before replying.

"Oh, he's all right. Hey, look at the time and I've got the table to lay yet!"

Ann's eyes followed her as she jumped up, collecting the sandwich-making paraphernalia.

"Are you still losing weight like you said in your letter, dear?"

There came the sound of water running on to dishes in the sink.

"I don't think so." Julie looked over her shoulder. "But *you* are. Not on a diet, are you?"

Ann cleared her throat, conscious again as she did so of the wedge of pain it was getting harder and harder to deny.

"Well, I've always been a bit on the heavy side. 'Well-upholstered' my brother used to say."

"Ah, but today is your birthday," said Julie, bringing in the sideplates, "so you must let yourself go."

Ann smiled and began the long business of getting to her feet.

"I think I'll just pay a call, dear. Get it over before we begin."

In the bathroom she nibbled two capsules off her palm and swallowed them with difficulty, water hardly helping to wash them down. It had been easier at first when she had asked for capsules instead of tablets but now they were a problem too. She looked at her face carefully in the mirror. It was true about losing weight. Bones she had not seen for years were beginning to poke their way to the surface. She would have to make herself more soups and milk puddings and tell the nurses who changed her leg bandage she *was* on a diet.

"There!" Julie stood back from the table and made a flourishing gesture, "How's that?"

Ann stopped in the doorway, leaning on her zimmer, and

wondered whether it was worth lowering herself into the easy chair now only to have to struggle up again to the table in a little while. She could not help noticing that, unusually for Julie, some of the sandwiches were clumsily cut and one or two pieces of cutlery were not quite straight.

"It's lovely," she said.

Julie settled the question of the chairs by punching a cushion and saying: "Now sit down and let me give you your present."

Obligingly, Ann shuffled forward, turned and lowered herself into the chair. She would have liked to blow her nose and wipe her glasses but, instantly, a parcel was produced. As gaily as she could, she tugged at the string. Julie, sitting on the edge of her chair, leaned forward and Ann sensed the energy and impatience vibrating through her body.

"You do it, dear."

With two brisk movements Julie revealed the contents of the parcel. It was a headsquare, lavender with a pattern of leaves in yellow and gold.

"It's about the right weight for this weather, isn't it?" she gabbled. "You could wear it round your neck over a blouse or on your head if it's windy."

"I'll wear it right away, dear." Ann draped the scarf carefully over her shoulders. Julie tied it with a loose knot at the front. Even the scent of her close up seemed urgent, sharp.

"I'll take a picture," Julie announced and bouncing up, grabbing her camera, snapped away. Never before had Ann felt so conscious of her own slowness and uselessness in Julie's presence and suddenly she longed for the afternoon ahead, something she had looked forward to for weeks, to be over. She smiled shyly again for the camera but Julie was already putting it away.

"Time to fetch Miss Abbot."

While she was gone, Ann sat without moving at all, eyes closed, looking forward now only to sleep. But she was worried about Julie. Why had she not said more about Mr Hodge? Had something gone wrong? And why was she so brittle in her speech and movements today? She wished she could find out what the matter was and try to help, but now there was this rigmarole with Miss Abbot to go through. Never mind, probably be for the last time. The truth of this uninvited thought hit her and her eyes sprang open blinking in fear. Suddenly she longed for distraction, any distraction, and on her face was a big welcoming smile when, a few minutes later, Miss Abbot, leaning on Julie's arm, appeared.

Although she had only come from two doors away, Miss Abbot wore a heavy green overcoat and a large brown hat skewered on to her head with pins.

"Come and sit down, dear." Miss Abbot's face was blank, mouth ajar. "Julie will put the kettle on."

Julie steered her silent charge to a chair and mouthed at Ann.

"I think her hearing aid's gone wrong."

"What, dear?"

The girl made gestures and Ann understood. When Miss Abbot was settled, sitting stiffly and staring straight ahead, Ann bent forward and said clearly:

"How are you, dear?"

Miss Abbot's eyes, small and damp behind round rimmed glasses, blinked.

Ann tried again, bending further forward and straining her voice.

"I was wondering how you are, dear. HOW ARE YOU KEEPING?"

Miss Abbot put her head on one side and her mouth twisted as she fiddled with her hearing aid. There was a sudden, agonisingly loud whistle and Ann sat back with a jerk.

"Chilly out, yes," said Miss Abbot, still staring straight ahead.

Ann let her glasses slide half an inch down her nose and rolled her eyes upwards at Julie. The look they exchanged then was the first real communication she had felt since the girl had arrived that afternoon. Miss Abbot, cut off, vacant but somehow a necessary part of the proceedings, gave them something to share. Her private loss – on this one afternoon, for she would never be invited again – was their gain.

"I'll go and make the tea," said Julie, behind the still firmly skewered hat, and she and Ann smiled, at the same time and in the same way.

Miss Abbot kept on her heavy coat as well and soon shreds of 'salmon delight à la Julie' flecked its lapels. Ann indicated that Julie should fetch a napkin and used the opportunity while she was away to cover her own barely begun sandwich with a tissue and slide it into her bag. Both of them used Miss Abbot as a focal point, at first trying in turn to converse with her and then, conceding that this was impossible, attending closely to her physical needs.

"Pass Miss Abbot the sandwiches again, dear. I'm sure she could manage another one."

Conveniently, Miss Abbot's appetite was large and there was only one sandwich left on the plate and the teapot had been refilled twice when the moment came to cut the cake.

Julie had stuck seven candles round the edge – one for each decade of Ann's life – and one in the middle representing the additional nine years. Ann had difficulty blowing them out so Julie did it with her and then sat back in her place to cut the cake. Her face went red and she stopped smiling as the first slice came away.

"Is something wrong, dear?"

This was the question Ann had been wanting to ask all afternoon, but not about cake.

Julie looked across the table at her.

"It's all gone wrong. It's just a mess."

Was she only talking about cake?

"Never mind. I expect you were in a hurry, weren't you? Trying to do too much."

An unconvincing smile came through Julie's flush.

"I expect so. Do for the bird table anyway. Do you want to risk a bit?"

"Of course. I'm sure it's all right really."

"What about Miss Abbot?"

"Oh, give her some," whispered Ann, suddenly irritated by her vacant guest, "she'd eat anything, greedy old whatsit."

Julie laughed and then stifled the sound. They watched in fascination as Miss Abbot picked up her piece of cake automatically and took a large mouthful of its almost raw centre. Her jaw worked steadily and there was no change in her expression. Julie looked away after the third mouthful had been absorbed.

"Ann," she said, "can I confide in you?"

Ann took a token raisin from the cake and nibbled it without swallowing.

"Of course, dear. It's about Mr Hodge, isn't it?"

Hodge

The white cardboard hat of dispatch worker (confectionery section) sat on Hodge's dark head like an upturned paper boat. He secured it at the back with a hairgrip, the packet he had picked up at the corner shop months ago having finally found a use. In the front pocket of his white overalls – black-streaked from rubbing against the metal trolleys he pushed – was a supply of ready rolled cigarettes and from time to time he would bend down near a gap under one of the loading stall doors and take a few swift drags. As smoking was prohibited in the work area he would pretend to be bent over coughing if anyone approached. But that was rare. The nightshift workers in dispatch took their instructions from printed sheets and were usually only visited by the overseer if it was their turn to go out on deliveries.

Light streamed into the dispatch area from a grid of striplights hung on chains. Every speck of dirt on the concrete floor was exposed by this white flood and one of Hodge's jobs, between loading the stalls, was to keep his part of it swept. His broom, bald in the middle and flattened into stiff cow'slicks at either end, made a soft thumping sound beneath the racket of metal crashing on metal as other workers flung their trolleys around. Perhaps because of the disconcerting quiet of the night outside and the lack of any other kind of communication, the workers used whatever was passing through their hands with loud, deliberate violence. Even the baskets of baked goods, containing row upon row of fresh, soft buns or fragile pastries protected only by cellophane, were always hurled rather than lifted into their allotted stalls. But the workers were expert and breakages few. Neither the noise nor the violence bothered Hodge whose eyes, the whites yellow and veined under the striplights' glare, were constantly focused inwards on his own world.

The days fell into a new pattern. Instead of painting Julie in the evenings Hodge was now ready to start, after a short sleep, at midday. On Wednesdays and Fridays when she was at her domestic jobs until one, he became restless, smoking and pacing in his room. It seemed to him unnecessary that she persisted in this work but he did not question her about it. He had expected to have to pay for her time. Now, sporadically, he gave, instead of paid her money. One day he would present her with something large. Perhaps a car.

Frequently, he took hold of her the moment she arrived, eating the lipstick off her mouth as he pressed her against door or wall. Both hands would be under her skirt tearing at tights and pushing her thighs apart. Then three fingers of one hand would be deep inside her as the other gripped her buttocks and held her still. As he felt her squirm he would grip harder and his mouth would leave her face and fall on her neck. And as she strained away upwards but also bore down on his hand, he would push in so high she was almost dangling from him. Only then would he loosen his own clothes and pull her towards the bed.

It was necessary to Hodge that Julie did not restrict or deny him physically in any way. Initially, it was she who had unlocked herself to him. Now, day after day, he tested the depth of that unlocking, pushing and pushing into her with his hands, with his penis, with his tongue until her gasps became guttural whoops and he knew that nothing in her was held back from him and that neither her mind nor her body were any longer under her own command. Frustrated that this condition must always be temporary, he tore at her again and again and again.

It excited him that she had to stifle her noise and seeing her twist away from under him to bite her own palms he would pull her by the buttocks to the edge of the bed, cram pillows beneath her and stand, a leg in each hand, knocking his bones against hers. And when she was exhausted and lay spread-eagled and helpless with the flesh on her thighs shaking, he would turn her on to her belly and start again, pulling her up by the shoulders so that, as he rocked her back and forth, kneeling behind, her breasts slapped the sheet and hung where he could hold them. It was often in this position that he came but even after he had, and had slid out, his hand still dragged whimpers from her, twisting in the sopping hair, a finger questing sharply as he detached the rest of his body and stood beside the bed looking down, his mind already beginning to paint.

As it had been in the early weeks after his release, Hodge's room was thickly layered with naked women. The difference now was that the breasts and vulvas and thighs covering walls, ceiling and floor were no longer anonymous and there were faces as well, or rather one face, repeated over and over. He had tried at first to paint Julie with her eyes open, looking straight at him, but something had always felt wrong. Somehow, if she was able to look at him, to hold a steady gaze, she was not as he wanted her to be. That was why more often than not he rendered her into the condition he did want before he began. Even if he was just painting a foot he wanted that foot to be Julie's foot after he had had his effect on her, not just, however accurately, her foot. And sometimes, even if she had not stirred for an hour from the position in which he had left her, he would lay down his brushes and return to the side of the bed, standing over her silent and motionless but for the thin sound of his breathing and the slight trembling of one hand. If her eyelids fluttered then or she started to speak he would command quietly: "Don't move."

Then, depending on the accessibility of her position, he would begin to work on her again, watching her efforts to contain herself while at the same time goading and goading her to lose control. And when she had lost it and lay stunned and wordless once again he would return to his painting. In some of the pictures her face looked almost dead.

At around five thirty Hodge would turn his current painting to the wall, throw a cover loosely over Julie and go down to the bar. He would drink a single whisky while the barman-manager, who raised his eyebrows in the same half conspiratorial way every day, gathered together his order of Sweethearts and ginger wine. Hodge sometimes bought the wine by the bottle, sometimes by the glass. The manager had had to order a case.

"What about the empties? Sure you don't want your room cleaned?"

"I'll do it myself, thank you," Hodge always replied and token carrier bags of empties and dirty sheets duly appeared. Hodge knew the minimum required, acknowledged certain rules.

When he came back with the drinks Julie would be sitting up, the bed cover tied toga fashion under her arms, attempting to roll a cigarette or tugging at her hair with a comb. He would hand her her ginger wine and open a can, folding himself into his chair by the gas fire, tobacco and papers to hand. Julie would begin to talk and, out of the corner of his eye – his main gaze essentially distant on nothing – Hodge would observe the process of her reassembling in herself the barriers he had broken down. Her face, so naked as he had painted it, would gradually assume the unconscious mask of self and her mouth especially, although still softened and somehow blurred by his earlier kisses and her own cries, would seem to tighten and become alien to him as she spoke. He gave her whatever treats he had stolen from the bakery – always the most luxurious things he could find – and watched that mouth become busy again with animal things. At first she had pretended to be modest about her hunger but now she fell greedily on brandy snaps, florentines or petit fours, lapping up the ginger wine afterwards with crumbs still on her lips.

Sometimes she would leave the bed and come, draped in her toga, to kneel in front of him. Speaking gently she would stroke his arm and try to look into his eyes. What she said washed over him leaving no mark but the closeness of her body brought him back from his distance and he would open his clothes and watch her head go down. Her mouth, moving like a thing alive on its own in her once more drowned face, spoke far more meaningfully to him then than when words came out of it and, occasionally, the hand not holding a cigarette would lightly stroke her hair.

At six thirty Julie would dress and walk part way to Perkins & Day with him, sometimes kissing the side of his long, bony nose as they parted by the river. Hodge would stand still, rolling a cigarette and watch her until she disappeared, often running, around a bend in the towpath. It would not be long now before he was ready to begin on a series of sketches that would culminate in a major painting, the most important painting he had ever done. The most important painting he could ever do. He would think about it on and off all night as he pushed his metal trolley, swept the concrete floor and stacked basket after basket of pastries and buns correctly into their allotted stalls.

Julie

C onfide in Ann? In *Ann*?
     I did not, of course, making up instead a story suitable
for her ears, while deaf Miss Abbot sat between us like some
ghastly joke figure, masticating uncooked cake and staring
straight ahead.

"I think you'll just have to be firm with him, dear," advised
Ann when my tale was finished.

I nodded and we had another cup of tea.

The Friday before, when I had mixed her cake in my room,
I had been so sore that I wore a flannel wrung out in cold
water between my legs and after work, instead of going to The
Chalet, took a long bath and lay down. As I had known he
would, Hodge turned up at about four.

"Why didn't you come?" he demanded. "Why, why, why?"
And before I could speak he was eating my mouth like an
animal and his hands were raking under my clothes.

I do not know exactly when or how the change took place
but it must have been some time after he went on to night
shift. One day, it seemed, my only ambition – my fantasy and
obsession – was to break through Hodge's reserve and to force
his desire for me – not just his wanting to paint me – into the
open; and the next I was almost ready to flee him. Almost,
but I did not. Not then.

When he went on to night shift he stopped coming to the
bedsit so often and all my memories of that era centre on his
room and the walks to and from it. The weather was becoming
milder but from winter habit I still put on a warm jacket and
scarf before setting out. Gradually, as I strode along the
towpath, I would unwind the scarf and unbutton the jacket.
I was so aware of every physical movement in those days, so
absorbed in my own body and its responses that even the

exposure of my throat to the wind seemed like the beginning of a sexual act. If I was so much as a minute early, I would slow down where the towpath turned into the residential area near The Chalet and deliberately saunter. There was something delicious about the suppressed energy beneath that casual pace when I knew that as soon as I reached my destination I was going to be whirled into a crazy storm of activity over which I had little, if any, control. I clung to what I did have in order to heighten the pleasure of giving it away. What I had never anticipated was that Hodge would take it all and still not be satisfied.

Passing the corner shop near The Chalet every day, I developed an odd little relationship with its owner. He had seen me with Hodge, I knew, and I could tell by the way he looked at me slyly from under his thick lashes, grinning to himself, that he had 'put two and two together'. It gave me a curious thrill to browse along the contents of the window outside knowing that those soft, alert little eyes were taking me in, detail by detail, with the imagination behind them working overtime. Or maybe it was my imagination. Whatever, it made me feel wanton in a way I had never experienced before and again, the anticipated pleasure of what would happen in The Chalet was increased. Once, I went in and stood baffled and then amused by a huge display of beachballs taking up half the shop while the March winds were still blustering outside and there was not a beach for miles. I laughed aloud and the Indian looked irritated, but when I bought one he grinned and grinned and, as he handed me my change, tickled my palm. I dropped the beachball behind someone's garden hedge before reaching The Chalet.

Pleasure. That was what it was, at first. No longer was Hodge a spiky back turned away from me that I had to seduce; no longer did he use my body as though it were a poor but necessary second to his painting. No. The backlit glitter I had courted was in his eyes again and again. Speech and all preliminary gestures were bypassed and there he was, above, behind, before me, relentlessly shoving all *my* reserve aside.

Sometimes I watched him shaving, which he often left until after the first time so I never knew whether he shaved for work or for me or just for himself. Stretched and sweetened on the bed, I saw vulnerabilities in him then which, in the first months, excited something more complex than desire. Hodge, hard Hodge, had tender little nipples, his back was white and thin and there was a momentary, private uncertainty about the way his fore and middle fingers checked for stubble on his chin that made me want to put my arms around . . .

Misguided tenderness.

He did not care about clothes or makeup and it took a while for me to realise this. When I did it was – again at first – a source of pleasure. I thought back to the pre-bedsit days when all my confidence had depended on whether I looked good or not and then how I hated the men who only wanted me because I did. Now I had a man who wanted to go far, far deeper than all that. And when he disarrayed me completely, washing the makeup from my eyes with his sweat, yanking aside my carefully chosen skirt and tearing my tights, I thought: at last, a man who wants to go *beyond*.

But that was the trouble. Hodge did want to go beyond and his beyond was not the same as mine. How is it that sex, an act with physical limitations and a great deal of inevitable repetition, can seem like a trip to infinity every time? At first I travelled there with him, or so I imagined, and the imagining was sweet. But when he began to stretch those limitations, I became unsure.

It is hard to believe now that back in the very first afternoons in The Chalet, when Hodge's use of my body was as sketchy and wild as his first scrawls, I sometimes left him with a flush of desire still on my skin and a hot, incomplete sensation flaring through body and brain. I would charge along the towpath then, hips twisting under my skirt, breasts aching. Back in my room I would lie on the bed in a half sleep, day and night dreams producing over and over the same vision in which Hodge's gaunt head lay on my shoulder while inside me he rested deep and warm: spent, happy, held.

Reality was never like that. He found ways of curing the flush of desire; he found ways of making me scream; and because I loved that – at first – the dreams of him adjusted and he became, instead of a man with whom I performed a 'precious act', a being, hardly human even, who bestowed on me through his own obsessive lust for something else, the irresistible gift of a thousand starbursts followed by sweet oblivion. That was how I saw him for a while, as a key to my release and in fear that each time might somehow be the last (". . . every hour bears off a fragment of our life, while we prepare to live . . . and suddenly we die") I reached out more and more desperately for that gift, opening myself wider and wider, bucking and sobbing. I even heard my own voice, choked, almost unrecognisable, pleading: "More! More!"

Then the 'gift' began to feel like a demand and when his body left mine and I left The Chalet I felt emptied – drained, turned inside out – rather than filled. I will never know how much of it was in my mind. God: when was it that I began to *mind* feeling sore?

Looking back, I cannot see into my head but I can see what I did. In April, grasping belatedly at all the little things that had ordered my existence before, I found myself buying muesli again and going for runs. I even, purely as a distraction from Hodge (who had originally been the perfect distraction from everything I now wanted to get back to), found myself telephoning Daley.

"How's Mr Bun the Baker?" I asked cheekily. "When are you going to take me out for a drink?"

Daley

Daley laughed when Esther told him she had made an appointment with Dr Sharp.

"What for?" He puffed out his cheeks and massaged his paunch. "Is it because I'm getting fat?"

"No, love. It's because I'm worried about how you are in yourself."

"In myself? *In myself?*" Daley mocked the cosy little expression and waved an arm at the television. The news was on: scenes of violence; a close-up of a terrorist. "I reckon God had something wrong *in himself* when he made this lot, don't you?"

Esther looked away, was quiet for a moment.

"Anyway, you'll go, won't you? I mean, you're *not* yourself are you, love? And you're not happy."

"Not myself? Who's anybody? And who's happy?"

Esther stared at her hands then stood up, responding to a shout from Jonathan upstairs.

"We used to be," she said and now Daley looked away, pretending to watch television. She left the room and his eyes slid back and followed her legs as she climbed the stairs. Her tights were rough from repeated washing and the heels of her shoes were worn into curves. The children's clothes were shabby too, but washed, mended, cared-for.

"I'll go," he called after her, "promise."

And he meant it. But two days later Julie telephoned and instead of sitting in Dr Sharp's waiting room at six thirty that Friday, Daley was pulling up outside the Red Lion.

He was half an hour early for their date – a word, teasingly, Julie had used – and he stood sipping a pint slowly at the bar, wondering where they would sit when she came, what she would want to drink, what they would talk about. He undid the top button of the clean shirt Esther had laid out for him and did up another which had popped open over his paunch, bigger than when he and Julie had worked on the boats. She would not be wearing her old boilersuit now. It was months since he had seen her. Christmas the last time. What did a girl like Julie wear on a date? It made him feel queasy with excitement that the date was with him.

He ran a hand over his hair and felt its unaccustomed fluffiness. Esther had smiled encouragement when he said he would take a bath after work.

"That's right. Dr Sharp might want to examine you."

There had been a cup of tea waiting for him when he came down smelling of baby soap. Leonie had made a game of combing out his damp hair.

Seven o'clock came and went and Julie was still not there. Daley was on his second pint and felt the effect. It smoothed the edge off his nervousness but at the same time made his mind feel loose and uneasy, thoughts swerving into one another like dodgem cars; like at the bakery before the conveyor belt started or when he was filling in time before fetching Leonie from school. Juicy Julie. His head was down, eyes absorbed in the bubbles at the bottom of his glass when she tapped him on the back.

"Hiya! You were lost in a dream."

She was by his side unwinding a scarf, unbuttoning a jacket.

"Hiya," he said, using the strange greeting carefully and then, because he could not think of anything else to say, repeating it.

Julie's hair was done in a style he had not seen before, a long ponytail flowing over one shoulder. She shook it as she shrugged out of her jacket and for a second it disappeared down her back and then came over the shoulder again.

"I'm more than ready for a drink," she was saying explosively, "what shall I have?"

Daley felt panic at the thought that he might have to suggest something but he need not have worried.

"Half of lager," she called to the barman, scattering pound notes on the bar, "and another pint in here."

"I'll . . ." he said, a hand moving slowly to a pocket, but

she waved the gesture away. "You get the next one. Where shall we sit?"

His mouth opened to reply but again she answered herself.

"There. Over there," and sipping from her lager as she went, strode to a corner table near a red shaded lamp. Other eyes besides Daley's followed her. Proudly, lumberingly, he crossed the floor in her wake, squeezing in beside her where she patted an upholstered pew.

She was talking, saying things like "What a week!" and "I'm worn out. Damn buses. Thank God to be sitting down." He did not follow it all, taking in more the way her hands twitched on her glass and a light flush, or it might have been the red shaded lamp, emphasised her cheekbones. She was wearing a pale skirt and a soft black sweater with a medallion between her breasts. And perfume.

"You've got thinner," he said as she stopped talking for a moment to sip her drink. "And I've got fatter." He giggled.

Her eyes, with turquoise shadow on them, looked at him over her glass.

"Yes," she said seriously, "we've both changed."

Then she switched back to her former, gabbling mood and fired questions at him, answering most of them before he could begin to think of the answer to one.

"How have you been? . . . OK? . . . What's the job like? . . . Boring, I bet . . . How are the children? Jonathan must be talking now . . . How's Esther? I never seem to get time to . . ."

"You're gorgeous," said Daley flatly and got up to go to the Gents.

On the tiled wall beside the urinal was a small sketch in red felt tip of a penis in a woman's mouth. Daley stared at it while he urinated. When he shut his eyes he imagined his head resting on Julie's black sweatered shoulder. Zipping up, he went further, conjuring between the dodgems an image of himself nestled between her legs; peaceful, happy, her arms around him. When he got back to the table he saw her drink was finished and bought her another before sitting down.

"Thank you," she said and gave him a deliberately tooth-paste ad smile. "Now come on, talk to me. I want to know what you've been up to."

Daley buried his upper lip in his beer and drank.

"Not-a-lot."

The excitement he had felt before she came had evaporated. In his mind's eye then he had seen himself 'chatting her up', a vision in which she had somehow been sitting back quietly, smiling at what he said. But he had nothing to say and it was she who was leaning forward, in command, while he sat back listening to his own vacuity. It made him feel so hopeless, he almost relaxed.

"At work," he told her suddenly, "me and this other bloke – they call us 'the wallies'."

"Really?" Her head was turned to him, elbows on the table, "What's a wally?"

Daley flexed his legs and twiddled the loose button over his paunch.

"You know: useless type."

Julie gave a small laugh and drank more lager.

"What exactly do you do there?"

Now Daley laughed, paunch shaking gently.

"Put buns into ovens. All day." He laughed again. "Hey Julie, shall we get drunk?"

"I don't see why not."

The Red Lion was beginning to get crowded by eight o'clock and Julie suggested moving on. A group of punks, faces young and vulnerable beneath aggressive hair-dos, stood near the door and Daley found himself weaving between them, eyes hooked on Julie's disappearing back. They did not look at him, even when, accidentally, he nudged one of their legs. It gave him the peculiar sensation that he did not exist. Outside he caught up with Julie, panting. She was already opening the van door.

"The Threshers," she said. "And let's get some chips on the way."

It was cool in the van after the pub and she asked him to switch on the heater.

"It's gone wrong," he said and laughed privately as they drew up at traffic lights. "Everything goes wrong with me."

He heard her giggle beside him and the low sound of it in her throat brought back his earlier queasy excitement.

"I know what you mean," she said. "Oh, I know what you mean."

She had had a glass of wine last thing before they left the Red Lion and he could smell it, heavy and suggestive, on her breath.

"Listen to this." He recited the piece of graffiti that had so impressed him in the swimming baths: "*When the bottom is falling out of your world take Andrews and the world will fall out of your bottom.*"

She rolled about beside him, squeaking with laughter.

"Say that again."

He did, then they said it together.

In the fish and chip shop she stood close behind him in the queue. There was a calendar on the counter, next to the pickled onions, showing a big breasted girl straddling a motorbike. Daley stared at it while he waited to put in his order, enveloped by Julie's perfume from behind. He wondered whether she had heard him when he had said "You're gorgeous" back in the pub. Perhaps he had not said it aloud at all, merely felt the words reverberate inside his head. The end of her ponytail touched his neck as she flicked her head impatiently when his turn came.

"Chips for two," she called over his shoulder as he dithered, "with plenty of salt and vinegar."

They ate the chips as he drove, Julie balancing the paper on her knees, his hand coming across at regular intervals to select blindly from the hot, greasy mass.

"Do you still see that old lady who wrote to you?" he asked, conscious of his hand, touching, through chips, paper and skirt, her thighs.

"Yes. As a matter of fact I've made her a birthday cake and we're having a little party this weekend."

"Ooh, a party, eh? Can I come?"

"Certainly not, dirty old man like you. This is girls only."

Daley drew his hand away sharply, without a chip in it. Dirty old man.

"I've got to phone Esther," he said.

"Why? Doesn't she know you're out on the tiles?"

"'course she knows I'm out. I've just got to phone, that's all."

In the Threshers Daley left Julie to order their drinks while he went in search of a telephone. Esther answered immediately.

"Is that you, love?"

"Yeah."

"What did he say? Are you in a pub?"

"Who? Yeah. Oh, Dr Sharp. I didn't go."

"Oh . . . !"

He felt the disappointment in her voice.

"But it doesn't matter. I'm fine. Having a drink. Nothing wrong with me."

"You'll come home soon, won't you, love?"

"Yeah. Don't worry."

He hung up.

Julie was sitting in front of a half-empty glass of lager and a full one of wine when he got back to the bar.

"I've been having 'an affair'," she announced abruptly. "You always used to think I spent all my time when I wasn't working with 'boyfriends'. Well for once that's been true. One 'boyfriend', anyway. Since Christmas."

Her words came as a shock to Daley. On his way back from the telephone through the crowded room his mind had been on bodies again; specifically, her body. Now, looking at her flushed throat above the V of her sweater and the way the medallion between her breasts glinted and swung, he felt a dizzying surge of jealousy. Without saying anything, he sank his upper lip in his beer. Julie did not seem to expect any comment and after playing with her wine glass and taking a few long sips of lager, went on.

"He's . . . unusual. Doesn't talk much."

"Oh yeah?" The words shot out of Daley. "What *does* he do? I suppose you've slept with him."

Julie seemed oblivious to his anger. She laughed.

"Of course!"

Daley sank his lip again, staring over the rim of his glass. In his mind he saw the stranger's hands creeping softly, like a tide, under Julie's sweater. He saw her leaning forward, offered.

"Good, is it?"

He was no longer angry. It was the question of a voyeur.

"Well, it *was*. Don't quite know what's happening now."

Daley

The tide in Daley's mind crept on, the stranger's hands becoming his own.

"Legend," he said softly, as he had in the bakery, then: "ledge end" and he fell off it slowly, in his mind, into her.

"What?" Julie was leaning right forward so that her perfume folded round him like an arm. Loud music started up close by and now, even when he raised his voice, reciting another piece of graffiti, she could not hear him or perhaps just did not understand. After a moment she gave up trying and they both sat back and finished their drinks, locked in private worlds. Trying to unlock hers, he clinked the bases of their empty glasses together, offering another. She shook her head and he fell off another ledge into the gap between worlds.

But when they parted a little while later she said, mocking the formality of the phrase: "We must do this again."

"Yes." He swayed as she gave his plump white Feeder Grade IV's cheek a fleeting kiss.

Her final announcement was: "Friday nights are good for me."

165

Ann

The nurses were not convinced by Ann's protestations that she was on a diet. There were tests, doctors' visits and towards the end of April, she was taken into hospital.

She abandoned the bird table with regret, saying to the porter who wheeled her to the ambulance: "They'll miss me. They all know me now."

"Never mind, love. You'll soon be back."

She did not nod.

The diagnosis was cancer of the oesophagus. It had been her companion for some time. Ann guessed but was not specifically told. Phrases like 'under observation' were used and they spoke to her slowly, kindly, loudly, as though she were simple or deaf.

"I didn't say goodbye to Miss Abbot."

"Never mind, dear. You can write."

Ann said nothing and the nurse looked quickly at her hands.

". . . Or a friend can write for you."

The nurse meant well and Ann smiled. She would write, not to Miss Abbot – what would Miss Abbot do with a letter, eat it? – but to Julie. When she had settled in.

There had not been much time to organise herself and when the warden had arrived to help her pack she was in a muddle, still not able to believe this was happening. Not wanting to believe it.

"I don't know what to take."

"Oh, you know," the woman said, hands folded in front of her in a gesture of controlled patience but eyes darting round the room eager to land on objects to stuff quickly into the grip bag on the bed, "just toiletries and a nightie sort of thing. Don't load yourself down. Everything will be quite safe here."

Ann nodded, repeating the words "Nightie, toiletries" and

moving slowly to point out where they were. But in her mind the decisions to be made were far more complex. She had somehow to distil in half an hour all that was valuable in her life that expressed itself in portable objects.

"It's just as well Freddy has passed on."

"Who? Come on, dear. I've got Mrs J's tablets to do. This your nightie here?"

"There's a better one in the drawer."

The drawer squeaked as the warden yanked it open. Folded clothes billowed up and Ann's eye was caught by a scrap of tissue paper sticking out from under a cardigan.

She gestured. "I'd like to take that."

It was the cotton frock she had kept, years and years old, to remind herself that, among all the dreams, half-memories and films, the day she had stood waving goodbye to Alec and his friend had been real. As her youth had been, wrapped up in that frock.

"Oh, you don't want to take that, love. Just basics. Nothing best."

Ann did want to take it but she did not want to argue. She would pack it herself, later.

She was exhausted by the time the warden left and all there was in the bag was – a nightie and toiletries. She struggled to open the tightly closed drawer and could not. In the end, the only item she took that meant anything special was the snap-shot of Julie with her plaits wound on top of her head. She carried it in her handbag and its bulky frame made a square bulge on one side. In the hospital she took it out and put it on her locker by the water jug, but facing her so that she was not constantly asked if that was her granddaughter. She was afraid she might say it was.

The move to hospital meant acceptance of current realities. Painful acceptance. Painful realities. Once established, she found ways of sliding backwards and forwards to other real or imagined eras – and there came a time when this happened whether she wanted it to or not – but during those first days she was forced to face her fear. It was a different kind of fear to what she had suffered during her four a.m. sessions, when she had imagined burglars, rapists, murderers breaking into her flat, but it made her feel helpless in just the same way, and talking about it did not help. The nurses' sympathy was there but it was distant, professional, and anyway no use because the murderer – the disease – had already got in. She felt it choking her silently before their eyes and the doctor, a pleasant, bearded man who touched her gently and gave her medication to ease the pain, was like the policeman who came too late. Death cannot be locked up.

When she had been a young woman hiding in an air-raid shelter during the war a mother holding a crying child had sat beside her one night. The child, not understanding the immediate danger outside, had kept whimpering: "Mummy, Mummy, never let me grow older or die." Those words came back to Ann now. "I am old," she thought, "and I am going to die", and it seemed unfair that her life had gone so fast – or so it seemed now – when at the same time it seemed never to have properly begun. Gone in the wave of a hand, a kiss carried on the fingertips. Gone in seeming. She felt the child's fear and also the helplessness of the mother. She was envious of the mother, too. She had never even had someone to helplessly soothe.

Fear and resentment made her irritable at times in a way she had never been before. One of the nurses jokingly called her Miss Misery to her face and Ann experienced a moment of raw hatred. "Stupid little whatsit. What does she know?"

In the morning, after her token attempt at breakfast and in the evening after her last cup of tea, Ann held the photograph of Julie and carefully examined the young, smiling face under the glass. Anyone passing her bed might have thought she was looking at herself in a mirror.

On the third day Ann asked for the shop trolley to stop by her in the afternoon so that she could buy some stationery. It arrived while she was dozing and, startled by its trundling noise, she glowered at the man pushing it. Without her glasses on he was just a small brown bobbing blur.

"Nice to meet you," said the blur. "My name is Gupta. What can I tempt you with today?"

The voice was high and boyish and the speech sounded rehearsed. Ann's voice was a croak. Her hand sidled, crablike, over her chest looking for her glasses. "I just want some writing paper, an envelope and a stamp."

"What a good idea!" cried Gupta. "Sending letters is just the thing to cheer you up when you are not feeling well."

He pulled open a slender drawer in the side of the trolley and displayed pink, blue and white writing sets, fluttering his fingers over them and continuing to talk.

"I myself do not know how I would manage without letters. Not a week goes by without two or three coming from home and every night I write a little and send one big bundle off at the end of the week. I save quite a lot of postage that way."

"How much is the pink paper?"

Ann had levered herself into a half sitting position and managed to get her glasses on. Even a small effort drained her now; did not seem small. She noticed that Gupta wore a clean white shirt and that his hair was neatly combed. A lot of the nurses were dark skinned, too. Like on television.

"Only sixty-nine pence, with six envelopes included. And would you like first or second class stamps? I can post the letters for you."

Ann looked unsure.

"Oh, don't worry," Gupta had read the look, "it is quite normal." He waved a slender hand to take in the far corners of the ward, maybe of the world (one old lady waved back). "All my friends give me their letters to post and I am happy to take messages, too, or fetch something I have not got right here on my trolley."

"I only want one stamp," said Ann and was about to say second class out of long habit of economy when, the familiar wedge of pain for a moment obstructing all other awareness, she was reminded of the possible shortness of her time.

"First class. And perhaps I'll take a new biro as well."

Gupta, happy that the old lady seemed less grumpy now, lifted the jar of biros from the trolley and offered it to her like a bunch of flowers, moving it this way and that so that she could admire the different colours.

"Which one shall I have?" she pondered, quite enjoying the comfort of shopping from her bed now.

"I myself always use black but blue is very popular too and –" he paused as though struck by inspiration "– it would go most beautifully with your pink paper."

"All right. A blue one then."

Ann leaned over and pulled her bag from her locker. She had difficulty sorting out the correct money and Gupta said: "Take your time. Take your time."

The little phrase, so ordinary, so well intended, upset her. Time again. Too late, she thought, dropping coins, my time is in the hands of other forces now. She was sorry when the exchange was finally made and there was no further reason to keep the trolley, with its cheerful, distracting owner, by her bedside.

"Will you be coming again tomorrow?"

"No unfortunately. You see I also have a business outside and I can only manage two afternoons a week here when the shop is closed – Wednesdays and Sundays. I re-open for evening sales. Never an idle moment for a chap to get lonely!"

Ann listened to his explanations politely but was worried now about when he would post her letter. She did not want to entrust it to the nurse who had called her Miss Misery, who would be on duty later. As if reading her mind, Gupta said: "If you write your letter now, I come back for it at the end of the afternoon."

"Thank you. That would be very kind."

Ann's former stoniness was totally dissolved but she was exhausted. She must rest a while before she started the letter. But not too long.

Gupta turned and waved to her when he was halfway down the ward. Weakly, hands as meaninglessly still as those of a deliberately stopped clock, she smiled.

Five

Hodge

On the last Friday in April, about an hour into Hodge's night shift, the dispatch overseer came to see him. It was his turn to go out on deliveries. Hodge straightened up from the basket he was pushing into place, scratched an ear beneath his paperboat hat and nodded to show he was ready. It made little difference to him what he did during work hours so long as he could go on planning the painting in his mind. He had ordered a large canvas and was due to collect it this weekend.

"Right then. Go over to loading now. You'll be on the road by half past nine."

The light outside in the loading area was gentle compared to the white glare in dispatch. Beyond the flour silos the sun was being crowded softly downwards by pink clouds. Hodge worked alongside the man who would drive the lorry, the two of them sliding wooden-sided trays like drawers into the back, then the driver standing inside and receiving baskets from Hodge which he stacked snugly into a specially designed space. The tail-board of the lorry went down with an echoing boom on their completed work and the driver shouted:

"OK, mate!"

Hodge, wearing the pork-pie hat of Perkins & Day delivery man now, pulled his long frame into the cab and sat silently outstaring the pinkening eye of the sunset. The driver whistled through his teeth and tooted as they headed for the main gate.

"Roll on morning!" he said with a smile and put a country and western tape on the cassette player by his side. Hodge took out tobacco and papers. Their first scheduled stop was several hours away.

That afternoon, Julie had telephoned The Chalet instead of turning up at the usual time. A friend was seriously ill and she was going to visit her in hospital. Hodge had said little but his impatience must have been clear. "I'll make up the time at the weekend," she had said and that had calmed him. She had even offered to go with him to collect the canvas on Saturday afternoon. Then he would paint her. Paint her and fuck her. In the after image of the sun, now invisible behind chimneys, he saw her body. He wanted to be inside it now.

Less than three miles from the bakery the driver lowered the volume on *The Best of Johnny Cash* and slowed down, saying he thought he could hear something rattling in the back.

"Better check." He pulled off the road at the next lay-by. It was meant for buses only but he reckoned they would only be a minute and left the engine running. Hodge waited, smoking, in the cab. Across the road was the Threshers where, months ago, he had sat one lunchtime thinking about the possible treasures of Miss Wainwright, deceased. He had not been in there since.

"Switch off," called the driver, tapping on the cab window and indicating that this was going to take longer than he had thought.

"My fault." He refused an offer of help. "Stacked one of the baskets lopsided."

He whistled as he jumped into the back again and Hodge heard the baskets crashing around. Winding down the window, he threw out the butt of his last cigarette and started to work on a new one. A car door banged across the road and a girl's laughter, high but at the same time throaty, rang out. Hodge's head turned slowly towards the sound and his hands, about to carry the cigarette to his mouth, paper ready to lick, stayed where they were. The girl was crossing the pub car park swiftly on high heels, followed some yards behind by a plump, slow-moving man. She stopped before the door of the pub and turned round so that her face, under the porch light, was clearly visible.

"Come on, slowcoach!" she called and stamped a foot in mock petulance so that her body, in a thin dress, shook. The man, to Hodge's vision now no more than a back with rounded shoulders, caught up with her and she reached out an arm, wrapping it round him flirtatiously for a second before, opening the pub door herself, she pushed him inside. The teasing laughter fluting out of her again was cut off as the door swung shut.

For a long time the cigarette poised in Hodge's fingers did not move. Then, very slowly, he brought it to his lips and ran his tongue along the edge of the paper. The tail-board of the lorry went down with its echoing boom and the driver climbed into the cab.

"Well, that's *that*," he said, breathing heavily, and switched on the engine and Johnny Cash, loud. As he drove away he scrabbled for a bag of toffees in his pocket and offered one to Hodge, shrugging when he got no response. Once on the motorway he sat back and mouthed the words of the songs, swapping his toffee from cheek to cheek. In his mind was a vision of the meal he would order when the bulk of the work was done.

In Hodge's mind was still the vision of his painting but, even unbegun, there was something wrong with it now, something distorted. In a private silence within the music and the engine din, he tried mentally to start the painting again but whatever was wrong with it would neither clarify nor mend. Broken lines, motorway and lights tore by the window, white and black and glaring and blurred. Hodge sat without blinking and water gathered in his eyes. Invisible to the driver his right foot, in its flapping mouthed plimsole, swung rapidly up and down, the movement trickling ash from his cigarette on to the cab floor.

At four a.m., after a number of deliveries – the work performed cheerily and with much whistling by the driver, silently, mechanically by Hodge – they stopped to eat. The place was large, the transport section of a motorway service station, but at this hour they were the only ones at the counter. The driver piled up his tray with fried food, sliced bread and pudding and flirted with the cashier. Hodge stood behind, tray empty, and ordered only a cup of tea.

"That all you want?" they teased him. "Never grow into a big strong boy that way." He repeated his order and his face, grim, gaunt, expressionless, choked off their fun. Behind his back they shrugged and grinned weakly. The driver read a newspaper over his meal.

On the back of the paper was a photograph of a woman

with long dark hair. Hodge, for want of any other focus for his stare, stared at this. The face was attractive even though it was distorted by tears and there was something familiar about it. His mother's face had looked like that years ago on the day she told him she was going away for a little while with Geoff's father and Geoff. In that handsome car. Hodge, fruit of an earlier liaison (a 'mistake'), was going to boarding school. It was not when she told him that his mother had cried. That happened later when she discovered her lucky rabbit's paw brooch torn and flattened with the glass of her dressing table smashed beneath it. At school, he had received just one parcel from her – foreign chocolate and salami – before the news came that she had died in an accident. But her death had only seemed like an extension of desertion. She had taken herself beyond his power either to worship or to loathe.

Hodge drank his tea and stared first at the paper, then at an image beyond it: that of Julie standing in the doorway of the Threshers, light catching on a thin dress that rippled against her body and falling over one shoulder in a ponytail, long, dark hair.

Julie

Mirabelle Ward,
Pemberly Hospital

My dear Julie,

As you will see, I am not writing from home. A kind Indian gentleman is going to post this for me. I got the paper and pen from his trolley.

I have been in here for three days now and they have not said yet when I can go home. It would be lovely if you could come and see me.

I am sorry this is such a short letter but I am not feeling very well.

Hoping to see you soon,

Love from Ann

In places, the new biro has failed to give out ink and the words are nothing but a faint indentation on pink paper, but the message is clear and I remember the shameful order of my feelings: one, relief because now I had a genuine excuse not to go to The Chalet that afternoon; two, guilt because I should have realised before how ill Ann had suddenly become. The photograph I took of her on her birthday held next to the one I took at Christmas tells its own tale. The eyes and the girlish smile are the same but the flesh around them is infinitely more frail. Lavender scarf against lavender skin. She was not on a diet; already then, Death was dieting on her.

I telephoned the hospital before going and made it sound as though I knew how serious the illness was so that, even though I was not a relative they were – albeit guardedly – open with me. But it was obvious what it was. Cancer. The word echoed when I had replaced the receiver and I felt momentarily overwhelmed with anger: "Dear God, what kind of a bastard are you to pick on someone like Ann?" I splashed out over three pounds on a jar of peaches in brandy. They said she could only manage soft food.

All the way to the hospital, sitting on the top deck of the bus, I thought, not about Ann, but about Hodge. And when I got there I talked about him too, inventing new details to add to the story I had spun before while inwardly feeling stunned and riveted by the changes in Ann. Soft, once heavy flesh like a burst bag; cheekbones like door handles. On the way back, less than an hour later – the nurse told me she tired easily – I sat in the same seat on the bus, staring out at the dull late afternoon in a state of subdued shock. I realised then that earlier, before the visit, I had been almost excited by the disaster of Ann's illness. Into my mind, as thin branches whipped the top of the bus, came a vision of myself in the shop where I had bought the peaches.

"I want something rather special," I had said to the woman behind the counter in a cosy, conspiratorial tone, and had ended up telling her, as she wrapped the jar in a butcher's parcel of brown paper and sellotape, about my 'poor, sick, elderly friend'. Suddenly I had added to a many sided image of self a kind of charitable facet, making the hospital visit into a mission of love and selflessness rather than what it really was: another little distracting game for Ms Julie Barton.

But it was not only that. There was another 'really' involved too. I really did care about Ann. And it was, of course, different when I got there. I can even forgive myself for chattering on about Hodge because Ann seemed so genuinely interested; because it was clearly painful for her to speak and because – this most of all – it was unbearable to just keep looking at her and nodding sadly in that useless, helpless way one does in the presence of the seriously ill.

"I think perhaps," she said, when I came to a pause in my tale, "you should do the dignified thing."

Be firm. Do the dignified thing. It was hard to think of dignity where my relationship with Hodge was concerned but even before she elaborated I knew what she meant. In the story-suitable-for-her-ears I had replaced Hodge's painting obsession with another woman with whom he was supposedly having an affair. Perhaps this was not so far from the truth.

His obsession with painting was like another woman. *I* was not what he wanted; just a receptacle into which he poured his fantasies and sperm. Ann was saying I should not compete, I should leave him.

"You're right," I said, "I'll tell him this weekend."

"Yes, dear. Then come back and see me soon and tell me all about it."

It was then that I put my foot in it.

"I will, if you're still here."

I would have done anything to erase the fear that suddenly appeared in her eyes.

". . . I mean, if they haven't sent you home."

I thought there was going to be a moment of terrible honesty then but there was not. We both kept up the game. Ann smiled and her gaze wandered over my shoulder to where a nurse was tramping briskly down the ward towards us.

"Of course, dear. It's been so nice to see you."

Her last words to me.

The shocked, sorrowful mood I fell into on the journey home broke when I got off the bus. I jumped off, in fact, and it was the physical jolt as my feet hit the ground that shook up a whole new set of feelings. Within seconds I was back on my distraction hobby horse, galloping after something to occupy the evening. I bought a can of lager and wandered through the burgeoning allotments down to the river. This was not fast enough, nor sufficiently distracting and I returned to my room, changed and went for a long run. The minute I got back from that, still panting, I telephoned Daley.

"Oy, it's Friday, what about it, cock?"

He sounded delighted, in his woolly way.

"Shall I come and pick you up?"

"Lovely. But not till about nine. I want to eat first and get changed."

I ate while waiting for the sweat to dry; Hodge cakes and the second dose of muesli that day, the unbalanced combination exemplifying the muddle I was in. Then I took a long bath, not too hot because I did not want to be flushed. The polythene on the still unmended skylight flapped as I soaped my legs but I ignored it, postponing the problem of Hodge. I wore a single curler in my fringe but not for him.

Back in my room I ran hands and eyes over the clothes lining the walls and was dissatisfied with them all. It was not that I was interested in being attractive to Daley. He was merely an innocuous companion in the pub and transport to and fro. No. What I was doing was dressing for myself and a faceless audience of men in general, needing almost desperately to rediscover that sense of physical confidence and invulnerability that is the hallmark of youth. And putting on a distracting mask. I wanted to be beautiful, to revel in the resilience of my own flesh while I still could. The birthday photograph of Ann was stuck in the corner of my mirror. Her almost coy smile; the tilted head. What is an old woman but a young girl involuntarily masked by years? I still had power and I wanted to use it.

In the end, after rejecting a dozen other garments, I put on a thin, silky dress I had not worn for years. Brushing my hair into a ponytail I shook my breasts at my image in the mirror, ready to play games. When the doorbell rang I thrust Ann's photograph into my handbag with one hand and squirted on perfume with the other.

"Coming!" I yelled over the banister and galloped down the stairs in stockinged feet, bending over and putting on high heels in front of Daley at the bottom. I had forgotten that it was quite fun to be alluring to him, too.

Outside, Daley asked which pub I wanted to go to and should we pick up chips on the way. This was only the fourth time we had been out on a Friday evening but already rituals had developed.

"The Threshers," I said, after weighing up the possibilities. I liked the anonymity of the place and the quality of the 'faceless audience' there. "And no chips." I wanted no greasy spots on my dress.

In the van, it amused me the way Daley's eyes kept sliding off the road on to my legs and when we got to the pub I almost danced across the car park in my high heels. I wanted to drink, flirt, turn heads and be entirely light. And Daley was such a perfect sidekick for my performance, ever attentive, obedient and so easily outwitted. I exchanged a dozen open-ended glances with strangers over his head.

All went well – as successful distraction, at least – until I went to the Ladies and Ann's photograph fell out of my bag as I was groping for lipstick. Why had I taken it at the last minute? To remind myself of the existence of another world even while I was on my flirting and drinking merry-go-round? It is hard sometimes to fathom one's motives for actions that are on the surface spontaneous. When I think back on all the things I said at that time – to Hodge, to Daley, to Ann and to myself – and all the things I did, I grow more and more confused about reasons and motives. To trace one's own history is not to unravel knots but merely to observe patterns in the tangles.

When I got back to where Daley was sitting with his upper lip buried in his beer, I produced the photograph of Ann. A man at the bar and another at a nearby table were giving me looks but I was not returning them any more.

"Guess who that is."

Daley looked dully at the picture and flicked the corner with his fingers.

"Dunno."

"It's Ann," I said, taking it away from him and looking at it myself, "and she's got cancer and she's dying."

He licked a bit of froth from his lip.

"Oh, you mean that old girl you go and see sometimes? Shame. Still, I suppose it comes to us all in the end."

I put the photograph back in my bag and fastened it with an angry snap.

"Bloody platitudes."

Daley's pale eyes wavered before me, non-comprehending, prepared to be hurt.

"Beg pardon?"

"Nothing. Just a life, that's all: birth, the bits in between, then burial."

Daley was hurt now, because I was angry. His doughy cheeks sagged and he looked away. After a long minute in which I drank and he just sat quietly with his hand on his glass, he said: "Can I get you some crisps or something?" A puny offering which evaporated my anger at a stroke.

"Yes!" I cried and all at once I was frisky and giggly again. Any moment I might lean over and ruffle his hair. "And peanuts and another drink!" I finished my lager and prepared

Daley

Esther watched Daley as he prepared for his Friday evenings out and she watched him when he came home. The first time, when he had missed his appointment with Dr Sharp, she had been worried but now she accepted his 'going out for a drink with the boys' once a week as normal. What was not so normal was the way his moods changed so inexplicably. He went out of the door singing and came back talking about suicide.

That Friday, he seemed to have drunk more than usual.

"Mr Bun sticks head in oven," he muttered, eyes closed, lying fully clothed on the bed with his workboots dirtying the counterpane.

Esther chivvied him gently as she tugged at the boots.

"Don't be so maudlin, love."

"Maudlin?" he said, grinning with eyes still closed and a hand on his fly. "Maud Lin? Who's she?"

He snored well into Saturday morning, oblivious to the shrieks and giggles of the children playing in the room below. Esther, washing the kitchen floor on hands and knees – the squeezy mop had been broken long ago by Leonie using it as a witch's broom – was glad that at least, lying up there, she knew he was safe. It worried her when he wandered out of the house in the afternoon, hands in pockets, not telling her where he was going.

"Wouldn't you like to come to the park with us, love?"

Looking down, he shuffled a toe on the front doorstep and stroked Jonathan's hair. Since the time he had fallen asleep in the park, there had been no suggestion that he should take the children anywhere on his own. Although he did still fetch Leonie from school, a responsibility he valued.

"I've got a headache. Better to walk it off by myself."

"All right, love, but you'll be back in time for tea, won't you? We're making a special cake for May Day."

"Yeah."

He walked away and Esther had to hold the children's hands tightly to stop them running after him. Not looking back, he echoed her words.

"Mayday mayday mayday."

As he walked, Daley thought back to the evening before. The worst moment had come when, after watching Julie giggle and chatter her way through three glasses of thick green ginger wine and pulling steadily at his own drinks, he started to tell her the truth. It was in response to one of those strange questions of hers. Earlier she had talked about her old lady friend.

"Well then, Mr Bun, let's get down to basics. *What do you really want in this life?*" She giggled, hiccoughed and repeated: "*Really?*"

"I want . . ." he said, and the dot-dot-dot pause seemed endless – or maybe it was the ledge end again – "I want to . . ."

"Yes?"

Her flushed face swayed close. Through her thin dress he could see her breasts.

"I want to go to bed with you."

He put his glass down at the end of the sentence and his hand remained on the table beside it, resting in a puddle of beer. His eyes slid away from her face but he was aware that the animation in it was suddenly frozen, like a mask, and that her fingers, previously playing restlessly with a sleeve, with her glass, along the edge of her neckline, were suddenly still. His head spun lightly and in the continuing silence he wondered, as he had on other occasions, if he had said the words aloud. Then he knew he had because she began to respond. And it was not just her voice that responded but her whole body. His plump hand in the puddle of beer curled slowly into a fist. She was laughing. And she went on laughing, hand to her mouth, rocking back and forth in her seat, for a long time.

During that time, black things seemed to dance in Daley's head and something hot and thick in his throat made it impossible to speak.

"I'm sorry," said Julie eventually, still shaking beside him, "I'm not laughing at you, *really* . . ."

She made an effort at control, lifting her glass and then, just as it reached her lips, started again so violently that the drink leapt out of the glass and splashed down the front of her dress. In the mopping up operation that followed – the dampened tissue dabbing, trip to the Ladies, table wiped – his 'truth' seemed to be forgotten. And it was closing time.

When they got into the van she asked him if he could drop her, not at her bedsit, but at some traffic lights near the river. "I've got a message to deliver."

"Oh yeah?"

"Oh *yeah*," she echoed, strangely grim, and disappeared, trotting on her high heels, down a side road. It was not far from where Daley found himself now, just round the corner from the Indian's shop.

Since he had started what he secretly persisted in calling going on dates with Julie, he had begun window shopping for girlie magazines again. After the fright he had had at Christmas, when lights had sprung on suddenly as he was staring in, he had for a while avoided the Indian's. Then, as the days lengthened, he had started to go back. The big newsagents in the High Street were busy and the few times he had tried to browse along the high racks there he had been jostled, like in the changing room at the bakery. It was quiet at the Indian's.

Passing the shop in the van earlier in the week he had noticed a new billboard. 'Coming to this shop soon! Video specials!' Behind the board, in the window, was a poster which, walking casually up to the shop now, Daley was able to inspect at close range. The sample film advertised was a desert romance. In the foreground a man and a girl were clinched together beside a burning jeep. Behind them hordes of Arabs waving knives were galloping about on camels. The girl, on whom Daley's eyes settled, lolled back in the man's arms, body spilling out of torn clothes. Daley, hands in pockets, fantasised himself into the man's position. After a moment he glanced up quickly to make sure he was not being watched and noticed that in the shop was a new display of magazines, too. Presently he would go in. There was change enough in his pockets for a couple of comics for the children if he needed an excuse.

Gupta, in the storeroom at the back, was sorting out new items to add to the wares he would take to the hospital on Sunday afternoon. It was hard work, so many boxes to pack and unpack twice a week and often for little profit, but he was confident that, in time, like the copying machine – used regularly now by a lady poet – the trolley business would prove worthwhile. Peppermint creams, he had discovered, were a big seller with both ladies and gents, with candied fruits a close second. Stationery was popular too. Impulsively he added a carton of coloured tissues to the pile in the centre of the room, then shook his head (too bulky and probably available in hospital anyway) and replaced them with a box of hand mirrors. *One must cater for one's customer*, he reminded himself and at that moment the new bell he had fixed to the front door jangled. Gupta automatically ran a hand over his hair, put on a welcoming grin and passed silently through to his place behind the counter. The corners of the grin turned down and the twinkle in his eye became a derisory glint when he saw who his customer was.

"Good afternoon," he said, deliberately omitting any hint of a 'sir'.

Daley, tearing his eyes away from the front cover of *Knave*, gave a small nod in Gupta's direction and picked up a copy of *TV Chatter*. The pages rustled loudly as he leafed unseeingly through them. Gupta, impatient at having to wait doing nothing when there was so much to get on with in the back, began irritably rearranging sweets on the display counter in front of him. He was pleased when the doorbell jangled again and a group of neighbourhood youngsters came in. They wandered round the small shop, crowding it with their presence and exchanging apparently very funny private jokes in loud voices. Gupta, who knew them all by sight, and most of their parents, was not put out by this and bantered with them as, one by one, they handed in soft drinks and crisps for him to pack in white paper bags.

"And twenny Marlboro," said the oldest, putting on an extravagant pleading expression when Gupta said "Tut tut".

"Go on, it's for me Dad. He'll give me hell if I don't bring 'em."

"I will believe you," said Gupta, twisting up the corners of a bag primly, "though thousands wouldn't."

There was a lot of good-natured elbow nudging as he reached behind him for the cigarettes. On their way out, two of the youngsters joined Daley at the magazine rack, sniggering and making rude gestures for several minutes. And it was the recollection of this that so frustrated Gupta when, at the end of the day, he ran an eye over his stock and found that an unpaid for copy of *Knave* was missing. He was convinced that the culprit was that sloppy, dirty-minded fellow in workboots but, unless he was caught red-handed with the magazine in his possession or the theft was witnessed by more than one person, there was no way of proving it. This much he knew from past experience with shop lifters and it was reiterated by a bored constable at the local police station.

"But it is disgraceful!" cried Gupta, not for the first time. "These people must not be allowed to get away with such things."

"I quite agree," said the constable, "but there's not a lot we can do about it. Anyway, I'll take down your details and you can let us know if it happens again."

"Oh, I will," vowed Gupta, "I most definitely will."

Hodge

Hodge did not find the note Julie had left him immediately. She had slid it under his door and it lodged in a slit of ragged Chalet carpet as he pushed his way in. He reached the bed in two strides and collapsed his thin length upon it but he did not close his eyes.

He had not completed the night shift. After finishing his tea in the motorway service station, staring at the photograph of a woman on the back of the driver's newspaper, he had walked away as though going to the Gents and simply not returned. Outside, he had crumpled his delivery man's hat into a ball and waved down the first lorry that passed, explaining that his own rig had broken down. He had been dropped within a few miles of The Chalet and walked the rest of the way through a mild May Day dawn. It was of no importance to him that he would probably lose his job. The only thing he regretted, and that minimally, was the loss of his trenchcoat, which would now hang for years to come in the dispatch workers' changing room at Perkins & Day.

The arrangement made on Friday, when Julie had telephoned about her sick friend, had been that they should meet in the café for lunch on Saturday and then go to collect the canvas. He could paint her in the evening, his 'day' off; all night if he wanted to. Still sleepless at mid-morning, Hodge saw no reason not to stick to this plan. Julie did not know that he had seen her last night. He could still paint her and fuck her; fuck her and paint her. For a moment he imagined that nothing need change, that her defection was an irrelevance. Then back came the vision of her smiling, impatient face lit up in front of the pub door and the way her body shook in that thin dress he had never seen before; the long hair. He wondered if the man had had a big car, like the one that had whisked another woman out of his life.

Grief, suppressed for over thirty years, did not surface visibly now. After another hour of staring expressionlessly at the ceiling, Hodge creaked his legs stiffly off the bed, stuck a cigarette in the corner of his mouth and started sorting through paints and brushes. He did not find Julie's note until a quarter to one when he was on his way out to meet her.

Without his trenchcoat and with the white overalls he had worn last night stripped off and bundled under his bed, Hodge looked exposed, like a hermit crab without a shell. On the way to the café he stayed close to the garden fences away from the road, the note in one hand, cigarette in the other. His long grey sweater hung loose as a skirt round his bony hips. Gupta, waving – he had lost Hodge as a customer because the bakery canteen stocked tobacco but bore him no grudge – was momentarily concerned for his health.

On reaching the High Street Hodge stopped at an off licence for a half-bottle of whisky and by the time he arrived at the café, Julie was already seated at their usual table.

"Hiya," she greeted him, "I've ordered mine already."

Hodge stood by the table, a hand in his trouser pocket looking for tobacco; fumbling. The already begun half-bottle was in a brown paper bag under one arm and he laid it flat on a side plate before sitting down. Julie was smiling. Behind her the waitress wandered into view.

"Tea-and-a-salami-sandwich, is it?"

Hodge ignored her and stared at Julie. He spoke as though reciting an alien code.

"I don't understand."

The other man did not explain everything. Julie had not even mentioned him in her note. The waitress scratched a bulging hip and rustled the paper on her pad.

"I think just tea at the moment," said Julie brightly.

Hodge's elbows displaced cutlery as he sought space for them on the table.

"*Why?*"

The waitress shrugged, moving away.

"Look," Julie spoke without looking at Hodge, "there's no point causing a scene."

"*What's the matter with you?*"

She played with the base of one of the plaits wound on top of her head and smiled sadly, almost wistfully.

"These situations are always impossible, aren't they? All I can say is 'I'm sorry'. And I know that isn't much help."

Hodge's lips closed, trembling. There were uneven spots of red on his cheeks. He remained silent while Julie's order – a toasted cheese sandwich – was placed in front of her. His tea came at the same time.

"But I meant what I said about sitting for the painting, if you still want me to."

She started her sandwich, neatly catching up gluey skeins of melted cheese with the tips of her fingers and folding them back over the toast. She nudged the sugar bowl towards Hodge.

"Drink up before it gets cold."

"I want to fuck you." He was not whispering. "*Fuck you fuck you fuck you.*"

Julie flushed and her chewing became mechanical.

"If you must know," she said softly but clearly, "that's the trouble. That's what it's been – fucking. Nothing else."

The waitress ambled to a table nearby and wiped its surface languidly.

Hodge was sitting back now, pinching tobacco on to a cigarette paper.

"You loved it." He looked up to watch Julie's flush darken and spread.

"*Maybe. But I didn't love you.*"

Suddenly she tossed her head and pushed the plate with the remaining piece of sandwich on it away.

"This is ridiculous."

Some tension seemed to fall from Hodge too and he leaned against the back of his chair, lighting up. He said nothing for a moment, eyes on a puddle of skin forming on his tea. When he did speak it was quietly.

"Let me do it one last time."

Furiously, Julie shook her head. She leaned towards him, mouth averted from the waitress who had wandered to a nearer table and was wiping a clean ashtray.

"For Heaven's sake, I've made it clear. It's over. If you want me to sit for the painting I will but not if you're going to be impossible."

She was threatening him. Hodge stabbed a hand into a pocket and flung money on to the table. He looked at it wildly for a second. Not enough for a car.

"Bill," he commanded the air. To Julie he said: "All right. Just let me paint you."

He picked up the half-bottle, unscrewed the top and drank. The waitress was approaching with the bill.

"Here, this isn't a pub, you know."

He did not look at her but shoved pound notes roughly in her direction so that several fell to the floor. Julie stood up. As they reached the door she said: "What about your change?"

"Fuck it," he said and went out.

Hodge walked straight past the place where they would have caught a bus to collect the canvas.

"What about the canvas?" Julie was taking two strides for his every one to keep up.

"Fuck it," he said and headed for the towpath, a short cut through to The Chalet.

Still staring after them through the café window, the waitress counted the pound notes one last time before tucking them into a pocket over a fat breast.

Ann

Energy was an entity outside herself with whom she once had had – was still sporadically having – an affair. Who kept brushing off whom or was it just the work of Father Time? Ann made an effort to conjure an image of Time she knew should be familiar. He was stooped and carrying something. But the effort was too much. All she could see was a broom. Dust accumulated before its bristles in long, thin lines. There was a little square of gauze in the middle of one of the lines. Hospital.

Most of the time she kept her eyes closed. Or at least they were closed. It no longer seemed deliberate, involving decision on her part. This lack of conscious control applied to other bodily functions, too. Distantly, she was aware of tubes, plastic bags, a sloshing jar. God had not answered her prayer.

Images appeared constantly, unsummoned, on a screen inside her head. Only occasionally could she muster the strength to 'change channels' to something of her own choice. She had lost the ability, it seemed, to switch off completely and yet she sometimes had a sensation of waking up, which meant that the screen must have gone blank for a while. Would the final slipping be like that – so strangely *uneventful*? Would it make any difference to know?

All knowledge now and all experience were becoming obsolete. Everything that had ever happened to her, everything that added up to form the being that was her, Ann Evans, seemed like a bag of currency that no longer had any value. The very cells that made up her body, cancerous or non-cancerous, were coins of no worth where she was going. It seemed pointless that she could still sweat, suffer, smell.

But there were other sensations too, particularly after injections. Sometimes what was on the screen soothed and the bed seemed to hold her very gently, like a buoyant sea. At those times she would have liked to talk, or so she imagined. Who could she talk to? The cleaner with the broom? The Indian with the trolley? Where was Julie? She wanted to talk about when she was young. Only now, lying finally helpless, did she feel able to revisit the real world of might-have-beens taking somebody with her. "Look, that was me," she wanted to say to Julie, pointing to the image on the screen in her mind: a young girl in a cotton frock waving goodbye to her brother and his handsome friend.

More recent physical images slid into view uninvited: a yellow toe, corned and horned as an Irish donkey's hoof, being washed in a nurse's hand; a breast like an empty reticule hanging beside an enormous rib. These were hers. But that other body, soft, young, shyly held, was no less hers. It was just not visible anymore outside her head. If the boys had come back and she had married Alec's friend (Oh God, why have you taken his name away from me?) that young self would never have vanished completely, because in the very fading there would have been renewal: breasts slackened through feeding new life, not sucked empty by nothing but the appetite of Time.

Over the May Day weekend there was a sharp acceleration in Ann's decline and day and night, as well as everything else, became less distinct. The days lost their familiar punctuation marks as though the mechanism of the clock which up to now had governed the passage of her life had suddenly been over oiled so that the hands were slithering willy-nilly forwards, backwards, fast, slow. As she searched for firm outlines at least to recent time, it seemed to Ann that one moment she had been laboriously pressing blue biro to pink paper:

Dear Julie ... not writing from home ... not feeling very well ...

and the next, the girl had been there. Was that yesterday or last week? The visit had taxed her but she was aware – as a man might be, nearing his last gasp on a hill he had chosen to climb – that this was something on which she wanted to spend her diminishing strength. She was aware also that it was thin:

cherishing the attention of a young girl met through a club, known for only six months. But what else was there? The girl had brought her peaches in brandy, had talked to her, confided in her, sought her advice – unwittingly given her what perhaps she had missed most in her life: something to give. Someone to helplessly soothe.

There had been questions on her admission, a nurse holding a pen tied with string to a board. "Just a few little details."

"Religion?"

That was not difficult.

"Next of kin?"

Pause.

"Miss Evans, we need the name of your next of kin, dear."

Ann had chosen that moment to fall into a doze. There had been whispers.

For the past twenty-nine years, Ann's life had been wholly occupied with detail. She had been fifty when, coinciding with the confirmation that she was suffering from M.S., all remaining ambition had died. Ambition to Ann did not mean wanting to achieve something special; to her it was more an indefinable pull forward – hope combined with will – when the future was still full of possibilities. Possibilities on a scale larger than what she might treat herself to for supper at the end of the week.

Concertina'd in retrospect, the process of the take over of detail seemed fast. One morning she was musing about the possibility of a foreign holiday on her way to the insurance firm where she had worked as an office 'girl' for twenty-four years; the next she lay in bed musing on the prospect of living alone for X number of years with a disease which, although varying in severity and effect, would gradually reduce all possibilities until nothing but the certainty of being old and ill was left. She marvelled, looking back, that that morning – or any other – she had bothered, eventually, to get up. Some instinct told her early on how vital it was to keep going. Vital: necessary to life. Keeping going was her life.

Living at first on a small annuity granted by the insurance firm and later on the benefits of the State, Ann had woken up, got out of bed, gone to the toilet, washed, dressed, shopped, cooked, eaten, watched television and listened to the radio, undressed, got back into bed and gone to sleep – for almost thirty years. When the days and nights in hospital had begun to slide together a cartoon scene had appeared on the screen in her mind. There were three characters in it: two mice and herself. She was wearing an old familiar cardigan and skirt and an old familiar night dress – not together but in quick succession. That was all that happened in the cartoon: getting dressed and undressed, lying down and getting up again. The mice mimicked her actions and, unable to switch off or change channels, this upset her. A nurse, seeing a patient moaning and restless, had come to smooth sheets; check tubes.

"What are you doing? What are you doing?" Ann had cried out hoarsely, eyes remaining shut.

Of course she had done other things. That was where the detail came in. For some years she had remained able to walk unaided and pull herself up on to a bus. She could recall clearly the many mornings she had sat over her breakfast informing Freddy and his predecessors of her plans for the day. She made lists. Date and day would be pencilled in at the top, then it might read:

49 to High St.
Brown's – 4 rashers, ¼ mince
Walton's – pots. Carrots, 2 bananas, a Bramley(?)
Samuel's – matches, wire wool. Ask re. soldering kettle.
Morris's – s.s. white
Lavery's – mints. Book?

Going over such a list she would put a line through *Walton's* and transfer those items to the end because potatoes and carrots were heavy and it would be more sensible to get them last. Over the years s.s. white (small sliced white) became s.s. brown because the nurses who came more frequently as time went by and the health column in her 'book' (a women's magazine), said it was better for her. Not on the list were things she knew she would do in the course of her outing: window shop in Honniger's the furnishers, exchange notes on the weather with Mrs Morris in Morris's (Mr Morris passed on in 1972) and rest for five minutes on the bench by the 47 bus stop. Back in the flat it was often a rush to have the shopping put away and lunch ready by half past twelve. But she liked the rush. Being busy, being attentive to detail, was being alive.

"Do it *properly*," she said to herself (or Freddy), day after day as, day after day, she performed the knife test on two properly scrubbed and peeled potatoes boiled for twenty minutes in her little-old-dented-bottomed pan. It surely did not count as cutting corners to put the carrots in the same pan or keep her bit-of-fish or mince warm in a covered dish resting on top instead of the (proper) lid. What she would have for pudding, what she would watch on television, what small adventure her shopping trip tomorrow might bring – these were the questions. The answers – the details – were hers to fill in.

Then the walking became more difficult and the step up to the bus impossible.

"Why don't you put in an order for your shopping?" the nurse, who by then was coming once a week, suggested. So she did. Once-a-week list collected and box delivered at no extra charge.

No more "bit warmer today, isn't it?" with Mrs Morris. No more window shopping in Honniger's where once she had gone so far as to imagine sitting on the big red sofa with Alec's friend enjoying their 'autumnal years'. No more five minutes' rest by the 47 bus stop where, spring after spring, the sight of the first daffodils, even on that scruffy little patch of grass used by the dogs, had given her pleasure. Soon, no more going out at all unless she was taken.

It took a while for her to comprehend the profundity of this change. She got up as usual, washed, dressed – these things were taking longer and longer – and sat over her breakfast making plans. The lists she made were different now.

"What have they got?" she asked the boy who came for her order, just as her mother had asked the greengrocer, years and years ago, "What's fresh today?"

On the first occasion the boy, lanky in the doorway, had shrugged, anxious to get on with his rounds.

"Everything."

He worked for a large supermarket chain.

Ann had blinked up at him.

"What kind of bacon is there?"

The boy's feet had moved impatiently.

"All kinds."

Seeing that she was still waiting he had sighed, loudly. "*Own brand, Danish, Canadian, back, streaky, smoked, unsmoked, Halls, Walls, Bowyers, Ayrshire middle, thin cut, thick cut, off cuts, vacuum packed . . .*"

Ann had got the message.

Four rashers of Bacon, she had written on her list. She would wait to see what they would bring.

At first, it had been quite exciting waiting to see what they would bring. There was almost a touch of the grand lady in being brought an order box, even though she carefully counted out notes from the sheaf folded into her pension book to pay. They got some items wrong: 'own brand' instead of her usual Brown & Polson cornflour; plain chocolate Homewheat instead of milk. She had assumed that in time, these things would correct themselves. Some did, but there were always others. The grand lady feeling wore off and soon, it seemed – although it might have taken years – Ann found herself looking for the mistakes first, instead of any nice 'surprises' she had put on the list for herself.

It was loss of power that was hardest to accept; the simple power to say: "This is what I will do today". It became a matter of: "I will tidy out that drawer if nurse can just lift it on to the bed for me", and later, as she lost more and more dexterity, "I will wash my hair if I can just get that delivery boy to fix on the shower spray . . ."

Asking people. Relying on people. And sometimes they said no. "Who'll put the drawer back for you, dear?" the nurse might say, "Better leave it till another day." It got left. More and more things got left until, after thirty-five years in that flat, it was agreed by the various forces that flitted in and out of her life in the shape of social services, doctors, nurses, that she would be better off in a flat with warden care.

So she had moved. They had moved her. And the scope for Ann to perform the details that made up her life had been reduced. Although the simplest activities – washing her hands, making a cup of tea – now took up a huge amount of time, she could no longer pretend to be busy. Once, the gaping spaces in her day were brutally revealed.

It was soon after they had started bringing meals-on-wheels. The woman had said they would be dropped off around twelve thirty, "Sometimes a bit after, sometimes a bit before." Ann looked forward to the arrival of the lunches, each week brought by a different volunteer. There would be the sound of the van drawing up outside, and if it was Mrs Barnes or Susan Langley the clack-clack of heels followed by a cheery "Hello" or "Me again!" If it was Mrs Warwick or Mr Bain there would be the spongy thud of brogues instead and a "Dinner's up!" or "Shepherd's pie – must be Tuesday!" Ann was irritated when they shouted out what it was; it took away the element of surprise.

That day had started badly. When, on waking, she had switched on the radio as usual, she had inadvertently knocked the tuning knob and some loud, muddled thing had blared at her while she tried to readjust it. This had made her late for her first 'call' of the day, which meant that her nightie had got wet. It was only a little but she hated that smell; hated the powerlessness. And after the extra washing – she did not like to put those things in the laundry bag – and getting dressed and doing her hair, she had sat down exhausted. Almost ready to go back to bed. The cartoon.

The plan had been to make her bed after breakfast which, with a dust round, would take her up to the next call. This might be a strenuous one and then there would be the longest part of the morning to face. To outface it she planned to reread an article on Princess Diana. Then there would be the daily service on the radio and after that she could have another hunt for her spare glasses which she might need at any time. If she made herself a cup of coffee it would probably mean an extra call. Not feeling up to any of this, shortly after the nine o'clock news, she had slipped into a doze.

It was pleasure she had felt, pleasure and relief, when she woke to find that the meals-on-wheels had already arrived. For once the morning had gone by effortlessly with none of the dreary grappling with empty hours she did not like to acknowledge. She experienced a stab of dismay so violent it was akin to horror when, having eaten all her lunch (stew and dumplings, treacle tart and custard, she could still see the scraped containers), she had switched on the radio expecting to hear the lunchtime news followed by *The Archers* and instead there was the time signal for eleven o'clock.

Dear God, what was she going to do with all that time? In panic she had vented her anger on the meals-on-wheels people. How dare they mess up her morning! The food would have been stone cold by midday. Trembling, she had switched on the television. Thank you, God, for giving us our daily bread. And the schools programme. That afternoon she had wound all her clocks. Time must not be allowed to play this horrible trick on her again.

Must not. Julie was a great one for that sort of ferocious emphasis.

"I *must not* let it go on," she had said, referring to what had 'gone on' between her and Mr Hodge.

Ann had wanted it to go on, had been sad that the daydreams about weddings and outings and babies would have to come to an end.

"Do the dignified thing," she had advised, seeing that the affair must end and the only thing left to do was terminate it gracefully.

There had been an injection shortly after Julie left; many more over the holiday weekend.

I will be ready soon, too, Ann thought – sinking, floating, the hands on the clock sliding willy-nilly backwards, forwards, Energy failing once more – to acknowledge the end of the affair. But not quite yet God, please. There are still a few details to fill in.

Julie

When it is quiet at the sauna I make myself orange juice. I say orange, but it can be grapefruit or lemon as well, all fresh and very expensive to clients. I get it free and have tried every combination. Four oranges with half a lemon is best but when I am upset with myself I use only grapefruit and lemon. Last night was a grapefruit and lemon night. I was thinking of Daley and the way I used him. And Ann.

I laughed at Daley when he said he wanted to go to bed with me. Not just laughed but rocked and guffawed, and I was wearing that thin dress that clung when I moved. Even as I was laughing, feeling bad about it and trying to stop, I was aware of a man at another table taking in my back-flung throat and shaking breasts. I had not made any decisions about going celibate again after finishing with Hodge. Surely a man could give me starbursts without tearing me apart? I still have not found out.

Way back, I think there was a kind of innocence in the games I played. Vanity, insecurity and innocence can be curiously linked. Preparing for an evening out in pre-bedsit days, I used to lift my skirt, checking the lie of my underwear in the mirror. Sometimes I was not satisfied and changed at the last minute. Frills? No frills? And I used to wear lipstick that was faintly scented, enjoying the way taste and smell mingle on a mouth at their most suggestive. To offer a scented mouth felt voluptuous and to wear it alone lent decadence to the most workaday nakedness. Foolish, or worse, pathetic, when what I longed for was a man who would gently wipe it off, saying: "I want to taste *you*."

God (the ultimate), can I never get away from fantasies? One does not get that sort of lover on a whim.

Maybe I should not feel guilty about Ann. Our use of each

other was probably evenly matched. Still it seems callous to say that: she was an old lady, dying, searching for a little pleasure in dreams and I was a healthy young woman playing games. I think I used her chiefly to exercise feminine urges that were not directly to do with sex; someone to bake cakes for, give flowers to, wrap scarves around. But I genuinely cared for her too. There is a fine line sometimes between love and use. Or abuse.

On the towpath that Saturday afternoon, Hodge abused me. Not conventional abuse but nevertheless abuse. Whatever else he had done to me, or I had felt about him – or imagined I had felt – faded to black in that long, long moment out of time. Any abusing I did at least left no visible scars.

We left the café and headed for The Chalet. There were big green fisherman's umbrellas up at intervals along the towpath even though it was not raining. They use them, perhaps, for territorial purposes, along with thermos flasks and cans of worms. It was odd, hurrying like that, the way things my eyes skimmed over when sauntering sprang vividly into focus: a tree split at the fork, torn wood like an inner organ glistening against the elephant grey of trunk; litter chucked roughly in the direction of bushes showing up no more or less drab than the few flowers. There were small boys riding on bicycles, something about the weak shine on their handlebars, their streaked, unevenly socked calves and the flat whirr of thin tyres on the towpath epitomising Saturday afternoon.

A short way past the last fisherman's umbrella, Hodge disappeared. I saw him veer off the path on to a strip of grass that widened out at that point. There was a bench with a litter basket beside it and beyond that, a broad slope thickly covered with bushes. Bright green, almost plastic looking leaves swished for a moment. I stood still looking at the river, surprised to be stopped. He called out.

"Come up here."

Why did I go? These are the mysteries. Why did I let Hodge into my room after he had crashed through the bathroom skylight? Why did I let him tear me apart in The Chalet? Why did I follow him into the bushes?

From where I sit now – drinking cocoa at six a.m. to counteract the bitterness of all that citrus at the sauna – it does seem like madness. But it is too easy to dismiss chunks of the past like that: 'I was crazy in those days' as if there were neither cause nor effect, as if it were all somehow 'just a phase'.

I let Hodge into my room not just because I was lonely and curious but because – despite the return of my little urges which I feared in any case to be circular, leading eventually back to the pre-bedsit dilemma – I had reached a stage where I did not care – or thought I did not care – about living very much. (Ann, Daley, running and seven-thirty-on-the-dot muesli were not enough.) Therefore, whatever the conse- quences of my actions, nothing mattered. I then discovered – created? – in the very object of my possible end, a brand new interest. It was like deliberately getting myself shipwrecked – a reckless gesture with potentially fatal results – then enjoying, temporarily, being a castaway. Hodge was my fantasy island and I latched on to him in the same way as Daley latched on to me. To a lesser extent, Ann and I did it to each other. The problem was that the fantasies couldn't always be controlled.

I let Hodge tear me apart in The Chalet because I loved the starbursts. Perhaps, for all my whims and strangers, I had never had an orgasm before. I, Julie Barton, independent, individualistic, did not exist for him but my essential female- ness, my animality, did. He touched something at the core I could not reach alone.

And Hodge, ultimate stranger, was the ultimate distraction. Distraction from what? From *nothing*. My own Private Nothing. I followed him into the bushes for no better reason than wanting to postpone a return to that.

I walked across the strip of grass, skirting the bench with the litter basket beside it, to where the bushes began. The strained exchange we had had in the café was in my mind. (Him: "I want to fuck you, fuck you, fuck you." Me: "For Heaven's sake, I've made it clear. It's over.") Despite the agreement we had then come to about doing the painting and nothing else, I suppose I assumed he was going to have one last try. Wrong.

My behaviour in the café had, I know, incensed him. First I was brittle-bright, then soft ("These situations are always impossible, aren't they?") and finally, when backed into a corner by his vehemence, threatening. I knew how much his painting meant to him. Perhaps the implication that unless he 'behaved himself' he would be denied the chance to do it was the last straw. I am procrastinating about what happened in the bushes because I find it so disturbing to recall.

It is the running that I remember. That needs no detailed recollection because I have relived it involuntarily a thousand times. I had never run like that before, did not know I could. Almost airborne, it seemed, I hurled myself along that same stretch of towpath where, at Christmas, walking back from Ann's, I had felt so secret and potent as a woman and at the same time so empty. My leg caught the spoke of a fisherman's umbrella and I heard an indignant cry and knew that, behind me, a big green circle spun. Grey path and brown river streamed by, both appearing to move. Breath stretched my chest like unuttered screams. I was terrified Hodge was following.

Madly I raced, madly towards two small boys, legs dangling over the water, bicycles propped against a wall. One of those small boys is frozen in my memory. His legs stopped moving, stuck out over the water at forty-five degrees. There was a splodge of – I presume – bicycle oil on his forehead. His eyes were blank but the attitude of his body was amazed. I felt nauseous trying to run up the steps to the bridge. They were steep and I was afraid I would trip. Hodge, in my mind, had assumed the proportions of Death pursuing me by then.

At the top of the steps I looked back for the first time. He was not there. I had a snapshot vision of a calm Saturday afternoon river scene: lumpy brown water caught in mid-trundle; tree trunks and boat houses a similar grey; patches in bushes of that surprisingly bright leaf green. And from somewhere on the other side of the river came the bland, churned tinkle of an icecream van.

When I parted the leaves where he had disappeared, Hodge called again, quite softly. I followed his voice, bent double, using hands to pull myself upwards on branches. At that stage I was still aware of thinking, even examining the foolishness of my actions. Then I was grabbed and forced down close to him on the slope, the undersides of leaves above us, beneath our bodies dry earth and all around the elbows and knees of branches and roots digging in. He did not speak, was suddenly, I could see, beyond speech. I expected some sort of sexual assault and was prepared to acquiesce just to get it over. *(Was that the only reason?)*

But Hodge just held my face. He held it like an object, not a living thing, fingers gripping jaw and cheekbones as though they were handles, thumbs pressing into flesh as though it were cloth. His own face had set into something unrecognisable, something like a stubbled animal mask: red eyes, yellow teeth, no longer fantasy but nightmare. One hand was on my throat. In the other was the small, brutal-looking knife he used for sharpening pencils. I expected the knife at my throat. Wrong. He cut off my plait, one plait at its base. Then he tried to cut off my fringe and that is how I got the scar because I started to fight. The knife skidded into the skin of my scalp; a needle pain and the horrible impression that my head was being sliced open like a boiled egg. I struck at his face and the hand with the knife.

Incredibly – I don't know, maybe he let me – I got away. Then the airborne running, blood welling and the plait only held on by hairgrips to the top of my head where it wound round the other one.

Fear does strange things to time. When I started to run again on the bridge I can't have kept going for more than fifteen minutes, yet the feeling is that I ran for hours: a panic-stricken girl who has just realised how much she wants to stay alive running and running and running, one plait flapping, on a calm grey, green and brown Saturday afternoon.

Daley

Waking was his enemy. In fighting it, his body, heavy with the torpor of depression, was an ally. On weekdays, when Esther woke him at five to get ready for work, his movements in rising were automatic, dreamlike, almost as though he was not awake at all. A spring in the middle of the bed made the same complaint every morning as he heaved his bulk to the edge; the groan he uttered on the toilet was always the same and the van went through the same performance of clearing its throat feebly three times before agreeing to start. Sounds and movements were repeated: the children laughed and cried; meals appeared and were cleared away; bakery shifts ended and began, somehow hauling the weekdays past. But at weekends, when the opportunity for a prolonged dose of oblivion presented itself, Daley closed and reclosed eyes and mind against the nauseating vacuum of time without form. He had long ago abandoned the idea of imposing structure on the hours through decisions of his own.

The day after he had stolen the magazine, Daley woke late morning to two sets of tears: Esther's and Jonathan's. It had in fact been Leonie's voice that broke through the thick surface of his sleep, prodding him to partial, reluctant consciousness with cries of: "Why, Mummy?" and "Mummy, why not?" He rocked deeper into the gully his body had made in the bed, drew his head deeper under the blankets and, hunching his shoulders like a small child, pressed belly and groin into the mattress.

"No, darlin'," came Esther's voice, nasal with tears. "Give it to Mummy." A wail of protest from Jonathan, sound of paper tearing. "*Why* not?" from Leonie.

Daley's hand found the opening in his pyjamas and he cupped himself drowsily. He tried to shut out the voices, reaching for an image to lull him into a sensual limbo. He thought of the magazine he had so far only flipped through and fantasised the mattress into a warm sea of breasts, belly and large, slowly opening thighs. But the fantasy flattened within seconds to a wrinkled undersheet and his arousal died. Inside his head, outside his head, Esther was crying.

He rose on one elbow and called out.

"What is it, love?"

Leonie's feet scampered on the stairs.

"Jonathan's torn a book," she cried, dancing into the bedroom, "and Mummy won't let me pick it up." Her eyes shone.

"Oh," said Daley, slumping down on his back, both hands above the blankets now. He could not understand why Esther was so upset. He wanted to go back to sleep.

"Jonathan, give it here!" came a sobbing cry. He could hear soft grunting as Jonathan struggled up the stairs.

"What's going on?"

No reply. He sighed at Leonie, who smiled at him, and slowly, bed creaking and blankets sliding to the floor, he got up.

Daley stood on the landing, pyjamas awry, holding Leonie's hand. Esther was at the bottom of the stairs, gripping the banister, head down, Jonathan was halfway up. Clutched in one hand as the other helped him from step to step was a torn and bunched sheaf of papers. Breasts, belly, thighs.

"Oh God," said Daley.

Esther's face turned up towards him, its normal expression – warm, slightly anxious – broken like a wrecked jigsaw.

"Take it away from him."

Daley hitched at his pyjama bottoms.

"Give that to Dada." Letting go of Leonie, he held out a hand.

Jonathan stared up at him, no readable expression on his plump face and clutched the pages tighter, crumpling a red garter on a white leg. Leonie hopped from foot to foot by Daley's side.

"Give it to Dada! Give it to Dada!" she sang.

As Daley moved towards him, hand extended, Jonathan retreated down the stairs. Awkwardly he tried to hurry, backwards, and pages fell from his hands. Daley's feet dithered among them.

"Come on, darlin', Dada will find you another book."

Then quickly, clumsily, he snatched at the sheaf held close to the small chest. Jonathan lost his balance and an angry wail broke from him as he tumbled into his mother's waiting arms.

Daley stayed where he was, watching Esther soothe the child while at the same time wrestling the last page away. When she carried him into the kitchen with promises of biscuits and juice, Daley followed and stood in the doorway, heavy paunched and dishevelled, half the magazine trailing in tatters from one hand. Leonie bounded down the stairs kicking the pages dropped there like leaves, before bending to gather them carefully. She joined Daley by the kitchen door.

"All right now, darlin'? That's nice, isn't it?"

Esther had Jonathan settled in a high chair, a picture book, beaker of juice and small pile of biscuits crowded on to its plastic tray. Seeing this, Leonie demanded a biscuit too. Esther gave her one, holding a hand out simultaneously for the pages. Reluctantly, but with a delicately self-righteous air, Leonie let her take them. Not looking at Daley, Esther opened the pedal bin under the sink, lifted a handful of damp potato peelings from inside and pushed the pages down, replacing the peelings on top. Shuffling forward, Daley proffered what was left of the magazine and, still without looking at his face, Esther took it, creasing a lipstick-painted nipple here, a pair of spread thighs split by silk there, as she squashed them into the bin. A tea pot with last night's leaves swollen in it stood on the draining board and Esther emptied it on top then let the lid fall.

"Cup of tea, love?" She reached for the kettle.

They drank the tea in the front room, Daley slumped in his chair, the children playing happily with bricks and toy ponies.

"They're going to a party this afternoon," said Esther.

Daley's head remained sunk over his tea.

"I'll be taking them down about three then fetching them about six."

She took a sip of tea and tapped once more against his silence.

"It'll give me a chance to get some washing done in peace while they're out."

A minor squabble took her attention to the children and Daley, leaving his mug half-full, got up and left the room. She heard his heavy progress up the stairs and then the creak of springs as he got back into bed.

"Lunch in an hour," she called, almost a plea in her voice as, a few minutes later she set up the ironing board in the hall and started on the children's party clothes. "Your favourite – pie and mash."

Daley did not come down for lunch and Esther fielded Leonie's persistent *why?* by telling her Dada was not feeling well. She took him up a tray but the lump under the blankets stirred only enough to shake its head.

"I can always warm it up if you're hungry later."

Silence.

"I'll pop in just before we go." She hesitated before adding: "They'll be dying for you to see them all dressed up."

The lump shifted slightly and the head made a movement that could have meant yes or no.

In the hours before they left, Daley coasted through a dim, tunnel-like region between sleep and consciousness. Groping upwards from what was not quite a dream he rehearsed the words he would say when Esther brought the children in to show off their party clothes. "Lovely" and "Like a real prince and princess". But they did not come. Only the slam of the front door announced their departure and he struggled for a moment to sit up, thinking he might run to the window and call the words after them. He ran nowhere, falling back instead among flattened pillows. Weak spring light through half-open curtains pointed up the night disorder of the room. His own disorder.

"Hara kiri takes a lot of guts," he said, and giggled. Then was quiet.

He lay with eyes open, hands limp by his sides. In his mind he was visiting the contents of the kitchen drawers: tea towels; tin-opener; cutlery. Esther had told him some time ago that they needed a new carving knife but he had only said "OK, love" and forgotten about it. Now he wished he had not. There was only a small vegetable knife and the bread knife, which was blunt. It'll hurt, he thought, and wished he had an anaesthetic. He remembered Esther's collection of family medicines in the bathroom cupboard and got up.

Beechams, Calpol, Benylin. He read the labels and touched each bottle and packet, lifting some down to check what was in them. The Calpol, a thick pink syrup for children, contained paracetamol and this, along with half a bottle of junior aspirin and a dozen foil wrapped Vegenin, he kept out. He held them all in one hand while he urinated then made his way downstairs.

The ironing board was still up in the hall, a plastic laundry basket full of crumpled clothes on top; dolls, bricks and colouring books underneath. In the kitchen the lunch plates and cutlery were washed and draining but the sink was full of saucepans left to soak. Daley stirred the greasy water with a potato masher, looking for the vegetable knife. It was not there. He opened and shut drawers, examining and rejecting an apple corer and the pair of scissors Esther used to trim bacon. Finally he found the vegetable knife still stuck in the remains of the pie. He wiped it perfunctorily on a pyjama leg.

In the front room, he looked for something to write on. A woman hurried by on the pavement beyond the tiny front garden, body bent forward, face blurred through net curtains. I could give her a flash, he thought, suddenly aware that, if he was going to die today, he was free to do anything; nothing mattered. It was living that held him in restraint: the requirements; the failure. But he did not flash and his new found sense of freedom, meaningless when he realised there was nothing he wanted to do with it, mocked him. Setting knife and medicines on top of the television, he unscrewed the cap of the Calpol and took a swig. It was sickly sweet but he drank it all, then picked up a green wax crayon. There were no clear spaces in any of the comics lying about the room so he went into the hall and leafed through the colouring books under the ironing board.

I'M SORRY LOVE, he wrote in inch high letters over an outline of a donkey wearing a hat and, unable to think of anything else to say, tore out the page and placed it on the ironing board, anchored by one of Jonathan's shoes. Another figure went by outside, head and shoulders framed for a second in the glass above the front door and Daley was reminded that Esther might return at any time. With a lumbering attempt at speed he gathered up his bits and pieces and went upstairs.

On the landing he had a vision of Esther's face turned up towards him as it had been earlier when Jonathan was clutching the magazine. There had been no accusation in that face, no blame, not even a complaint: just sheer unhappiness. Daley shut himself in the bathroom, filled a tooth mug with water and sat down on the edge of the bath.

He swallowed the aspirin first, then the Vegenin, hoping they would act quickly as the anaesthetic he needed. After five minutes he felt nothing but a faint nausea and there was a bitter taste on his tongue. He unbuttoned his pyjama top, loosened the gathered waist of the bottoms, and poked with the vegetable knife at his belly button. He was cleaning it out.

Thoughts and pictures wandered into his mind like guests he had not invited but could not be bothered to turn away. They sat down with him on the edge of the bath and joined him in watching tiny black gouts of dirt emerge from his belly button on the point of the knife. His head felt both crowded and empty. Crowded with emptiness, he thought and congratulated himself on inventing the sort of phrase Julie might find amusing. Julie. Black sweater, breasts, belly, thighs. He groaned. The knife was drifting through a sea of little hairs now, too blunt to cut them. He needed a razor blade.

Daley stood up, more faint nausea rising with the movement. On top of the bathroom cupboard was a full packet of Wilkinson's Swords. A bit on the small side for hara kiri, he reflected, a weak grin playing around his bitter tasting mouth; have to be a wrist job. He liked the professional ring of that and said it aloud: "Wrist job." As he broke the cellophane on the packet – reminded for a second of his image of Christ, vapour misted, among the loaves – he heard the front door open. Instantly, his nausea increased.

"I'm home, love," Esther called. "You awake?"

She walked straight past his note.

Eyes tightly closed and head thrown back, Daley pulled a razor blade across the inside of his wrist. It hurt much more than he had anticipated, a horrible, wire-thin pain. He gulped like a child.

"I'll just put the first wash on then I'll make us some tea."

Daley dragged the blade across his skin a second time. Tears burst from the corners of his eyes.

"Help me!" he cried raggedly as the wire pain cut through him again. "Help me!"

Esther sat with him for an hour and a half at the hospital, then had to leave to pick up the children from their party. There had been a flurry of activity when they first arrived, porters meeting the ambulance with a stretcher, nurses attentive and a doctor quizzing Esther on how many tablets he had taken. But when the empty containers were produced and it was learned that Daley had already vomited, comprehensively, en route and was quite able to walk unsupported, the flurry ceased. Doctor and porters vanished and only one nurse, who glanced dismissively at the small blood stains on the handkerchief binding his wrist, remained.

"Take a seat in the waiting area," she said, pointing to a benched alcove to one side of the Accident and Emergency entrance, then she vanished as well.

There were about a dozen other people waiting, some with bandages on, one in a wheelchair and one woman with her legs apart and head in her hands. They were all quiet, only a few murmured comments passing between them from time to time. Daley and Esther joined them, filling a space in the middle of the longest bench like birds melding into ranks of their fellows on a wire. They both sat hunched forward, her hand resting lightly on his uninjured wrist.

Daley hardly noticed her touch during the time they sat together but he was acutely aware of its absence once she had gone. Ignored as he was by the others, he nevertheless felt exposed. What would he answer if someone asked why he was here? The waiting seemed endless before the nurse, who knew why he was here, came to fetch him.

"Doctor will be along in a little while," she said and left him alone in a large cubicle. A lemon yellow curtain flecked with orange dashes screened him off from the rest of the world.

He sat on a black plastic chair and waited again, hands in his lap. Footsteps sounded outside the cubicle and he tensed, expecting the doctor to come in. But the footsteps went by, followed after a short interval by more, this time accompanied by female voices, chatty and unhurried. How long is a little while? Daley's mind began to play its games again. Long as a piece of string. Purse string, draw string, G-string. He grinned suddenly, fantasising a pretty nurse with big breasts bending over him. He was still fantasising when the doctor, young, black and brisk, appeared round the flecked yellow curtain.

"Well, I think you'll live," Daley was told as he was examined, the slack grey pallor of his skin in sharp contrast to the controlled pink and brown fingers probing it. Brown eyes, witty behind glasses, looked up. "Or is that the wrong thing to say?"

"I don't know," said Daley slowly, shuddering at the minor sting of swabbings, "what's right or wrong."

"Now that is serious stuff!"

The doctor explained that he was going to put in two small stitches. As he worked, he asked questions. Had Daley done this sort of thing before? Had something happened to upset him suddenly or had he been feeling generally low?

Daley could not watch the stitching. He looked at his trousers, hastily pulled on by Esther before the ambulance came. His pyjamas had been old and torn.

"I feel terrible," he said, a general answer to everything, and then, remembering Esther's concerned questioning in the past, added: "In myself. I feel terrible *in myself*." The repetition of this made him grin, despite the soreness of the stitching.

"Look, I'm going to arrange for you to see another doctor," this doctor said, "so you can talk some more. Nurse will come and put a dressing on this."

Daley went on grinning, backsliding into fantasy.

"Big tits," he whispered.

It was after seven when he got home. Esther, who had been supervising Leonie's bath, ran down the stairs.

"I didn't know what to do – bring the children to the hospital or what. Did they send you back in an ambulance?"

"No need." Daley slumped into his old chair. "Be wasted on me. Got a bus." The grin was becoming a fixture.

Leonie was calling from upstairs. Esther stood in the doorway, hands, red from the bathwater, twisting in her apron.

"What did they say, love?"

Leonie yelled again.

"Mum!"

"I saw two doctors and they said I should see another one. They're writing to Dr Sharp to fix it up."

Esther called up to Leonie that she was just coming.

"But I won't go," said Daley.

"Oh, love, why not? You must!" Her hands twisted and twisted.

"Mum! Mum! Mum!"

"Oh goodness, I think I'll go mad."

"Na." Daley slumped down further in his chair, the grin weakening, then dead. "That's me."

Hodge

Hodge finished the half-bottle in the bushes. The whisky moistened, temporarily, his dry, whitened lips and brought back their colour. Long fingers ran through his hair displacing twigs, bony elbows nudged a space between those of the branches and his rump found a narrow groove between roots. From the towpath, only the soles of his plimsoles were visible and nobody took any notice of those.

In the tussle, his cigarette papers had disappeared. His trouser pockets, unlike those of the trenchcoat abandoned at Perkins & Day, were shallow; things fell out. Patiently, he ran his hands over the area where their two bodies had been. He turned over to do this, crouching. Dry earth accumulated under long, yellow fingernails. Moisture not far below the surface dampened his trouser knees. Above him, bright green leaves rustled and above them, a block of lightly massed cloud hung like a grey bag in the sky. His fingers, moving like the tines of a rake, found the papers and he hunched back into a sitting position to smooth one out. An icecream van tinkled in the distance. Fragile, wrinkled skin at the corners of Hodge's eyes twitched. She was gone.

At about tea time, when the fishermen were packing up or reaching for second thermos flasks and the small boys on bicycles were heading home, Hodge moved. He came down from the bushes in a way that a man barely out of sleep might emerge straight from bed into a garden, limbs stiff, eyes blear and the weight of his movements uneven. One leaf and a V-shaped stain of earth patterned the back of his sweater. Quietly, unevenly, his plimsoles flapped.

When he reached the bridge, he felt in his pockets for money. All the loose notes were gone and the roll he kept tucked deep down was getting thin. He urinated under the bridge before climbing the steps. The upward movement, forcing the muscles of his thin thighs to strain, snapped through the remaining whisky blur so that when he was on the flat again, he fell into his old stride. Stopping at an off licence, he bought four cans of Sweetheart, two ounces of tobacco and a bottle of White Horse, thinning his roll of notes to one. He was stocking up.

The decisions Hodge made were dictated by simple needs. He did not draw conscious conclusions and, wherever possible, sidestepped what he saw as the complications, the superfluous details, of civilised behaviour. He had no gods and therefore no guilts. In the past, when he had been good at it, it had been easier for him – more dangerous but essentially easier – to burgle than to get a job or fill in DHSS forms. It was easy, too, to use prostitutes or paid models. Women who were paid yielded automatically, giving their bodies – but only their bodies – at a flat, even rate. Julie was exceptional in that way as well as for her face. He had given her money – offered it originally to back up the painting proposition – but it had never been a commercial exchange. She had not – or he had thought she had not – needed to be bribed to stay with him. But beautiful women vanished in big cars. That was one pattern in Hodge's history's tangles.

In his room at The Chalet, Hodge tossed the drink and tobacco on to the bed. He sat beside them as he had sat during the first days of his release last year. It had been cold then and he had wanted coins for the gas meter. Now what he wanted was a canvas, a large one, but he was no longer prepared to go through the civilised motions of getting it. He was beyond going to collect pay packets, catching buses, filling in forms.

He rolled a cigarette and opened a can. The dark beer streamed like a ribbon over his tongue and slid around in his empty insides. His eyes bore beyond the metal honeycomb of the gas fire. Apart from the occasional movement of can or cigarette to mouth, he sat perfectly still, concentrating.

In Hodge's mind was the outline of the painting he had been planning for so long. Julie's body and Julie's face. He saw her pelvis, open as a cupped palm as she half sat, half lay, back propped with pillows, on his bed. Her hipbones, delicately visible, were braced square, supporting open thighs. Their angularity, echoed by other lines – fingers and the wishbone tendons at the base of the throat – gave emphasis to the roundness of buttock and thigh. Small breasts rode on the torso, the soft triangle of one, apexed by pale nipple, making the highest point of the pose. The dark hair around the back-flung head was loose, one hand rested lightly on lower belly, the eyelids were not quite closed.

Hodge drank more beer. He could see her mouth. Sometimes, when he had been on top of her, not inside but the tip of his penis close enough to tease, he had played a thumb just where the pubic hair ends and buttocks begin. He had watched her mouth as he did this, the lips full and open but a tension around the upper one as if there might suddenly be an indrawn hiss. There had been, when the thumb moved. Breath, with its little familiar odours and the small sounds which he knew could rise and rise, had driven him inside.

He got up, a dribble of beer from the discarded can staining the bed. He stood by the window, one hand holding the cigarette close to his lips, the other gripping his elbow. No steam on the windows now, no rain, no Julie behind him sipping ginger wine. The only way not to lose her completely was to paint her, to somehow contain that buoyant, yielding but subtly resistant body between four pieces of wood. Julie, portable on canvas, legs forever open. His.

Outside, a half-caste jogger appeared, trainers inaudibly thumping on cracked paving stones, hands paddling the air. Hodge turned round abruptly to face the room and, sticking the cigarette between his lips, began to search for something on which to paint.

He foraged under the bed, first shoving aside the compressed Perkins & Day overalls, pieces of already well used hardboard and canvases too small to be of any use, then raking out sheaves and sheaves of early Julie scrawls. Every one of them had been rejected for a reason and the vertical furrow in his brow deepened as, flipping through them in the hope of finding clear space, he was forced to witness again his own incompetence. Line after line hit his view as wrong: a breast had shape but no weight, meaningless as a dry tear drop; a calf hung over the arm of a chair, flat as an empty sock. Half-finished faces floated up, expressionless as bubbles; eyes without sockets, sockets without eyes; tongueless mouths. The essence of Julie was the hair, hips, throat, shoulders, vulva, eyes . . . it was everything. To capture her all on canvas, to *pin her down*, seemed impossible. But he was going to try.

In the wardrobe, the pictures were torn and old. None of Julie. Hands pausing in their rummaging, Hodge was struck by what seemed to him now a complete lack of flesh in the figures here. Some were painted, colour spread on thickly as if the texture of pigment could make up for absence of volume suggested by line. Hair flowed, lips hovered, thighs gaped. Nothing lived. And there were no large free spaces to work on. Angrily, he stood waiting for his own actions, hands clenched into fists by his sides. When at last his shoulders relaxed and fists uncurled, the backlit glitter in his eyes was in place but calm, a controlled burn. Necessity had created decision. Quietly and methodically, Hodge removed the wardrobe door.

He propped it on the bed, pillows placed strategically so that it lay at a slant. The wood was cheap, thin, but luckily, on what had been the inside of the door, unvarnished. Hodge primed it as he would a canvas, the paint just stretching to one complete coat. He lit the gas fire to help it dry faster and settled down, as though keeping a bedside vigil, to wait.

Julie's hair. The first time he had seen her it had been roughly gathered into a bun for the bath. Later, it had been invisible under a hat, then pleated into a chignon. He had seen it in a loose ponytail that sometimes appeared over one shoulder and he had seen the bun made tidy for day-time wear. Then she had taken to wearing it in plaits, the long, tumbling mass of it neatly divided at the back and split into six even strands. She said that that was how she always used to wear it 'before'. He could see her fingers making the divisions, the unthinkingly caressive way she handled her own hair, the way she handled her body. When the two plaits were formed and swinging down her back or flicking forward to brush breasts, she could still seem accessible. But when she wound them on to the top of her head, opening hair-grips with her mouth and pushing them into place with a carelessness that did not disguise precision, it was as if she were putting herself away. She would wear it loose when he asked her but in recent weeks he had sensed a reluctance. Once she had said: "It gets in the way – I lie on it. *You* lie on it.'' Only her fringe was always loose, fluffy and taunting.

Hodge opened the bottle of whisky, drank, and set it on the floor without replacing the top. He sat far forward on his chair, elbows on thighs, cigarette held downwards between middle finger and thumb. The blue flames of the gas fire, purling evenly over the metal honeycomb, made a blurred backdrop for his visions. Again and again, his thumb retraced that soft, divided triangle where pubic hair ends and buttocks begin. And again and again he saw her hair as he would paint it, tumbling loose. He did not dwell on the image of the knife, the severed plait, the blood, the fringe. That was now irrelevant, a small, clumsy episode which could be discarded like a torn sketch. The painting would be something permanent. A painting can neither desert nor defect.

The blue flame dwindled in the early hours and went out. Its small, dying eructations woke Hodge. He had not drawn the curtains and through the now fugged window a blotch of yellow light from a street-lamp shone like a giant thumb print on the glass. He drew a finger along the edge of the wardrobe door. No primer came away on the skin but he knew it would be hours before it was properly dry. He wondered what time the Indian opened his corner shop. His rent being due, he did not want to see the barman-manager. Once again, he needed coins for the gas-meter.

Opening a can of Sweetheart to quench the thirst whisky had left, Hodge stood looking at the white blank on the bed. He was aware of a rising tightness inside his head, a renewal of the tension of the day before. But he was also beginning to feel the presence of something else, a dinning sensation like a constant, nagging demand in the background. He knew what it was. It was the complications, the details of the outside world clamouring; the fiddling business of having to go out and find ten-pence coins. He would not go. He would simply wait for the door to dry naturally.

When Hodge had come out of prison, he had gone through all the usual post-release discoveries. He had enjoyed the freedom to sleep whenever he wanted; to open a door and walk straight out on to a street; to drink Sweetheart; to uninterruptedly smoke, dream, doze. But liberty also brought constraints. Not all the details could be sidestepped. And after a while they always began to din at him, the burdens of freedom outweighing the pleasures.

He started to pace. Three strides and about turn, a regular creak from a floorboard close to the fire. The tightness in his head became an ache which, periodically, he blunted with Sweetheart. When that was finished he went back to the whisky. The last time he had drunk like this had been at Geoff and Bea's. Christmas: spangled woman on trapeze; gin; molten icing steaming in the cold. In the cupboard where he had found the cake (cake, pudding? Pudding, cake?) there had been old family snapshots. Two little boys; man with handsome car; long hair across the camera lens. He had painted out memory then in mauve lipstick and eye crayons, Christ and a geisha coupling. Soon he would paint it out again. Julie captured. Woman with long hair never to go away again. For hours he paced, pausing only to test the drying door. Finally, at one thirty p.m. on Sunday, when the barman-manager of The Chalet was sitting down to roast beef and along the road Gupta was setting off with his trolley wares for the hospital, Hodge was ready to begin.

He stood as far away as possible from the wardrobe door, a chipped Elmgrove Project plate and two brushes in one hand, cigarette in the other. The cigarette went to his lips and one of the brushes changed hands as he crossed the room. When the first streak of fleshtint carved into the white there was a moment's panicky hesitation. The brush made feints and shook. Then suddenly, and without a break for many hours, Hodge was bending, straightening, kneeling, balancing, holding back, rushing forward, swooping, stroking and dipping. By evening, the butt long dead, damp and flattened between his lips, he was crouching astride the door.

On the chipped plate now, were crimson, magenta and blue. Brushes were scattered around his knees; gouts of paint were caught in the rumples of the counterpane. Working close like this, Hodge's movements were sharp as a pecking bird's. He gripped the brush near its loaded head, stabbing it upwards, downwards and in tight, swirling curves. Beneath him, the white blank of the wardrobe door had vanished and in its place bones, blood, muscle and moisture grew.

Long after the barman-manager had settled down in front

of the evening's feature film and Gupta was back at the corner shop counting cash, Hodge eased his cramped knees off the bed and, keeping his back to the painting, rolled a cigarette. He postponed the moment when he would have to look by shaking each of the empty Sweetheart cans in turn. Nothing but the dry rustle of ring pulls. Then, long body braced, one hand gripping an elbow, he looked.

The head was wrong.

Hodge remained braced, looking, for a long time. The body lived. It was there as it had been in his mind: cupped pelvis, fingers low on belly, high, beached breast. And between the open thighs was texture, shine and depth, the colours melded into rich, beckoning swirls . . . Above which the head was a nothing. The face, correct as to angle and proportion, had less poignance than the farthest knee. And it was not hers.

His narrow shoulders relaxed. Hodge, who never consciously drew conclusions, had confronted himself with one in paint. The past could not be righted by being frozen and the present could not be pinned down. From now on his women would all be faceless once more and, to perfect nothing more than a body on canvas he might as well abandon the complications, the details of liberty and return to a cell.

But Hodge did not think in these terms. He only felt, could not directly interpret the conclusion. What he thought was that perhaps the moment had come to have another go at the Wainwright house. This time, he would get the right one.

Six

Ann

Snowdrops. Once Julie had brought her snowdrops. Holding them together was not a ribbon but wire, a practical twist. Ann had held the posy in her hand while Julie talked, meaning to put it in a cup of water when she had gone. But she had forgotten and, next day, had found the flowers at the side of the chair where they must have fallen when she stood up. Alone in the night, the white, fragile petals, deckle-edged with brown to mark their sudden plummet to old age, had folded into an exquisite death.

"This is Julie," said Ann, capturing a nurse's hand and trying to bring it to the framed photograph that lay on her chest. It was an immense effort to speak. The nurse gently rubbed the old woman's hand before pushing the gripping fingers back to release her own.

"Try not to get yourself worked up, dear."

"Look at the picture," commanded Ann. Her head refused to raise itself off the pillow. Weakly, her eyes stabbed at the pretty face above her. Dutifully, the young neck craned.

"Very nice. Is it your . . . ?"

"*It's Julie.* I want you to recognise her."

The nurse's brow was wrinkled above her smile. Ann knew she was in a hurry but she reached out again for her hand.

"I want her to have some of my things."

She had said it. For a few seconds her eyelids fell. Then she forced them open again to check that the nurse was still there. She was, masked behind professionalism now, doing things with blankets and drips.

"Don't you worry about that, dear. I'll get matron to have a word with you later."

Ann nodded and again, her eyelids fell. She tried to make the screen in her mind take her on a tour of the contents of her flat. Isolated objects appeared before, hazily, there was a general view.

Wrapped in a housecoat at the back of the wardrobe was a smart black jacket. In the drawer there was the cotton frock. The cabinet in the front room was full of bits and pieces, some precious to her, she knew, but it was a long time since she had seen them properly. A large embroidered tray cloth had slipped down over the front and on top of the tray cloth were piles of papers, folded underwear, tea cosies. It had occurred to her many times to tidy up. But there was so much. Too little, too much. And now she could not remember what most of it was.

The nurse sent for matron and matron sent for the Chaplain. He spoke of God, comfort, prayer but Ann, conserving strength, responded minimally. God knew her life and His will had presumably been done where it touched on her. When the fear and the pain struck, she prayed. Perhaps using him like this was wrong but she could not help herself and if there was a Heaven, and she was destined for it, she would find out soon enough. Better to concentrate on the few remaining details of earthly things now. Matron appeared towards the end of the Chaplain's visit and, as Ann had anticipated, the subject of next of kin was raised again. She was ready.

"I've got cousins."

There were nods, smiles, a pencil poised. For less than a second her head came up off the pillow as she strained to make the next sentence loud and clear.

"And I want nothing to do with them."

The grip on the pencil slackened so that it wobbled, redundant, in matron's hand. The Chaplain still smiled but looked uncertain.

"Never visited," said Ann, her speech becoming telegrammatic in the effort to save breath. "Only *Julie*."

Again, the photograph was produced and in what seemed to Ann a final, significant move, the girl's address was taken down.

But they needed more, wanted to help. Framing the question as gently as possible, they asked if she had made a Will. She wanted to talk about that but she was exhausted. She would rest now and hope that Energy would visit her one last time, long enough to make one last list.

"No," was all she could say and all they saw of that was a

slight rounding of the lips and a small, effortful movement of the jaw.

That afternoon, the shop trolley came round. The ward, between the after-lunch beverage and visiting time, was quiet: three patients asleep, one knitting and one sitting up and staring at the wall. Screens were drawn round a bed at the far end. Gupta's shoes, small, black, padawaxed, squeaked between soft snores and the trolley rumbled. He drew up at the knitter's bed.

"Hello, my dear!"

The old lady put down her knitting and removed her glasses. She looked grim, shrunken, the humanity somehow drained from her face through the plug hole of her mouth. But Gupta was not put off. He knew that as soon as she had her teeth in, she would smile. She did. She was his best customer in this ward.

"Hello, duck. I'm glad you're back. It's been quieter than the grave in here lately. Been getting on my nerves."

"Well then," Gupta's hands made passes, as though to magic jollity from the air, "we must do our best to cheer you up. Let me show you some nice surprises I have today. How is your son?"

He moved the trolley close so that she could inspect the items on top one by one. While she did, they chatted, the old lady about children, grandchildren and in-laws, Gupta about nephews and cousins. From time to time the old lady would interrupt the flow to exclaim "Ooh, Maltesers!" or "Got any nice soap?" Their voices roused two of the other patients who sat up, waiting for their turns, and began to chat to each other. The ward seemed suddenly alive. A smiling nurse came in – the same one who had called Ann Miss Misery soon after her admission. She did not call her that any more.

"You seem to bring the sunshine with you," she said to Gupta, stopping for a few seconds to admire the old lady's purchases before moving on to rouse the remaining sleeper for medication and help the staring woman focus her attention on what was going on. No sound came from behind the drawn screens round the bed at the far end.

Gupta stayed in the ward for a full twenty minutes, happily dispensing chocolate, soap, stationery and cheer. He was outside in the corridor restocking the top of the trolley from an inner compartment when the nurse came out. Could he pop back to see another patient? This one was 'very poorly' so better not stay long. "What, back already?" called his knitting friend as the trolley rumbled into the ward again. The nurse helped to guide it behind the screens then left, saying she would be back shortly.

Gupta, who never forgot a customer, was taken aback by the changes in Ann. He recalled how, only days ago, he had cajoled her out of a grumpy mood and brought out the little girl side he knew was just a scrape below the surface of most old ladies. She had been able to sit up then, had enjoyed choosing – what was it? – a biro. Now she lay flat, looking as crumbly and breakable, he could not help thinking, as the pale wafers that came with the new Continental De Luxe icecream. He gave a sensitively toned down version of his professional grin.

"Hello, my dear. How can I help you today?"

Deep creases around the mouth bunched together and words Gupta had to stoop to hear rustled out.

"I want you to write something down."

He started to straighten, hands turning palm outward as if to say this was not his territory, but the rustling whisper dragged him down again.

"And I want the biggest box of chocolates on your trolley."

Behind Gupta's listening eyes appeared a picture of the confectionery display shelf in his shop: the best of Cadbury's as well as some interesting foreign lines. He wished he had brought the most extravagant box. Thinking hard and grinning reassuringly for Ann – he had to assume she could see him through those barely open eyes – he bent down beside the trolley.

"Write list." The whisper shook with the insistence of a command. Or a plea.

"Yes, yes," Gupta wished the nurse would come back. "I am just getting some paper."

He thought hard about the chocolates. It frustrated him to have to compromise, selling only one of the modest boxes on the trolley when he had the ideal one, cellophaned and beribboned, sitting idle in the shop.

"Listen," he chattered as he perched on the edge of the bed, legs crossed like a secretary, "if you can wait for the chocolates until Wednesday, I can bring you the perfect thing. Let me just take down your list now."

"Thank you," whispered Ann. "Write: 'for Julie'."

The nurse did not come back to rescue Gupta for some time. When she did, he handed her the scrap of paper discreetly. They both smiled at Ann, now silent and exhausted once more and, between themselves, exchanged a grave, significant look.

The box of chocolates was not included on the list and nobody ever knew who it was for, because Wednesday was the day Ann died.

"Maybe it was for herself, a treat, like," suggested one old lady.

"Quite right," said Gupta, and sensing the subdued atmosphere in the ward, decided to make a grand 'spontaneous' gesture. With a flourish he brought out the huge box – ribbon and cellophane dusted just that morning – and presented it to the ladies of the ward in general. It was quite old anyway and the space it had taken up on the shelf had already been filled.

Julie

Perhaps he hated the curl. That would be ironic because after concluding that makeup and clothes were irrelevant to him, that little lift of the fringe was all I persisted in cultivating in the beauty line.

I expected to be horrified when I looked in the mirror. I was, but I was also intrigued. I got up slowly from the bed where I had collapsed for an hour after the mad running. The mirror was a small one over the wash hand basin and as I approached it my hands were already fiddling with hairgrips. They stopped when I saw my face. It looked wiped, blank, devoid of self, no meaning to it but a stare. Blood and mess of hair struck as secondary to that blankness. It was as though Hodge's peculiar act of abuse had exposed a layer of me I had never seen before.

One by one, I removed the hairgrips. The unsevered plait fell down forward of my shoulder, ordinary, taken-for-granted. The other came away in my hand. What was left on the severed side arranged itself in jagged hanks around one half of my head. Where the lowest strand of the plait had been was no more than a toothbrush stubble of hair. I laid the plait down on the shelf above the basin and there was an odd moment when, automatically, I checked that it was not lying in the soap, getting smeared – as if it mattered, as if it was still attached to my head.

It would have made sense to have had it all cut. A telephone call, a short walk to the nearest salon wearing a scarf and that same afternoon I could have emerged through the tunnel of the whole crazy experience of Hodge as 'a new woman'. It was not awkwardness in the face of a hairdresser's inevitable questions that prevented me; it was reluctance to make the total break with past self that I imagined a radical cut would

mean. I was afraid that with the new, naked face I seemed to
have acquired and without my hair bar a vestigial cap – the
only style that would have matched the shortest hacked bits –
there would have been nothing of the self I knew left to
recognise. Not even its shell. It is not uncommon to cling to
something – or someone – you do not particularly like.

Scalps bleed a lot. My hair had absorbed most of it but
there was a long, dried stream, rat's-tailish, behind one ear. I
pulled aside my clothes and saw how the red-brown stream
divided on my shoulder, ugly against the skin. Had I had a
very lucky escape?

It was as I stood bent over, with crown soaking in the basin,
that I made my plans. I knew I would not sleep that
night and there was no reason why the next should be any
easier. Hodge might come at any time. I would have to go
away.

I went on Sunday afternoon, leaving a fortnight's rent in
advance under the landlady's door. The things I took were
minimal but strategic – makeup, underwear, running shoes,
post office savings book, one pair of high heels and the dress
I had worn to the Threshers. I wore several spare T-shirts and
a jacket and trousers that could pass for smart but were also
comfortable. Thus equipped, I got on a bus and headed not,
as I had first thought, for some retreat in the country, but
right into the bright, loud, anonymous heart of town. I did
not know it then but the bed and breakfast place I booked into
was just round the corner from the sauna. I found that out
during the week when, having put together an attractive
collection of scarves – mostly from second-hand shops – plus
one realistic wig, I started to look for a job. I dropped postcards
to the women for whom I had charred, explaining that I had
been called away suddenly, someone was ill. It might have
been while I was writing the cards that I thought of Ann. But
I did not do anything about it. I know I thought about writing
to my family but I did not do anything about that, either.
Some known devils do not inspire clinging.

For that whole fortnight I was busy, treating it partly as a
holiday into which everything must be crammed – after I had
secured the sauna job I went to a museum, a gallery or the
cinema every day – and partly as planning time. The job, due

to start in three weeks, paid better than anything I had done before, so I felt confident enough to look for a bedsit in town. There was nothing affordable close by but half an hour's walk away – that walk I now know so well – I found my current place.

It unnerves me rather to know that I have been here a year and although I have slightly shortened one side of my hair and the other is growing, I am still, beneath wig, scarves and lopsided chignon, as unbalanced or perhaps just as undecided as before. Worse, as unchanged. I keep wondering whether, going over this now, I am trying to make sense of something or exorcise it.

One cannot exorcise death and I doubt that it is designed to be made sense of any more than life is. When, at the end of that fortnight, I went back to the old bedsit to start moving out, I found two letters waiting. One was from Esther, the other looked official. Assuming that the one from Esther was something inconsequential – an invitation, maybe, which I would almost certainly refuse – I read the other first. It told me in formal terms – thin grey typing on cheap paper – that Ann Evans (Miss), aged seventy-nine, had died twelve days ago in hospital; that attempts made to contact relatives had so far failed and that, in the absence of anyone else responsible, the funeral had been handled by the Health Board. The letter was from a Mr J. Phillips, a solicitor appointed by the Health Board to deal with the matter of estate ('as is customary in such cases'). Miss Evans, wrote Mr Phillips, had died intestate. There was, however, an informal note listing bequests and it was in connection with this latter that I was advised to contact, etc., etc.

What had I been doing while Ann had been dying? Wandering round a bizarre exhibition of modern art? Watching a Woody Allen film? I had meant to telephone the hospital to ask how she was, had meant to visit again. Meaning to means nothing when you don't act. Crying came easily and went on for a long time.

When I had washed my face and made myself a cup of tea – God, I could see Ann doing that, looking after herself after an upset – I telephoned the solicitor. I do not know what I expected. This person had no real connection with Ann – an official appointed by a board – but was my only connection with her now. The first thing I asked was where she was buried. He had to send for a file and I had to put more coins in the box. Not buried, he said, cremated, and told me where. I must have gone quiet because into a silence came the information that there had, of course, been a proper funeral. Efforts had been made to contact me by telephone. I had never given Ann the number of the coinbox in the hall and it was not in the book under individual bedsit tenants' names. It would have made no difference anyway because I was not there and had left no forwarding address, not even letting the landlady know when I was established in the bed and breakfast. Because of Hodge. I was less traceable during that fortnight than I had ever been in my life.

Mr Phillips mentioned the bequests. He said that during her last days, Miss Evans – state of mind vouched for by the hospital staff – had brought several people's attention to the fact that she wished to leave certain items to a Miss Julie Barton. I would need to bring some form of identification when I came to see him. Absurdly, the first thing that popped into my head was the severed plait. (Holding it up to my head: "Look, Mr Phillips, it matches, I must be me.") He said my post office savings book would do, and an appointment was made for two weeks' time. Efforts were still being made to trace relatives.

Upstairs, I had a long list of things to do, a list made sitting on the bus on the way from town. There were boxes to be collected from the packing areas of supermarkets then carefully filled with my possessions and transport to the new place arranged. There were books to be sorted into piles – some to move with me, some to be sold. Same with clothes. I would have to get some newspapers for wrapping fragile things. It was hard to think of any of this but it was harder to just sit still and brood about Ann, so that evening I started on the sorting and next day, planning to collect boxes on the way back, I bought some flowers and went – too late, uselessly and for the last time – to visit her.

Beside the crematorium – large, modern, an architectural marriage between brutalism and discretion – was a chapel. It was here that the man in the office suggested I should leave my flowers. He stood behind me, plump hands predictably clasped, as I read the entry in the book which said that Ann had been cremated here.

"Why cremation? Why not burial?" I asked. I would have liked to sit by her for a last time. Just sit quietly and I suppose, in my own way, 'pay respects'. Mourn.

The official opened his plump, clasped hands.

"Space," he said sadly. Further north and in rural areas burials for such cases were apparently more common. Such cases. The solicitor had used the same phrase in his letter. That was Ann.

I could not sleep that night, or others. At two, three, four a.m. I sat up eating apples beside half-packed cases – the room was now an obstacle course of things half-packed – and thought about all that still had to be done towards the move. And I thought about Ann. And Hodge. The landlady had assured me that while I was away there had been no callers but still I worried and the trips I made to the bathroom were hasty. I could not look at that by now many times restuck polythene without thinking of him: the shattering skylight; the flailing plimsole. What would the next tenant make of it, I wondered. Lucky for me the landlady had arthritis in her knees.

During the days, I was busy. With books in a duffle bag I made trip after trip to shops that would pay ten, sometimes as much as twenty-five pence for paperbacks. Most of my clothes from the pre-bedsit era (low necklines, split skirts) went to Oxfam or Nearly-New. I only kept things that would do for wearing under my sauna receptionist's overall. It was thoughts of overalls and the progression to sorting boilersuits, that brought Daley to mind. In the after shock of Ann's death and the flurry of moving preparations, I had forgotten Esther's letter. Even now, not wanting to interrupt my sorting, I waited until I was relaxing with coffee and yoghurt at midday before reading it.

Dear Julie,
    Please excuse me writing to you like this but I felt I had to tell someone. I have rung your place a few times but no answer. It's about Jim.

Jim? The handwriting was careful, rounded, only the punctuation marks crossed out or smudged in places. Jim Daley.
He had only ever been Daley to me.

> . . . You might know that he has not been very well for a while,
> well he got worse. He was depressed and everything was getting
> him down. I tried to get him to see the doctor but he didn't
> want to know. He tried to take his own life Julie and ended up
> having to go to hospital. I am sorry to go on like this but I just
> felt I had to tell someone.

I put down my yoghurt spoon. I could see Esther with
those little children. Did Daley have his stomach pumped in
hospital? Or had he tried to do it with petrol fumes?

> . . . It's funny because I thought he was getting on all right at
> work. He called himself Mr Bun the Baker and would have a
> laugh. But he wasn't happy Julie, and there's something else.
> He got in trouble with the law. In a way it was a blessing in
> disguise, but it did not feel like it at the time. They did not
> know about him not being well until I told them. Jim was in a
> terrible state. But the thing is that they did get him to see a
> doctor. They said he was obliged to, which I thank goodness
> for really because I know he needs help. He is on tablets for
> the moment and we are going to a clinic next week. I was
> wondering if you could stop with Leonie and Jonathan, Julie,
> just while I go with him to the clinic . . .

She gave the date of the appointment. Nearly a week ago.
It had all happened while I was away. Wandering round
bizarre exhibitions. Watching Woody Allen. Esther would
have had to take the children. *I am so useless!*

> . . . I know they would really like to see you.
>   Hoping you are well,
>   best regards from Esther
> P.S. Leonie and Jonathan each send a kiss.

I threw my coffee into the wash hand basin and – uselessly
– kicked a packing case.

Daley

Gupta had still been in a state of excitement when he went to the hospital. As he handed round the chocolates, watching the old ladies coo and posture, taking their time over the luxurious selection, it was all he could do not to blurt the story straight out. Already he had told it to a dozen customers. But in the hospital, respectful of the atmosphere, he held himself in check and when the patients had each had four chocolates and nurse was beginning to remonstrate, he resumed his normal rounds. Patiently, he parted with pens, plastic wallets (new line of the week) and boiled sweets. Patiently, he waited while the old ladies dilly-dallied over their choice of magazines. But when he reached his friend who knitted and she said: "What have you been up to then? Anything new?" Gupta could no longer contain himself.

"Well actually," he said, bubbling but at the same time conspiratorial, "something quite extraordinary has happened."

"Oh yes?"

She was interested.

"Yes!" Gupta paused for effect, "I hardly know where to begin."

"Get on with it."

"Well, my dear, what would you say if I told you that you are looking at a thief catcher? Yes, I myself have caught a thief red-handed and assisted the forces of law and order!"

The little shrunken face goggled, thrilled.

"Go on! Where?"

"In my very own shop. Right under my nose."

"What did he pinch?"

Gupta, who had been swaying about and waving his hands, went dramatically still.

234

"My dear, I am ashamed to tell you."

"Go on, you can't shock me."

So he told her everything. The tale he spun was not entirely accurate, but it made the old lady's day.

Monday felt like the longest day in Daley's life and one of the strangest. He had expected, somehow, that after the drama of Sunday, everything would change. Nothing did. The small dressing on his wrist was all that was new. He woke to the sound of his children playing. It being the May Day holiday Leonie was not at school. At ten Esther brought him up a cup of tea and he felt the usual guilt at seeing her tired, anxious, sympathetic face. At one she brought him up lunch.

"Are you trying to hide me from the kids?" he said, hardly a question. "Am I that bad?"

"Don't be daft, darlin'. We'd love you to come down, and it's a lovely day out."

"Na-a." He pushed potato into one side of his mouth and stared at the lump of his body under the blankets. He did not get up all day.

The afternoon felt endless to Esther. She wanted to take the children to the park but did not dare leave Daley. Leonie became restless, bored after a while even with a cardboard box made into a train, potato stencils and plasticine. Esther sent up a prayer of thanks when a Walt Disney film came on the television.

On Tuesday, Daley insisted on going to work.

"But you're not well, love. You could easily get a note if you went to the doctor. You're supposed to go to the doctor."

"I'm all right," said Daley. "Leave me alone."

Mid-morning, Esther telephoned Perkins & Day. Her husband had not been very well over the weekend, she explained, and she just wanted to check that he was OK. The man she spoke to was brisk. The bakery employed a large number of staff and it would not do for all their spouses to be ringing up every day. However, just this once he would send someone to check on Mr Daley. Something in her tone made him suspect that 'not very well' had nothing to do with flu.

When she rang off he went through the report made by the

company nurse after her visit last month. Nothing sinister under Daley. In fact, if he recalled correctly, this Feeder Grade IV had been described by one of the overseers as an ideal worker, although not a big mixer on the social side.

Daley's feet were planted almost a yard apart in front of the prover and with each couplet of dough pieces plopped safely in their tins, he swayed forward, a small movement repeated over and over. His body rotated slightly from the waist after each sway, turning to face the new dough on the belt. His arms moved but were stiff, only his fingers flexing on the breasts of dough. His face was empty of all thought.

Here at least, Daley knew what he was doing. The prover did not intimidate him any more and he even felt, stepping up to it as though powered by the same current as the conveyor belt, a sense of release. Like sleeping, like masturbating, it was a known act and by now his body performed it for him, bypassing the confusion in his mind.

In the changing room, during mealbreaks and on the walk to and from his place, he suffered. Pulling on the white tunic – a squeeze over his paunch now – he felt buffoonlike, sure that the other workers, bantering and loud with hairy, aggressive arms flashing in and out of sleeves, saw him as stupid and slow. He knew they did. They called him a wally. And when he walked past the cooler he felt that the din and juddering of it entered his brain. The door opened and vapour puffed out like a monstrous sigh. That sometimes felt as though it entered his brain too, or even came from it. The rhythm of the divider chipped like a chisel at his precarious calm.

It was shortly after a mealbreak that the overseer came to check on him. Daley's comrade, the other wally, had not appeared so he had sat alone. He used the food – thick rolls, doughnuts – to drug himself against what he saw as the stares of the other workers. In the urinal afterwards he had leaned his forehead, sweaty from hot tea, against the tiles and when he had put his cap back on he had crammed it down low as though to protect ears and brain. Only when he reached his place did he begin to calm down. And then, just as he was relaxing into the sway – the slight rotation, a thousand breasts in his palms – his shoulder was clasped. To Daley, whose fingers spasmed, destroying two pieces of dough, the overseer's hand felt like the grabbing beak of some giant mechanical bird.

"All right, are you, mate? Understand you wasn't too well over the weekend."

What was the man saying? Daley, locked under the protective carapace of his cap, stared at him with shocked eyes.

"Beg pardon?"

The man's face cracked into speaking shapes again.

"I say: Are you all right?"

"Eh?"

Daley's hands, empty, were moving in slow motion panic over the conveyor belt. It was still moving but there were no dough pieces coming. Startled afresh, Daley looked to where the man operating the moulder stood. He was staring at Daley with a hand on a lever and, staring back, Daley felt the absence of one sound in the general din. The moulder had stopped. No dough pieces emerged, sleek, bomb nosed, from under the roller still dripping with vegetable emulsion. They were all waiting for him.

How could they stop the moulder? What was happening back at the divider, the first prover, the mixer? Was the other wally, way up in his eyrie in the flour store poised with a sack over the funnel? Was the entire bakery waiting for him?

"What?" Daley shouted suddenly and at that moment, felt a nudge in his side. Dough pieces appeared. The moulder was working again. Someone was taking his place. And the overseer was beckoning.

They stood with their backs to one of the walls, in front of them a redundant slicing machine: neat rows of saw-edges frozen above another still conveyor belt; empty metal sleeves dangling.

"Nothing to worry about, mate. Just your wife phoned, said you wasn't well over the weekend."

Daley's feet moved among waxed wrappers.

"I'm all right."

The overseer's feet moved too.

"Well, that's all right then," he said, quite jolly, and Daley was allowed to go back to work.

But his rhythm was destroyed. Mechanically, his hands moved, his body rotated, but they were out of sync. Again and again dough pieces fell off the end of the conveyor belt or slopped over the sides of the tins. Daley's face was red under the white cap. How dare she? How dare she interfere with him here? This was his work. He got on all right here. Hung on by the skin of his teeth. What was she trying to do? When the next break came he fled to the urinal, missing his tea rather than facing any more questions or stares.

At the end of the shift Daley got into his van and drove. He kept below 30 mph, bumbling at traffic lights, dithering at a roundabout. Shops, pedestrians, zebra crossings, looked different somehow to the way they had before – new, strange, looming up as vivid conglomerations of colour and shape, everything slightly out of kilter. He leaned close to the window, trying not to make mistakes, and drove at his snail's pace around Crescents, along Avenues, down cul-de-sacs. What if he was still in this state when it was time to fetch Leonie from school? He thought of her protectively – how could he protect her from himself?

But it was all right. Esther was there. At the same time as feeling relief at the sight of her waiting by the gates, Jonathan in the buggy, he felt a resurgence of anger. First she had telephoned his work as if he was a child to be checked up on and now she had shown she did not trust him by taking over his job of fetching Leonie. He pulled up on the opposite side of the road, far enough from the other parents not to get involved.

"All right, love?" asked Esther, helping Jonathan into the van. Daley got out to fold the buggy. He did not look at her.

"All-bloody-wrong."

Leonie sang into a silence all the way home.

After supper, Daley sat in front of the television, not watching but with the sound turned up loud. When she had done the dishes, Esther came and sat down too.

"Anything good on?"

Her hands were folded on stockingless knees.

"Not much."

Daley watched Esther out of the corner of his eye as she tried to get interested in a chat show. The distress he had felt at work, the anger, the odd moments of relief, were all locked far down inside him. His belligerence had not lasted long. It took too much concentration and, other than flinging out swear words, which he knew upset her, he did not know how to express it. He did not know how to express either the soft flood of feeling he experienced when Esther bent forward and unself-consciously scratched a vein in her calf. Her feet, small, bunioned, half in and half out of old slippers, touched him too. He shifted in his seat.

"Would you like a Coke?"

She turned and looked at him, smiling. Like Leonie when he offered her a sweet.

"Where are you going to get that at this time of night? It's nearly eight."

He got up, the weight of his paunch making him cumbersome as a pregnant woman.

"The Indian's."

Esther came with him down the front path. The evening was cool and she handed him a jumper.

"You're feeling better now, aren't you, love?"

The anxiety was there again. Why did it make him so angry?

"No!" he said loudly, and banged the van door.

It came and went, that was what was so frightening. Sometimes he felt almost normal, and when he felt like that, he wanted to forget everything else. But then it all broke up, all went wrong, and he knew that normality was only held together by the finest threads, frayed, in his case, to easy breaking point. And when one broke the strain on the others increased. And if too many broke . . . Finding himself bumbling again at the wheel, Daley stopped some distance away from Gupta's and walked the rest of the way.

He did not – consciously – intend to steal any more magazines. Jonathan finding the one he had brought home on Saturday, and all that followed, was lesson enough. He did not know why he was coming back to the same shop now except that he had told Esther he was going to buy her a Coke. He would still buy her a Coke even though she had made him angry. He went in with money ready in his hand – enough for Smarties for Leonie and Jelly Tots for Jonathan too, a treat for the morning. Then he saw a blonde girl with a red leather harness dividing tanned breasts and a black girl lying with a white girl on a pink bed and another girl with long hair wearing half a lacy dress and he bought the Coke and the Smarties and the Jelly Tots and he stole the magazines.

Outside the shop Daley turned, not in the direction of the van but towards the High Street, where he wanted to buy some beer. He passed a woman walking a dog who stared at the bulge in his trouser pocket, clearly more distracted by that than by the way he walked with one arm across his belly as though cuddling it. The Coke can had been the most awkward thing. He had needed both hands to stuff the magazines under his jumper. Now he took it out of his pocket and carried it casually, his alibi. He shifted the magazines round a little so that, with one arm clamped to his side, he could walk more naturally. On the High Street he slowed to a dawdle, staying close to the shop windows and peering in. He was trying to think of somewhere private to go. If he went home now he would have to wait until tomorrow before looking at the magazines. He could not risk taking them into the house again. He thought of the last boat he had abandoned working on in the winter. It would be damp and chilly but there might still be a memory of Julie there. Julie as she had been. The zip of her old boilersuit slid down in his mind and breasts divided by a red leather harness appeared.

He moved less hesitantly now, mind on one clear track. He passed typewriters in a shop window, then soft toys, their glass eyes dull without the spotlights that were trained on them in daytime. He paused and saw something unusual moving in the window. A blue light, silent but urgent, spinning and spinning. Amazed but not at once alarmed, he stared, moving on clumsily. Then there were two flashes, white and peremptory and a sound escaped from Daley, a sigh. He stood still. A car door opened and footsteps approached.

While the policeman spoke, Daley stared at the broken laces of his workboots. He was being asked to say what he had been doing during the last half hour.

"I haven't done anything."

"Then you've got nothing to worry about."

Again he was asked what he had been doing.

"Nothing."

Where had he just come from and where was he going?

"Nowhere."

"Name and address?"

When Daley failed to respond he was warned that he was liable to arrest. He went on looking at his workboots.

"All right, get in the car."

Daley lifted his head as though it were the first time he had ever made that movement. As on Sunday night, when he had sat on the edge of the bath having drunk the children's Calpol and swallowed a dozen or so pills, he had a sense that at last something was going to happen. The difference now was that forces outside himself were in control. And somebody else's hand on the razor might mean more than a scratch.

"On telly," he said experimentally, addressing the air over the policeman's shoulder, "they sometimes call you lot the pigs."

"In the car, mate."

Daley moved and the three magazines slid from under his jumper, slapping the pavement hard. The black and white girls on the pink bed lolled, pouting up at the policeman. Where a centre spread had fallen open a fleshy redhead mooned. Daley was told he was under arrest.

After a search at the police station – he swore that he had paid for the Coke and sweets and told a lie about the dressing on his wrist – he was taken to a cubelike room and told to sit down. His chair, the red plastic seat nicked in two places and bleeding grey foam, matched another behind a scratched table. The only other features in the room were a grey metal filing cabinet in one corner and a small window high up. A policeman, head up, eyes blank, stood by the door.

"Just like *Kojak*, isn't it?" said Daley, setting the can of Coke beside him on the floor.

There was no response.

Daley waited, as he had in the hospital, hearing footsteps approach along a corridor, tensing himself for someone to appear, then hearing the steps go by. The light in the room was bright, not, as he might have expected, from a naked bulb, but from a yellowish striplight which emitted a steady buzzing. Like a bluebottle, Daley thought, glancing at the policeman by the door, and wished Julie had been there to share the joke. But Julie had her own jokes. Julie laughed when he said he wanted to go to bed with her.

His chair was close to the table, but sideways on, not pushed in squarely like the other. Even with nothing on the table and nothing to distinguish between the two chairs besides the pattern of nicks in the seats, it was clear which was meant for interviewer, which for interviewee. Looking down, waiting, both hands limp on his thighs, Daley noticed one more feature in the room: a large, rectangular floor ashtray. Something about its metal slopes and slits reminded him of the machinery in the bakery but it was the silence here, only underlined by the light's buzzing, that seemed to enter and do things to his brain.

"What about a cup of tea, then?"

Daley did not raise his head to say this and the policeman by the door did not indicate he had heard. Esther would have had a cup of tea ready when he got home. She would have had her Coke and he would have had his tea. And a beer. The sweets for the children were back in his pocket after the search, Jelly Tots pressing up like warts through the stretched material. He felt the beginnings of a need to urinate.

An officer came to question him after half an hour. To Daley this felt more like two hours and then the presence in the other chair seemed sudden. The table between them became a desk as soon as notepad, pen and elbows rested on it. The officer had just had a cup of tea and three custard creams. He licked his lips and scratched the bag under one eye lengthily before speaking.

"Do you understand why you are here?"

Daley looked up. His voice, seeming to come from some-where outside himself, was loud and rude.

"Do you think I'm daft?"

The officer's heavy features were kept deliberately void of expression. To Daley he looked like a typical television policeman, not real and therefore not threatening.

"What I may or may not think about that is my business. What I know is that you have been brought in under suspicion of stealing property from a Mr Gupta Seth's shop – and for failing to give your particulars – and that this property, as described by Mr Seth, was discovered on your person by the arresting officer."

He lifted his pen.

"Name?"

Daley felt a peculiar calm invade him. He did not recognise it as despair. His body seemed to spread like something melting into the chair.

"You mean those dirty magazines?"

The melting calm had spread a grin into his voice.

"I'm not here for a chat," said the officer quietly, "I'm asking you for your name."

"All them tits."

There was silence. Daley knew that a change had come over the atmosphere in the room but he did not know what it meant. He turned away from the heavy, waiting eyes across the desk and addressed the figure by the door. Again his voice, somehow out of kilter with himself, was loud and rude.

"What do *you* do when you want a piss?"

When they told him that he was going to be detained and that he could expect to appear in court in the morning, he did not react, just gazed out of pale, babyish eyes, a faint grin splitting a dough grey face. But when they touched him his calm collapsed. All at once two sets of big, efficient hands were pulling him to his feet. His flesh, his brain, wobbled with the shock.

"Hey, get off! Leave me alone!"

Their eyes, above small moustaches, were inaccessible. Daley, feet in undone workboots tripping over each other, stiffened and flailed.

"Get off!"

He felt the loose knitting of his jumper stretch and his shirt come untucked. The loose flesh of his paunch appeared, a baglike, clumsy, shaking thing. The noise of the struggle seemed suppressed, his staggering feet just a shuffle, Coke can rolling across the floor, but when they opened the door and pulled him into the corridor all three sets of feet seemed to echo and there was a thud as one of his own movements knocked a body against a wall and loud, ugly clattering as they jostled him down some stairs.

"Get off! Get off!"

They did not speak. One of them had a grip like a slowly tightening tourniquet on a bicep. A crack came into Daley's voice.

"You're hurting me!"

They let go of him in the cell as carelessly as dropping a towel on a bathroom floor and were gone before he could cry out again.

Daley did not fall but stood swaying, hands flopped by his sides like useless paws. Then he ran to the door, pressed his face, his hands, his body against it and screamed.

"You pigs! You bastards! You filth!"

He screamed abuse for the next twenty minutes. Then he screamed to be let out. Then he just screamed.

Hodge

The weather, dull over the weekend, brightened on the holiday Monday, bringing out crowds. Women, limbs like peeled fruit in their first light dresses of the year, strolled unhurriedly with bags or buggies; men, ties abandoned, pushed buggies too and peered as at mysteries into shop windows. People hovered, chatted, paused. Between them, head down, the wardrobe door wrapped in Perkins & Day overalls under one arm, Hodge strode.

He was on his way to Geoff and Bea's. This walk, last undertaken on empty streets in the cold of a Christmas Day dawn, today took over three hours. From time to time Hodge paused to switch the wardrobe door under the other arm but only stopped once to roll a cigarette. The last part was the easiest; long, gently sloping suburban roads free of clutter, just the odd Geoff and Bea type car sliding by. On the crowded streets he had avoided bumping into people by instinct, carving a way forward without consciously trying. Obstructed by nothing now, he still seemed to be carving a way.

His mood was familiar but its familiarity, like the repetitions of eroticism, did nothing to make it less intense. Hodge was going through a process – a process he had gone through many times before – designed to bring about change. The end result was not specific in his consciousness, but the component parts were. The first part was to leave the painting with Geoff; the second, to reconnoitre the Wainwright house with a view to burgling it soon. All else was forgotten. Painted out. Where regret, where frustration, where hope might have been, were – parts of a process.

He heard Bea's voice from several houses away, swanning and assured. They were in the back garden and there were scrapings as of metal on concrete. Garden tools or a barbecue. Hodge's eyes, red-rimmed, the whites dull, examined the front of the house. No one visible through windows and at the back they sounded well occupied. He went silently to the garage and, resting the painting against a wall, swung the door open, controlling it so that it did not make a noise when it touched the roof. He eased the Perkins & Day overalls off and positioned the painting, naked, on the bonnet of the BMW. Lips, hair and the wetness of vulva glimmered weakly under the windscreen's voluptuous shine. Silently, Hodge closed the garage door and walked away. Not to have abandoned the painting in The Chalet when he went to do the Wainwright job could have been a last mark of his feelings for the woman he had failed to pin down. It was equally possible that he thought the painting might in time acquire value and that leaving it with Geoff was a small insurance policy for the future.

Hodge was caught at one fifteen on Wednesday morning, the new burglar alarm installed by Harry Wainwright causing a commotion in Gormley Gardens. But the arrest was without drama: a gaunt man with thin black hair getting quietly into a police car and being driven away.

At the police station, where his history was known, Hodge was permitted to smoke. Paperwork completed, the CID officer interviewing him sat back, expression neutral. Referring to the burglary he commented: "Bit clumsy for you, I would have thought. Losing your touch?"

"Maybe." Hodge's lips twitched. "Or maybe I'm just getting old."

The officer, who was of a similar age, nodded, as near to a smile as he would allow himself. Then he waved an arm wearily.

"OK, take him away."

He hitched up his trousers when Hodge had gone and wandered back to his office, where he spoke into an intercom.

"Better take old Hodge a cup of tea. Looks like he hasn't had a square meal since he was last inside. Charlie's screamer stopped yet?"

Charlie was the name of the officer who had interviewed an unco-operative shop-lifter earlier.

Over the intercom came the information that the screamer

had quietened down. Hodge's sleep was only interrupted by the occasional sob from the next cell and, an hour or so later, its occupant was removed.

Julie

I went to see Esther. We took the children to the park after collecting Leonie from school and sat on a bench watching them play. Leonie insisted on wearing a scarf, "Like Julie". With her hair hidden she looked very like her father.

"I didn't know what to do when he didn't come home."

Esther's hand was on the buggy, jigging it mechanically even though Jonathan was not in it.

"He said he was just going for a Coke so I thought he'd be back in twenty minutes – half an hour at the most. I got his mug out for tea."

"It must have been awful," I murmured, hating the commonplace words. Remembering other words to Daley: 'fucking platitudes'.

"Then I told myself he'd probably stopped at a pub. He'd taken to going to the pub sometimes, you know, but generally just on a Friday. But I kept thinking about what he'd done at the weekend. At the hospital they said it wasn't a serious attempt, more like a cry for help. That was the worst bit of it, Julie. I didn't know how to help."

She paused and waved to Leonie who was bouncing up and down at the top of the slide.

"Anyway, when it got past pub closing time and he still didn't come, I rang the hospital. They took ages to see if he was there and then Jonathan woke up and it took ages to get him down again. It must have been past one by the time I dialled 999 and then they had to get on to all the local police stations."

A policeman had come to the house – waking Jonathan again – and taken down Daley's description. Esther had waited by the telephone and at about two thirty a.m. she had been told that a man answering the description had been brought in earlier for theft. Her first reaction had been "Oh no, that can't be him." But the old trousers, the jumper she had made herself and the undone workboots argued that it was.

"They said he would have to go to court in the morning but when I told them about him trying to take his own life it was different. They must have had a look at his wrist and checked with the hospital because they were quite kind after a while."

I kept wondering what Daley had stolen but when I asked I wished I had not.

"It was hardly anything, really. Just some magazines."

Her attempt to throw the line away did not work and I did not have to ask what sort of magazines; remembered Daley standing mesmerised in the fish and chip shop; calendar girl with big tits beside the pickled onions.

Esther left the bench for a moment to fetch Jonathan, who had been straying dangerously close to the swings. When she came back she explained that Daley had eventually been brought home under sedation by a doctor. She repeated the words in her letter, voice tight and high: "Jim was in a terrible state." I started to say something but she went on.

"His face was all puffy, Julie, like he'd been crying for hours and hours and when I took his shirt off to get him into his pyjamas there was . . . there was bruises on his arm."

She was rocking Jonathan fiercely on her knee and I could see that she was crying inside but Leonie was running towards us, smiling.

"I'm sorry to go on like this, Julie. You'll come home for a cup of tea, won't you?"

The rest of the story came out in snippets while Esther supported Jonathan over a pot, spread margarine on bread and searched for radio music for Leonie to dance to.

Another doctor had been out to see Daley the next day and prescribed more 'tablets'. Daley had hardly spoken. The police had found the van – keys left carelessly on the seat – and brought it home. It was over the following few days that Esther had tried to contact me, not knowing how she was going to get him to the psychiatric out-patient clinic with the children. I felt sure that she could have got help from somewhere – a social worker or someone at the clinic. But Esther was not like that, not pushy. She would not have liked to ask 'them'. So she had asked me. I said how sorry I was not to have been around to help. (*I am so useless!*)

"Oh, we managed all right. It wasn't that he was difficult or anything, just like a big baby really. And the tablets made him dozy."

It had apparently been decided more or less on the spot that Daley should go into St Bride's. 'They' had been very good to her after he had gone in. A community nurse and a social worker had been round.

"And he is better off in there, I know."

She looked at Leonie and Jonathan, watching television now, plates, cups and toys higgledy-piggledy round them on the floor. "I just wish he didn't have to be."

A year later Daley is still in St Bride's. The notes come, big, wobbly words influenced by, I suspect, if not directly quoted from Patience Strong. Esther, whom I telephone occasionally out of guilt, pity and a kind of fascinated admiration, tells me that he is gradually getting better. He is allowed out sometimes at weekends but he gets tired easily and the tablets still make him dozy. He makes raffia baskets in Occupational Therapy. The children miss him. "These things can't be rushed," says Esther. "Of course not," I say. She always finishes by urging me to go and see them. "I'll try," I say, but I know I won't.

Ann tried. Can someone like me measure the effort that went into the minutes, the days, the winters and springs that made up that long life? I can only imagine, basing my ideas on the evidence of struggles she went through during the short time I knew her. The struggles were so basic. She had to fight to get the lid off a teapot; twist and grope to find a tissue in her pocket; battle down the corridor to 'pay a call'. And I, discontented, fidgeting in the luxury of youth, 'struggled' through her teas.

What did she imagine about me? Was it more or less what I fed her: glimpses of gaps in family background – offering a slot to her, perhaps – evidence of solitariness; visions of romance? She was not stupid. Her picture of me must, by the end of our acquaintance, have been a lot less pat than at the beginning. Families were mentioned early on but something made us both cautious on that subject, which is surely unusual. Old ladies often talk of nothing but relatives. And the fact that she stopped asking after mine seems significant. No, she was not stupid. I was an imperfect subject for her imaginings – why did I do odd jobs on boats and charring, why didn't I spend Christmas with my family? – but I would do. And she had little choice. It turned out that the only other person to pick her name from the Treetops Club Contacts list was a partially sighted man in Glasgow who wanted help with Airfix kits.

Ten days after moving up to town I went back to keep my appointment with Mr Phillips, the solicitor. He told me that Ann did have relatives still living. He had managed to trace some cousins, although not through information discovered among her things. Their address had been scribbled over in her diary and she had made it clear that she did not wish them to receive anything. The cousins had not, it seemed, been able to meet the funeral expenses so – as was customary in such cases – these, plus solicitor's fee, had been met with monies raised by the disposal of the estate.

I sat in Mr Phillips' office thinking about the contents of Ann's small flat: the chairs we had sat on, the seat of hers bottom-shaped through long use; the cabinet with the traycloth hanging over the front; the vase I sometimes put flowers in – her estate. What remainder there was – Mr Phillips implied there was not much – had gone – as was customary etc., etc. – to the State. I sat nodding, watching sunlight on leaves through the window behind Mr Phillips' head. It was a lovely day, perfect for walking by the river. But I did not live there any more. He asked if I had a car and I looked at him, surprised.

Ann's things, the 'bequests', were produced from behind Mr Phillips' desk in a grey dustbin liner. The list, he told me, was on top and I was welcome to check the contents. I looked at the list, just a few words and a lot of parentheses jotted down in an odd, tight little hand, but declined to go through the things then and there.

"I'm sure it's all OK," I said, "I didn't expect to get anything."

"I'm sure you didn't," said Mr Phillips, seeing me out,

leaving the horrible idea, like a stain in the back of my mind, that he, or 'they', or someone had thought I did.

I had managed to get the new bedsit into reasonable order by then and the dustbin liner, cuddled like an oversized child all the way up to town on the bus, sat on the newly swept carpet looking out of place. I untied the knot I had made in the neck and gently shook the contents on to the bed. All present and correct as to list, which also described where to find some of the things.

4 handbags (2 black, 1 white, 1 brown)
In wardrobe (in housecoat) 1 black jacket (smart)
In 2nd drawer chest of drawers (in tissue paper) 1 cotton frock (dress)
1 traycloth (on cabinet)

I opened the handbags. In one, black patent, was a pair of black webbing gloves so fine I thought at first they were a lace handkerchief. The scent that came from the lining of that bag – of powder, old perfumes, old silk – was so strangely alluring I held it close to my nose and had a sudden unpleasant vision of myself doing that – peering into and actually sniffing Ann's handbag. I rested it on my knee and took out an old fashioned decorated tub containing what must once have been loose powder. It was the source of most of the scent – sweet, baked, biscuity. When had she worn the gloves? At a concert? A funeral?

The brown bag was stuffed full of coupons torn out of magazines. '10p off new formula Swish'; 'Save 15p next time you buy Chirp'. Had she bought bird food for that rickety table I made? I wondered if the next occupant of the flat would leave it there. Some of the coupons were years out of date but one, advertising a cut price Baby-gro (what did Ann want with a Baby-gro?), was dated as recently as March. In the white bag were photographs, some of which I had seen before: Ann on a coach outing to Wingate in 1980; Ann at the Elmgrove Project Christmas coffee morning the year before last. But there were a few much older: two young men in uniform – that must have been during the war – and one of Ann in an old fashioned dress and white shoes, smiling, not wearing glasses, leaning against a wall. Ann pretty. Ann young. This and a close-up of one of the young men in uniform were clipped together.

I recognised the black 'everyday' bag. This was the one that used to bang against her, dangling from the zimmer when she struggled along the corridor. In it were pens, tissues, biscuit crumbs, an empty glasses case, a compact, boiled sweets and an unopened pack of assorted Christmas cards – left over from last year or the year before? For next year? For whom? Her old, falling apart purse contained bus tickets and a pass that went back decades. Mr Phillips, I presume, had weeded out pension books and other documents and made sure that any monetary content of the purse had been returned safely whence it had come – to the State. But he had not weeded out my letters to Ann. I had not realised how many there were, dating back to that first one in which I introduced myself so carefully and continuing, on and off, right up until a few days before she went into hospital. Perhaps, to her, there were not many. God, what did she see in them or in my visits? All those not-quite-lies about Hodge, the cosy stuff about working on the boats, critiques on Perkins & Day cakes. Did any of it give her pleasure? Did she look for pleasure? Is there a special valve in old ladies like Ann that stops them giving up? Will I have one?

I did not know what to do with the things and for a long time they sat, neatly returned to their dustbin liner, on top of the wardrobe – all except for the letters, which I put in a drawer to reread gradually. The greatest luxury of this bedsit as compared to the old one is that it does have a wardrobe. No more boilersuits and lacy bras battling it out for supremacy on the walls. Confusion can be hidden. And the bathroom is down the hall. No danger of unexpected visitors dropping in through skylights.

I wonder about attraction and how much of it is dependent on need. Look at Ann, look at me, a most unlikely combination. And what about Hodge? Would I have ended up in bed with him if he had been a neighbour or did he have to enter my life through smashed glass to qualify as potential lover? How might I have seen him differently if we had met buying toilet rolls at that Indian shop near The Chalet? I would have looked at him longer than at most people. He was so exceptionally gaunt and he had that urgent backlit glitter in his eyes . . . but I doubt if it would have gone further than that. He would have been just an interesting oddity, like a picturesque tramp encountered on a walk. And Daley? A lower middle-aged man going to seed – grubby, paunchy, very likely a secret lech. I would probably have pushed past him to pay for my toilet rolls first. As it was, I played with him a little, then pushed past.

The small daily pleasure of the walk back from the sauna is increasing with the early light. I would enjoy the walk in the evening, too, but there are still crowds about then and the streets, so unlike the different planet they become at dawn, feel like the grooves of some machine – the shops, the offices and pubs the working parts, the people the energy. Take them away and the machine rests. Only a little current trickles through it now and then to show that it is not dead. The people who visit the sauna in the night are part of that current, as are the odd cars and taxis on their way to or from a nightclub or the airport, and the early milk van.

At night, behind my desk, beneath my overall, under my makeup, my wig or scarf or carefully lopsided chignon, I am calm. The routine is reassuring and the occasional bantering of the clients does not bother me. I am earning a living and back in the bedsit my muesli awaits.

But beyond the routine and the rituals, something is happening; something I recognise. In the last part of the walk back from the sauna I go up a hill out of sight of the silent shops and offices. Some of the houses there have gardens and to left and right of the main road are Avenues with trees cracking the paving stones. I run my fingers along railings and acknowledge the dusty aubrietias that flounce, despite pollution, from rockeries, the primroses that, bashed by the wind of buses during the day, still have a few soft petals to offer the dawn. There is a rhododendron bush outside one house, no flowers yet and spots on the leaves. My ignorant town self wonders if this might be a disease and then, not knowing, forgets the question. The leaves are still attractive. And there is a young tree with half-scrolled leaves like tiny brussels sprouts and another with large, tight buds, red-tipped, puissant . . . And there is a man.

I have seen him four times now and have begun to watch for him. He comes down one of the Avenues, tall, unhurried, and it is his pace and one hand in a pocket that makes me think he is on a solitary wander, not shuttling from point to point. He, too, is tasting the dawn. And there are lines in his face and grey hairs among the brown, telling some tale.

When I get back to the bedsit I make myself a cup of tea. Until these last few days I have always gone to sleep after my bowl of muesli but I find it more difficult now. I take off my bra and am conscious of the luxury of breasts released, take off my pants and confirm the smoothness of a hip with casually running hands. The banal, the repeated movements have something new in them. An old newness; the stuff of whims.

Yesterday, tidying up, looking for things to throw away in my restlessness – could I be avoiding Private Nothing again? – I came across Hodge's one letter in its H.M.P. envelope.

Hi Rabbit,
    Hardly a thrill a minute in here but thinking about you helps. I wonder what you are doing with yourself in the afternoons these days. It's fun to imagine. I do a lot of imagining, especially at night (!) Helps to pass the time you know.
    I was wondering if you could send . . .

. . . tobacco and salami. That is what he asked for and that is why he wrote. *Rabbit*. Who was he talking to? Certainly not me. And the language was not his – borrowed, trivial, cheap. But why am I indignant? He was a stranger and I have always been attracted to strangers. He had his imaginings and I had mine. And now I have imaginings about another stranger.

Still sorting, tidying, I found myself unfolding Ann's clothes. The cotton dress rustled out of its tissue and hung limp, creased, passé from my hands. The sleeves, just above elbow length, are modestly puffed, the collar neat, pattern of small flowers on a pale background – a frock. I can see Ann saying the word. It is the same one she was wearing in that old photograph clipped to the one of the young man in uniform. I had meant to try it on but I did not. Carefully, I folded it away. Somebody else's memories and maybe somebody else's imaginings.

But I did try on the black jacket. It has padded shoulders and a curious little peplum. I tried it on with nothing underneath and liked the effect of naked skin against the dark material and military cut. For the first time in a long time I let down my lopsided hair. Just one hairgrip made the scar invisible.

What am I going to do about the new stranger, my new fantasy, new distraction? I have no doubt that, sooner or later, I will do something. Or rather, *let something happen*.

Unless twenty-seven is not too late to change.